Family Illusions

Michael Tadman

First Edition

Printed in the United States of America
Print on demand may include various locations

First Printing: April 2013

Lake Vista Publishing
Box Bow Books

ISBN- 978-1-300-91823-3

10 9 8 7 6 5 4 3

MMXIII

Dedication

To my wife

Barbara Anne Tadman

And special mention to

Renee, Kim and Cassidy

Books in the Illusion Series
by Michael Tadman

Family Illusions

And look for future titles

Hidden Illusions
Unfolding Illusions

Family Illusions

Author's Note

Characters in Family Illusions are fictitious: creations only in the mind of the author. The story's geography blends reality and imagination: Burlington, Vermont exists, Clearville, Vermont does not. My apologies to the State of Vermont for adding a town without their permission... but Clearville is such a fine, upstanding addition, I'm sure Vermonters will welcome the village. As for what I've created in California, well it's difficult to enhance the Golden State.

Prologue

Murder is not difficult! Believe me, not difficult at all. Simply a life choice... one of many choices you and I make every day. Murder is like choosing a razor for cutting hair, or changing its colour, style or length. It's that easy, and it's always an option. If teeth can be changed, eye colour, even height altered, then anyone can shift from mouse to manic. Anyone, any deserving person can become an international celebrity just by the plunge of an ice pick. It all starts with knowing how to spell. Understanding that murder starts with R is crucial. One swift stroke will eliminate a dangerous enemy and achieve lasting fame means revenge. I should know. I'm famous now.

Maplehurst Correctional Complex
Remanded in Custody - Women's Section
Milton, Ontario

Chapter 1

Months ago, when the phone woke me in the darkness, I had no idea it would end in death. Groggy with sleep, my only thought was this call had better be important to wake me and risk Allan getting mad at being disturbed. Over thirty, and married for ten years to the volatile man grumbling next to me, I knew that neither my husband's moods nor the ringing phone were my fault; yet, still, I would be blamed for both.

"Sue! Sue, are you there?" My ditsy sister shouted from her end of the line.

"It's Anna," I whispered to my husband's back. "I'll talk in the kitchen."

Slumping in a kitchen chair, so tired, I spoke with my eyes closed, and said the obvious, "This better be good Annie, for waking me at 2 in the morning?"

"Well, you can sleep anytime, Sue Charter, but cancer doesn't rest."

My eyes suddenly opened wide, "Have you found another problem?"

"I'm fine, but breast cancer is a family disease, and it's time to protect ourselves. Cancer is in our genes, Sue, and we all need to be tested. All of us need a DNA test now and use that as a clean marker for our future health. There's an internet site I've been reading for weeks."

"Annie, are you crazy? We're the only two girls in the family, and we both take care of ourselves. Mom died years ago."

"If I'm crazy, then you can't count. There's five of us Stevens alive. You, me, dad, and our brother's Peter and Harry. Five. Men can get breast cancer too."

"It's not likely, Annie. It happens to men but not often."

"That's exactly what dad just said, but I told him he had to get a DNA test anyway. If there's a chance it can happen to him then we all have to have the test."

"You woke dad at 2 in the morning?" Annie, you're beyond help.

"It was only midnight. I called dad first, then Peter. Peter hung up on me, then I called Harry too, but he wasn't in. Sue, mom died years ago and I was never told what she died of. Family's keep secrets and mom could have died of cancer and, remember, back then you didn't tell the little kids anything. Dad still won't talk of her death. So I want everyone to get a DNA test. I sent you an email of how they cross check all our family genes for future problems..."

"Annie, you're my hero but not this late when Allison has school tomorrow, Allan has work, and I need sleep. I'll check your email in the morning. Love you sister but you're a pain in the butt at this hour. And don't call back because I have enough trouble with Allan as it is."

He was quiet, when I slipped back in bed. Too quiet, which meant he was priming for another fight. So like his dad, overly quiet until he exploded. My sister Annie was the twice lucky one - she had beaten breast cancer, and she was single.

I knew I would read Annie's email in the morning, take the DNA test, and badger my dad, and brothers' Peter and Harry into doing the same. Our family was close and caring. No secrets. Harry would tell Annie his troubles, she would tell dad, and dad would tell me. Peter was the odd ball who wouldn't tell any of us anything. We all still live close to each other even today. My home in Clearview, Vermont is across Lake Champlain from my oldest brother Peter and his second wife in Plattsburgh, and Annie lives a little south of them. Siblings are no trouble. My trouble is the angry man lying next to me; he shows less love and feeling than a large mound of soggy potatoes.

*****

Yesterday was bad. Allan found my results from the DNA firm. First he laughed, then he wanted to know how much it cost and, then, on reading it again he turned angry. "Susie, have you seen what they are saying. What do they mean saying your test is different from the rest in your family? Don't believe it! Someone's trying to cheat you out of family money when your dad dies? I'm taking these garbage pages down to the bar, and talking to a guy who's an expert in DNA. Don't wait up for me!"

Today is worse. Sue sat dead rigidly, holding a cold coffee, her thoughts fixated on the slightly cleaner area of kitchen wall indicating where a little picture had recently hung. She was talking out loud to an empty house. "Why did you destroy it last night, Allan? And where the hell have you put the pieces? I want my picture back. I can't replace the picture. Did you smash it out of spite? While I was sleeping, you destroyed the one family picture I treasured." Sue didn't shed tears often but, today, her eyes kept misting over.

She was nine in the destroyed family picture - all six of them at a summer fun fair. Ice cream being sold in the background, her mom and dad standing tall in the picture and Sue, the youngest, was wedged in the front between her sister Anna and her oldest brother Peter. While Harry, the second youngest, stood with the family, yet separate, as some stranger snapped the photo. And that silly old black and white picture had become a treasured possession. When you're nine, the world is full of promise. Sue could still see them clearly, see them all in the missing picture, all smiling, while her oldest brother pretended to be choking her.

Suppressing anger her voice broke the house silence, "Just shut up, Sue, forget the picture! Forget everything! You can only stay sane by forgetting reality and everything Allan does." She realized she was talking to her self and said, "God, I'm even talking to myself now."

She repeated her new mantra, "Sanity over reality," with determination, but words couldn't stop her feeling old and ugly. "Today is a bitch. Frumpish house, frumpish world and frumpish me. I look forty, feel like I'm fifty, and I'm only mid-thirties." She spoke in the empty kitchen while staring at the faint outline of where a picture had hung. The happy Stevens' family gone. She could still see all the details of their good times, while she worried over the rest of the week.

Two days later, Sue Charter's shoulders twitched tight, as she concentrated on her husband's breakfast mess of scattered toast crusts, with blobs of ketchup slopped over the side of his plate and onto the table. She, consciously, restrained her hand from sweeping the mess to the floor while knowing, "That's how he'd get rid of it." Her fingers would enjoy pushing his dirty plate over the edge of the table and deliberately smashing it into pieces. But she didn't move a muscle. Only her internalized thoughts stemmed action, "Oh, smash it, easy, then what? Then I have another mess to clean, and one plate less, and a plate I can't afford to replace from the dollar store. And would it change Allan? Like pigs fly, he'll change. We have a fifty/fifty marriage; he makes the mess and I clean it up. In ten years, I can only remember him helping for a while when Allison was born. Bugger all since then."

Talking to her distorted reflection in the old chrome toaster, she said, "Every marriage can't be this bad or there would be more wives topping themselves. They would. And why not? Anyone in their middle thirties, in a bad marriage, getting worse, and no way out, would be dead depressing for anyone. And we're always, always broke. Never enough money to take Allie and go see dad in Atlanta. Besides, there's no way out in rural Vermont. How can I earn enough money to change my life? What can I do when he knows I'm afraid. Every day, the fear gets worse. Face it dummy... life is short but fear is forever."

She sat all morning, unsettled, edgy, with no energy to move even when her ringing kitchen phone disturbed her morning misery. First thought, "Maybe he's got hurt at work. No. Not likely, he has to work to get hurt at work. I won't answer." But the phone continued to break the silent morning in the little house north of Clearville, Vermont. Ten rings. Fifteen. Susan felt uneasy. Poor country folk don't get pleasant phone calls at ten any morning. Either Allan's booked off work to drink with his buddies, or Allie is upset at school again, and how can I reach her without a car? The thought of Allie made Sue pick up the phone and hear her dad talking.

"Sue, was your brother, Harry, flying to Buffalo yesterday? Wasn't it yesterday? "

"Dad? Slow down. Harry is always flying, but I don't know his schedule?"

"I do. Get your TV on, Sue. Get CNN breaking news. A plane crashed into Lake Erie last night. No survivors. None. Sue, my gut tells me your brother was on that flight."

"You're overreacting, dad. There are thousands of flights every day. Okay, I'm watching the TV now, and they say the flight's destination was Buffalo. It went down in Lake Erie. So no, no Harry wouldn't have been on that flight, dad. He's been commuting to Toronto. God, you got me so upset. My heart is still pounding."

"Well, there's cause to worry because he doesn't answer his phone at home, he's not at work, and people at his office sidestep my questions. So where the hell is your brother and why is his firm being vague with me." Her dad's voice cracked with emotion as he continued, "I'm worried Sue... damn worried."

" All right, dad. Let me make some calls to keep you happy. And then I'll get back to you. You at the condo?"

"Yeah, I'm at the condo in Atlanta, but the sunshine doesn't feel so great today. You call me back on my cell phone, while I call on the other line. Hope my gut feeling is wrong."

"You're just a worry wart, dad. Remember when Annie went to Aruba, and you worried because of problems in Cuba. Relax. Harry's just fine."

"Make the calls anyway and later we can laugh at old dad going paranoid, right. I know you have your own problems, but I just had to call. Thanks, Sue."

"Harry's fine dad," Sue repeated. "Just fine. Bye dad."

Sue took a deep breath and called the 800 special crash number flashing on the TV. After working her way past three phone check points she was, eventually, linked to the right person - an airline lady who spoke in slow, measured words, and immediately Sue feared her dad's instinct had been right. When they wouldn't deny her worst fears, Sue felt chilled. Her brother, her defender all through school, Harry Stevens, was on the passenger list for the doomed flight. Confirmed.

All Sue could do was hold the phone ever so tight and face her next looming anguish. She knew how to call her dad in Atlanta. Just had no idea what to say.

Chapter 2

God, Harry, why did you have to die? That screwed me. My one chance of leaving this damn marriage died with you. Who will help me now? No one can. Allan keeps pushing me down; isolated, depressed and crammed into a black hole, a place that you would have saved me from. Mistake to have depended so much on you, Harry. I should have acted, somehow made plans, reached for help months ago, demanded attention by throwing a brick through Sophie's Sandwich Stop window in Clearville and getting dragged off to the looney bin. That would have done it. Or even keeping a diary, anything, to help sort my brain. My mind is frozen in a soft cotton sense kind of way, no edge to hold, so my world drifts away in mush. What is sane, insane, what is sane? Most days I don't think. Or hear. Is the phone ringing now? Listen to the phone ring, or ignore it, means no more than bird calls. Only more annoying. Everything is more annoying.

The answering machine beeped, "Sue, for god's sake, when I call you, at least answer the phone." Her dad's voice boomed from Atlanta. "This is the third message I'm leaving today, and I'm not going to..."

I picked up the phone. "Dad, stop yelling at me! Did you call before?"

"How do you think my other two messages got on your machine this morning?" John Stevens softened his voice saying, "Sue, what's happening to you? Are you all right? I've talked to your brother and sister in Plattsburgh, and both Peter and Annie say you don't return their calls. What's going on?"

"That's a Peter and Annie thing. You know them. Especially Annie. The scatterbrain doesn't make an effort to reach me. If she just thinks she's going to call, then for her that's making contact. And I'm just too tired to play their games. Tired dad, all the time, go to bed tired and still wake up exhausted. Vitamins might help. Do you take vitamins?" Sue paused a moment and added, "How are you doing?"

John entered her conversation saying, "I'm fine... getting a little slower. But you're young and shouldn't be tired.. You're only thirty-three."

"Thirty-four dad, almost thirty-five."

"Whatever. The point is you're not old enough to be tired all the time. Get active, get out more. Take the ferry over to Plattsburgh and spend the day with Peter or Annie. Never mind, Peter's always rushed, I told him to make time for you. Get busy. Wash dishes you've already washed if necessary. Do things you don't want to do. I filled in the paperwork the airline sent me for Harry, and you and the other kids have to do the same."

"Don't nag me over the airlines. Already gave them paperwork twice and permission to look at my medical records. They replied a week ago for another DNA sample and that's been sent."

"A second sample? Why did they want one, Sue?"

"No idea, dad. I thought it odd when their lab called asking for a second test." Sue's memory drifted back a few weeks to the unusual phone request.

She remembered exactly what the lady had said, "Just confirming your DNA tests you gave us access to Mrs. Charter. On our form, you stated your exact relationship to Harry Stevens, that he was your brother? Now I need to verify that both his parents and both your parents are the same individuals? Can you confirm this?"

"Yes, of course." Look lady, questions of Harry's death exhaust me. "Is this enough for your records? Are you finished?"

"Almost ma'am. Unfortunately, our lab needs to recheck your DNA. The sample made before your brother's death, may have been contaminated and so we require a second sample from you? Would you be able to see the nurse at the Clearville Clinic sometime in the next few days? We will run a new test, and issue a second report to your medical records. "

"Fine. Just happens I'll be in Clearville tomorrow and can drop into the clinic. Will that work?"

"I'm sure that would work just fine, Mrs. Charter. I'll call the clinic to expect you, and a registered nurse will take this second sample. Thank you again for your cooperation."

Sue's mind, re-engaging with the present, heard her dad saying, "...so I don't even consider going into a depression. Life is to be lived, even the days I don't want to get out of bed." He continued in a hushed tone. "Worst part is how unreal Harry's death seems to me. Like he will be knocking on my door anytime now saying it was all a mistake. Just like Harry to joke and say the airlines made him wait in a security line for the last few months." John expected Sue to pick up his thread of conversation and when she remained quiet, he continued, "You know Sue, in one way, you had your brother longer than anyone else in the family. You were the last to see Harry alive, when he visited you a few weeks after Christmas. He told me he spent an afternoon with you in Clearville and I can't remember the last time he spent an afternoon with me. So be grateful for that."

"He didn't visit me, dad. Where did you get that idea?"

"Harry told me. And you told me after he had been to your home. Don't you remember?"

"No, I don't remember." Did he really come to see me?

"Dad, I'm tired. I've got to ring off. Talk to you later." As the phone clicked off, a vague image of Harry floated on the edge of Sue's mind. Harry couldn't have been here or I would remember. But there was an afternoon visitor, not Harry, but someone else came with a package. "It's not a gift; it's insurance. Want to buy an insurance policy, little lady?" It's funny because Harry always called me "little lady." Why can't I recall? If I wasn't so tired, I could figure all this out.

*****

The Sheriff's Department, in Clearville, Vermont, was a single storey, red-bricked flat-roofed building, except at the front where two rooms jutted up as a second storey with a sloped roof, and dubbed the ivory tower for its odd look. In one of these upper rooms, on a Wednesday afternoon in early April, Sheriff Henry Mantes argued against the factual information he had just been given.

"It's garbage. Sam, my office shouldn't even be involved in Sue Charter's DNA report. She's not a criminal and this is not a criminal matter." Henry Mantes, long-serving Sheriff of Clearville, Vermont, was finding it difficult to accept the indications of fraud involving Sue Charter. When you served a relatively small resident base for many years, you get to know the locals - the ones to trust and the ones he couldn't. And he knew Sue well.

Swivelling to face Burlington Vermont's Director of Forensic Science, Nelson Samuels, he repeated, "Listen Sam, this report is a mistake. I know her folks, the Stevens' family. I lived in their house more than mine when growing up, and I can tell you that the report's conclusion doesn't make sense. Susan Charter doesn't defraud people and I don't believe she is adopted."

"Heartwarming Henry, but I don't care." Nelson Samuels

shifted his bulk in the chair and continued, "How she came to be part of the Stevens' family isn't my business. But facts are facts. Susan Charter, nee Stevens, is biologically not related to the Stevens family."

Henry paused a moment before saying, "Then look at the facts again, Sam. Months ago, members of the Stevens' family and Susan Charter had DNA tests made because of their fear of cancer. It's not a logical act, but they did it. Then, when their brother is killed in a plane crash with bits of his body parts scattered all over Lake Erie, to identify the brother, the family offers their previous DNA tests. But now the Airline and Insurance Company are questioning Sue Charter's right to compensation because her DNA doesn't fit with the rest of her family. So, could it be that Sue's tests are just fine and the fraud is from the Insurance Company trying to stall a payout."

"Henry, you don't believe that. You know Harold Stevens, like many young guys, died without having any Will. Insurance companies have to be careful to who and how they pay benefits." Nelson, raised his hand to forestall Henry's speaking, saying, "Now don't interrupt me... you just listen. My lab performed tests on numerous relatives related to the crash victims of the downed airliner. And my reports are directed to all interested parties - State, Federal, Airline, Insurance, etc. - all heavy hitters - with big dollars involved. So, when her supplied tests showed Sue Charter as biologically not related to her parents, we ordered a second test taken at a clinic. Was she adopted, or kidnapped as a child, or dropped from Venus, I neither know, nor care, nor speculate on, but, to be prudent, we examined that second test again. It gave the same results. Sue Charter is not a child of Mr. John Stevens of Atlanta, nor of his deceased wife Joanna Stevens, and she has no blood relation of deceased Airline passenger Harold Stevens. Yet she registered for Harold Stevens insurance compensation as the sister of Harold Stevens. That suggests fraud and insurance companies do not like fraud."

"She's not a criminal, Sam. She hasn't committed any crime."

"Fine. Let's make sure this is handled with some compassion. Her heritage could have been hidden from her. Hell, people can live a long life and never know they were adopted. But the problem for the Criminal Justice System, which you are paid to uphold, is that Sue Charter filed an insurance claim against the accidental death of Harold Stevens and now we find she has no biological claim to profit by the death of Harold Stevens. So what should be done?"

"She's not a criminal, Sam, I know the family."

"Henry, will you stop repeating yourself. Based on our lab results, the insurance company is simply asking Sue to do one of two things; either prove she is part of Harold Stevens family or withdraw her claim. Now I know you are a friend of the Stevens and, as such, my office is offering you a chance to inform Sue of the test results and advise her of the seriousness of making a false claim." Samuels softened his voice, adding, "And I've been told, off the record, that if she drops her stated claim, the insurance company may be glad to drop her investigation. Quid pro quo."

Sheriff Henry Mantes didn't answer.

Samuels continued, "Henry, set aside the fact you know the family or she's your old girlfriend. Just do what the state of Vermont pays you for. Deliver the report and tell Susan the DNA facts can't be disputed. She is not a child of either parent in the Stevens' family."

"Sam, what about her mother's side of the family? They lived up Canada way somewhere, and her mom could easily have had an old boy friend we never heard of."

"Canadian DNA follows the same rules as any other DNA."

"I know that. But Sue could be a love child from an old

affair. Even in our religious, rural, Vermont - sex happens. And with her mom dead, how can you be positive she's not related to her brother Harry?"

Sam pointed a finger at Henry and asked, "What do you remember about my lecture on mitochondrial DNA?"

"It's female DNA. I was listening."

"I'm surprised you even remember the name, because you seem to have missed everything else that I said." As Henry shrugged Sam continued saying, "Well the mitochondrial comparison of DNA supplied by Susan, her father, and by her three siblings is why I'm positive Susan is not biologically related to this family." Sam stopped for a moment, then continued, "You still puzzled?" Nelson Samuels shifted his bulk in the chair and assumed his lecture voice, "Everyone has mitochondrial DNA, but, and this is the critical point, it's only inherited from the mother. For example, you and your sister will have the identical mitochondrial DNA section that your mother has, but, as a male, all your children will only receive mitochondrial from your wife. Sue's mitochondrial doesn't match her siblings. Therefore, Susan is not biologically related to anyone in the Stevens' family. And she needs to know this, so she doesn't go further with her insurance claim and get blown away by the facts. You're the messenger Henry, and it's your job to deliver the news."

"I'll do my job, Sam. But is there any rush? Hell, a man with your education must have a reasonable side." Henry tapped slender fingers on his chin. Just less than six feet, his wiry frame and sandy hair suited his intense concentration now as he said, "Anyone mind if I wait a week or so before giving her the results. Perhaps, a flaw in your thinking would be found?"

"Waiting's not wise. Why delay a legal investigation? What's the point?

Henry drummed his fingers on his desk, thinking, hesitating, then continued, "Sue and her family are going through a bad patch just now. Raising family questions will only get Susan confused and her husband riled. Allan's unpredictable. He's a loose cannon with a big mouth."

"So. Since when are you afraid of a loose cannon, Henry?"

"Also, her reputation could be shredded by small town gossip. Gossip is vicious. So why rush in telling Susan? She needn't know it's sitting in my inbox for a week or two. And Sam... you gaining a little weight?"

"Henry are you nuts? Set aside a report in an investigation, over fear of gossip. That's a bogus excuse. As for hurting the family, hell most of her family live on the New York side of Lake Champlain. Only Susan lives in Clearville. And if you really care about my weight Henry, I've not gained an ounce. Fact, I've lost some."

The lab director rolled an unlit cigar between his fingers in anticipation of leaving. "I remember the night when you were pissed to the gills and told me how much Susan and her family meant to you. If you're such a good friend then don't try a cover-up. The air plane crash that killed all the passengers, including Harry Stevens, is still big news. Although Susan's DNA is not a story on anyone's radar yet, all it takes is one phone call to CNN with a mention of a cover-up, and a mess of reporters will accuse you of favouritism and be pounding at her front door."

Henry forced a smile over Sam's frustration saying, "All right, calm down big guy. I didn't think you would agree to a delay, but I had to try. I'll get it started today."

"Henry. Shame on you. Winding me up for the last half hour isn't good for my blood pressure."

"No one's playing games, Sam. Look my friend, Susan's husband, Allan, is a scary kind of guy. Even when he's being nice, he worries me." Henry waved the report in the air, saying, "Science doesn't know all the answers. Dollars to donuts there's another meaning to this and buy you lunch at the Cracker Barrel if I'm wrong."

"I'll enjoy that lunch Henry, cause you'll be paying."

Ten minutes after Sam had left his office, Henry was still pondering the implications of the report on his desk. Mr. Stevens had treated him well, when he was a mixed-up teenager. Now he felt unsettled, somehow disloyal. But then what did he really know of Sue over the last ten years. She could have changed. Perhaps, she had been adopted. And Sam was right; he had to act. Reluctantly, he dialled Sue Charter's home. It's a bad situation of a job, when it gets personal but Sam was right, he had to act.

Sue heard the phone ring, and answering machine click on.

"Sue, it's me, Hank. There are complications from a DNA test you had, and the results have ended up on my desk. I need to explain in person. If you could come to the station then call me back. But if you can't make it to town, I'll come and see you on Friday afternoon. Around four when Allison is home from school. Hope this will work for you. See you Friday."

Susan heard the message and now looked at her reflection in the hall mirror. A slight frame, mid-thirties, with long dark hair - the image revealing none of the turbulence churning in her mind. "Just tight nerves. Hank is just doing his job, not coming to see me like a drippy teenager. So why am I uptight? For god's sake, you'd think being old, married, with a ten-year-old brat - would stop my daydreams. I'll look fine on Friday. A blouse will easily cover any finger nail scratches on my left arm." She pulled down her sleeves, moved to the kitchen, and started to make dinner for three, or perhaps, even better, perhaps just for two, if Allan was late home for dinner again. She felt better since hearing Hank's phone call.

* * * * *

Nelson Samuels often did his thinking while driving and, today, he was driving rather slowly back to the lab. He told Hank that the mitochondrial test for Sue Charters didn't match her siblings - a true statement. But there was a caution.

Not every woman has healthy DNA. About 1 in 6000 can have damaged mitochondrial sections that result in a family of serious disease. There is no cure for mitochondrial disease. However, many people have a normal life span with their disease well-managed.

The problem is when the mother produces a child, it will carry the same damaged DNA with its associated problems.

How can these parents produce healthy children?

There is an experimental procedure. It involves using cells from one female minus her damaged mitochondrial, plus, cells from a second female using only her healthy mitochondrial, and cells from a single male.

In effect, producing a child from two females and one male, the child would not have the same DNA as its mother.

Nelson pondered this, for it would answer the dilemma baffling Sue Charter where her mitochondrial DNA did not match her mother. However, there was no point in mentioning this procedure. It would only confuse the issue. And, besides, it couldn't happen in nature. No way it could occur naturally.

Chapter 3

Friday, North of Clearville, Vermont.

When Allan Charter moved his family into the old, unattractive bungalow six years ago, he bought the place because it was cheap. Set on a high plain, overlooking Lake Champlain, Sue immediately loved the location. The Green Mountains marched eastward into the distance, farmland unfolded toward the rural town of Clearville on the south and, below and to the west, ran the cold blue waters of Lake Champlain. True, her narrow kitchen window offered a limited view of Lake Champlain and South Hero Island, yet the view never failed to please. Sue felt connected today, a little edgy waiting for Hank to arrive, but still connected to life.

Sue shouted to her daughter in the living room, "Allie, are you watching for the police car coming from town like I asked you?"

"Sure mom. Are they coming to arrest you?"

The thought of jail time would certainly solve home problems. "Keep watching. Heavens, where did you get the arrest idea from. Allison Charter, you're watching too much TV."

"Cause Officer Mantes said so." Her thin voice continued, "He did so, mom." She flipped her straight blond hair saying, "When we saw officer Mantes in town at Christmas, he said he would only come here if he had to arrest you."

Sue, remembering Hank's kidding remark, smiled at the literal thinking. Oh to be young again. "Allie, the sheriff was joking. Henry Mantes is an old friend. We went to school together, when I was your age."

"Ya, ya, you told me ten times already, mom. So why is he coming today?"

"Over some test results." Susan brushed a wisp of long dark hair from her eyes while repeating Hank's explanation for coming in her mind, and still finding it made little sense. "Now keep watching for his police car while I cook." I don't want dinner late and set Allan off to brood all evening. So Henry Mantes, get here and get gone before Allan is home. Sue then muttered to herself, "Egg shells. Always walking on egg shells around here."

"Maybe he's not coming, mom." Allison yelled from the front room.

"Keep looking, sweetie."

"Okay." Allison carefully followed her mom's request- sitting at the living room window, looking past their long gravel driveway for a police car heading its way from Clearville. Then, when the phone rang, ten-year-old Allie was eager to answer, so she missed seeing the distant flashing lights heading their way.

Allie's phone conversation drifted over to Sue in the kitchen. "Hi, grampy. What am I doing? Watching for the cops to come. No, it's not sunny here. Want to talk to mom?" Then, shouting as if the kitchen were a block away, she yelled, "Mom, grampy wants you on the phone. He says it's sunny in Atlanta." Allison handed the phone while and looking out the window adding, "And I can see the cop car coming way down the main road, mom."

"You hear your granddaughter, dad? Good old Sheriff Henry Mantes is coming to visit."

John Stevens said loud and clear from Atlanta, "I remember that long skinny kid. " John Stevens' then asked the obvious. "Trouble with Allan again?"

"Not this stuff. I figure it's good news. Mante's coming to tell me the Airline got my second test sorted out. Did you have a hassle when you provided a second sample?"

"I didn't give a second sample Sue, and I phoned Annie back a couple of days ago, she never did a second one either. Look, Annie thinks you've gone into hiding. You've done it before when depressed, so call your brother and sister and go visit. Only a half-hour ferry ride away."

"Dad." Sue spoke with a hard edge to her voice.

"Now don't dad me. With Harry and your mom gone, there's only three of us. That's it. So stay in touch with family."

"Dad, you're lecturing again. I'm not a kid."

"No lecture, just worried. Remember, we're here for each other Sue."

"Well, Allan and Allie keep me busy dad, but I think of you guys all the time. Now I'm hanging up. Your granddaughter says Mantes is almost here."

John held his thoughts in check. Tons he could have said but, instead, keep it light, replying; "Go look after the Sheriff and email me later on what he says. And consider a visit to warm Atlanta. Paradise. "

"Sure, 'cept you've had a dozen Atlanta colds this winter, while I haven't caught a single Vermont sniffle. Sunshine must be weak in Atlanta these days. Good-bye, dad."

"Okay Sue. I'll call again." It was understood he would call before Allan got home.

Sue Charter glanced at her reflection in the full length hall mirror, flipped her dark hair back from her small boned face and smiled at her still attractive looks. She opened the front door to greet Henry Mantes, her old friend from high school days but he spoke first.

"Mrs. Charter," Officer Henry Mantes held a manila envelope while saying, "This visit concerns the results from your second

DNA test...”

"Aren't you a little reserved in greeting an old friend? Henry Mantes I swear you're getting too big for that shiny little Sheriff's badge.” She started to reach out, to touch her friend of many years, but changed her mind and simply waved him in saying, “Come in. The kitchen is always the best place to talk and coffee's ready. Still drink it black?” When he politely declined a cup, Susan continued, “Well, you have changed. You were always the sophisticated one back in high school drinking coffee, while we kids sipped coke. Remember those years? Wouldn't you die to have them back. Have a chance to do things different than we did.”

Hank tightened up a little when the past was mentioned, only muttering, “Those days are long gone, Mrs. Charter.” Henry polished one shoe on the back of his pants, “This is a letter on the results of your second DNA test and, if you like to read it, I can wait and answer questions? It's not the best of news.”

Susan read the page. Then, she sat in a kitchen chair to carefully read the single page again. Finally asking, “Hank, how can this mean what it says? Saying there is no biological connection between Sue Charter and Harry Stevens is wrong. He's my brother for god's sakes.”

"I don't like it either, Sue.” He paused a moment and added, “The lab is saying more than Harry is not related to you. They are saying your families' DNA matches, except yours. Burlington Vermont Lab says you don't fit their genetic family pattern at all. Not even close.”

"Hank, this is no time to pull one of your practical jokes.”

"I'm here on official business. The lab's report is valid.”

"Nonsense, Hank. How can a report be right, if it states I just lost my family?”

"Well they're saying just that Susan, and they are saying a lot more between the lines. Talk to your dad and tell him the test results. Perhaps, he has an explanation for your different DNA, but from here on in, you need to be very careful."

"You're ahead of me, Hank - why do I have to be careful?"

"I know you personally, Sue, but the insurance company sees a DNA that doesn't match as fraud. They want you to prove you're genetically related or stop the insurance claim. That's why you need to be cautious."

Susan held the letter in a shaking hand, tried to read it again and stopped, to suddenly rip the letter in half, fold the pieces and rip again, "Tell your insurance people they are nuts. I never made a stupid claim. When I called that very first day, they checked a box for an insurance claim. It was their doing, so how can I be guilty of fraud? And what pisses me off the most is their gall now to say I'm not who I am." Susan crumpled the torn bits of paper, walked near the sink, and tossed them into the garbage can saying, "Tell the leaches they can keep their money, and I'll keep my family. Tell them that." Sue was shaking, "God, Hank, I was so looking forward to today. I thought my luck was changing." Sue wasn't making a sound, but there were tears in her eyes.

Hank waited a good minute before replying, "Right, I'll politely tell them to stick it if that's what you want. I'll let them know you still figure their tests are wrong, but I would suggest you talk this over with family and get all your facts in line before you call them again." Hank waited, drawing small circles on the kitchen table with one finger, and then continued, "The lab in Burlington does suggest one alternate line of thought. Now don't bite my ear off Sue, but could there have been an adoption? If your DNA doesn't match, then adoption is one logical answer."

"That's just silly, but I wasn't adopted. None of us kids are adopted. Even my dumb sister is related to me." They're saying adoption is a bunch of nonsense. "Besides, why are the police speculating on me and suggesting adoption? Why are they so interested in me?"

"Frankly, you're not a police concern. The fact you don't match your brother's genetic profile is not a police matter. But, figure out what's wrong first before you tackle the heavy hitters that now see you as a false claimant. They see someone who contacted them and then failed two tests. However, they aren't pressing charges. The airline is content to set your paperwork aside and let you sort this out."

"Sure I called but they suggested testing. The lab and the airline got this screwed up."

"Sue, work it out at the family level first. I'll do what I can and try to keep it all on the quiet, so it doesn't upset Allan."

"It's too late to keep this stuff quiet. My ten-year-old already blabbed to her dad about you coming to the house today and he ragged me all last night. Allan wants you back tonight to explain this airline report to him personally or he's going to the station and talk to your superior.

Allan James Charter opened the front door just wide enough to effectively block Sheriff Henry Mantes' entry, and smirked his greeting "Bring your hanging rope tonight, Mantes?"

Henry Mantes smiled, knowing Allan was just another man who drinks a lot and appreciates his family too little, so why push the sorry sod. Rural law enforcement means ignoring almost as much as you paid attention to. A simple, "Evening, Allan" was a sufficient answer.

"Come in, Mantes. Susan's waiting in the kitchen. You know your way around my house by now, don't you?"

Susan called, "In the kitchen, Hank."

Allan Charter placed a finger to his lips, saying in a mock whisper, "Careful Sue. Always let the police talk first." Allan's comment was doubled-edged, poking fun at Henry Mantes while showing his innate dislike of authority.

Henry looked at Allan while he addressed Sue's test results, "Well, like I told Susan, I'm just delivering the second lab results. The lab saw a family mismatch after the first test and to be sure there was no mistake, they took your second test, and the results are the same."

Sue was impatient "Get to the point, Hank!"

He turned and spoke directly to Allan, "Sue is biologically different from the rest of the members in her family. Her dad, Peter and Annie all supplied their DNA and it matched. Sue's DNA does not match their DNA."

Sue spoke up, "But Hank, doesn't everyone have naturally unique DNA?"

"Unique, yes, but while your brother Peter and sister Annie have a linked DNA inheritance to your father John Stevens, and a common mother, your DNA shows no such genetic inheritance or link. No link to your family."

Susan blurted, "That makes no sense. Do you seriously think all my growing up memories could be false? My baby pictures? My birth certificate and all my childhood stories are forgeries? I was conceived in Georgia, born premature on a trip to Canada, and have spent all my life in the States." Susan groped to continue, her voice going an octave higher, "Adoption never happened no matter what your office is saying."

Henry Mantes deliberately spoke quietly, trying to move the emotions down a notch. "The law is not involved in this. We have no interest in your family heritage."

Allan must have planned his attack, quickly pointed his finger at Henry Mantes, and yelling, "You're lying, Mantes! If the cops have no interest in Susan, then why are you here? Why raise DNA garbage? The point is simple - either you're lying now or just causing trouble over nothing."

"Allan, I'm trying to prevent future problems. If some reporter sniffs around and finds a link between Harry's plane crash and Susan's failed DNA tests, you can expect to have a news-hound team bringing TV cameras to your front door. Keep the issue to yourself until you and your family sort it out. I'm only here to tell you what's obvious."

Sue folded her arms across her chest. "Okay, so now you told me. But that's the end of it because what can one girl in rural Vermont do against the law and insurance companies. There's nothing I can do."

Henry Mantes regarded Sue thoughtfully, wondering, where her brightness and promise of youth had been lost. This was not the girl he knew in high school.

"Hank, my dad doesn't need to be bothered by a crackpot theory of adoption."

"It's your choice. You could even personally review the tests with Dr. Samuels, Director of the Burlington Lab. Hell, he practically invented DNA, he was..."

Allan interrupted, speaking in a low voice that threatened to escalate at anytime, "We don't need your help, Mantes." He gestured toward the door. "Almost time you went, even past time you went. I look after everything here. Everything. Sue, tell Mantes about that knife rack on the counter; well I made that rack Mantes, and I keep all them butcher knives sharp, all the time, don't I, Sue. So we don't need your help or Sue's dad's help, or anyone's help. I have all the stuff I need, and I can do what I need. Now you leave us alone. Go plague someone else, Mantes!"

Sheriff Henry Mantes flexed his arm muscles and blinked. He could feel Allan's greasy hair in his fingers, feel his head slam down into the counter, again, repeatedly slamming his head into the counter top, his strong arm tight around Allan's neck, smearing his bloody nose across the counter top, while Allan's futile hands could almost reach the razor-sharp butcher knives, almost, but not quite. But the moment passed, the illusion morphed into reality as Hank politely said good-bye knowing it would be a long hard night for Sue.

In the morning, Susan lay in bed listening to her husband's angry banging round the kitchen, his usual tactic of noise and delay before heading out to work, noisy delay before another round of harassment. She had almost drifted into sleep, when Allan came noisily back to the bedroom shouting, "You kept me up all night, Sue. You being deliberately restless last night kept me awake for hours. I need rest for work this morning. You and the cops and their tests only cause trouble for me."

"Allan, talking adoption upset me, too. My dad will flip, when he hears it."

Allan was seldom sympathetic and this morning was no exception. He spoke, almost yelling, "Well, he doesn't have to know so don't bother your dad. I do the thinking in this house, not Henry Mantes, not his phony adoption story, so Susie girl, the only call you'll make today is to the airline and demand your part of Harry's insurance. Hanky boy said the cops don't care 'bout you, and your dad doesn't care 'bout you either. Leave them alone, hear me, you forget all their family nonsense."

"How can I call the airline when I can't explain anything about my birth? You want me to just forget the test results. They'll laugh at me."

"They just want to get out of paying the claim. We wait a few days, call them, and they will settle. Leave the cops and their test results alone. Just don't think."

Right, stop thinking on demand? "Can't leave this alone? If I'm not me, then who am I?"

"You're my wife, dummy. You have me, so what else do you

need?"

Allan stomped to the bed, pulled the blankets off his wife, and let cold bedroom air flow over her warm body. "You just ain't calling your dad. He doesn't care, so just face facts. You don't have much of a family." Susan felt trapped in the bed between the wall on one side and Allan on the other yelling louder, "You've just got me Susie Q, so start appreciating what you got."

"You are appreciated." Just stop constantly knocking my family.

"Stick to the plan. You just show me appreciation... and don't yap tonight when I get in late after bowling with the boys."

"Since when do you bowl?"

"Boys at the shop bowl and I support them having a beer or two, so I'll be home when I'm home."

"I'll talk to my dad when I want." Susan shouted, only after the front door had slammed and his truck had spewed gravel when backing out their drive. "Check the phone bills. There are ways around them."

Sitting at the kitchen table she waited for time to pass, watched her daughter dawdle over cereal, listened to Allie's ten-year-old patter, gave her a hug and watched her daughter straggle along the gravel drive toward the school bus.

Susan waited. Looking at the constricted view from her small kitchen window, Allan chose that tiny window to save money. I remember what he said when I asked for it to be larger, "Only have money for a bigger garage, Sue. Can't waste money on a kitchen window you'll hardly ever use." So, the window remained small. I scrubbed the old kitchen sink and bought new dish towels on sale, and he never said a word. Sue shouted in the empty kitchen, "A damn two-car garage that only holds Allan's new truck."

Sue found the phone card her dad had sent and dialled the sequence of numbers. Nothing would be recorded on her phone bill.

John Peter Stevens, sixty-six next month in July, answered in his Atlanta condo. "Hi, dad. Yes, I'm sort of fine, but not really. My second DNA testing is screwed up like the first one. Major problems. Well the lab results have the authorities convinced that my DNA doesn't match the rest of the family, and I don't understand it."

"Sue, say again."

"Hank came here last night and went into detail with me and Allan as to how my DNA is totally different from yours, and Peter's, and Annie's. You all match each other, but my DNA doesn't match any of yours. And I don't understand why it's happening?"

"You might think their results are surprising, Sue, but I certainly don't. Hell, it's almost to be expected isn't it?"

"Expected?" Sue gulped a breath. "You understand what's happening?"

"Absolutely. You live in Hicks town Vermont, where the cops are clueless, and the labs can't handle a urine test. Hell, the law there hasn't been able to stop liquor smuggling from Canada, in the last two hundred years. Why expect them to get correct DNA results? Have the dummies redo the test."

"Dad, they ran it twice, same results. No family match."

"Then the hicks made the same mistake twice. It's their problem Sue, not yours."

"Wish it were, dad? You make it sound so simple. The problem is the law, the lab testing, and the airlines are all saying my results are pointing toward adoption. That's what's upsetting."

"Adoption? Ridiculous. You can calm down, because, unless we're dealing with another immaculate conception for your birth, you're my daughter. Your mother and I planned on having you as the fourth child to complete our family. The only surprise of your birth is you came a couple of weeks sooner than expected. You know the story. Your mom was visiting her folks in Canada, when you popped out."

"Then, how can the lab tests say I don't fit the family DNA?"

"Beats me but, I'm your dad, you're my daughter and I'm going to be late for my morning coffee club. And if Vermont life gets too stressful, come spend time with me in Atlanta. Adoption. Wait till I tell my coffee bunch."

"Thanks, dad. Go. Dazzle your coffee shop bunch while I think if asking for a third test is worth the hassle, or just drop the test thing entirely. It might be best to forget trying to know why the test was wrong."

"Sure, might be best to leave it alone. Let them worry about the mistake they made. You okay now? I hear tiredness in your voice."

"I didn't sleep well last night, dad. Just need some rest now."

John hesitated, reluctant to say what he thought, but knowing he should at least ask, said, "You know, after a cold winter in Vermont, I bet you could use a break. I'd dearly love to have you and Allie spend a few days in Atlanta with me. My one bedroom condo will be cramped, but we can make do. Besides, I did promise Allie we'd see a Braves game this year."

"Allan wouldn't like it, dad. Life's a little rocky, but we've been through this before. It'll work out. Talk to you next week. Love you."

Sue would talk to her dad sooner than next week. While she prepared lunch and thought of what to have for dinner, her world was collapsing. Her sister Annie would soon phone and set Sue on an unforeseen path of discovery and danger.

Chapter 4

Sue followed her dad's sensible advice. "I'm not going to fight the test results for now. Allan is angry at everything, cops in general, and at Hank, in particular. So, until he stops finding fault with me and the universe, I'm going to accept his demands and let the tension cool down. What else can I do?"

A few mornings later, with Allan at work and Allie at school, her sister Annie phoned, and her sister almost never called. She was falling apart, crying and talking at the same time saying, "Sue, it's dad. He's had a heart attack. He's going to die."

"Annie. Where's dad now?"

"I don't know what to do. Dad's in the hospital, and I can't get in touch with Peter." Middle child Annie was never organized and often, when panicked or in a muddle, turned either to her oldest brother, Peter, or to her younger sister. "Sue, what do I do now?"

"Slow down, Annie. Who called you? Who said dad had the attack?"

"Just now, some bimbo named Sontag, or Sunny, from his building. Did you know dad has a lady living with him? Why is she living with dad?"

"Annie, stay focussed. What did this Sunny tell you?"

"She took dad to the Atlanta General with chest pains. Yesterday. Now she calls, wants to know who will look after dad. Could be released today, soon, and I can't go down there? Who's going to look after dad?"

" Annie, we can figure it out, stop blubbering. Just give me the damn phone number for this lady in his building."

"I don't know her number. She must be at dad's place, if she's living with him."

"You have call display, look on your phone and tell me the number she called from. Good, I've got it. I'll call her now and then the hospital. And calm down. If dad has heart problems then the hospital is where he should be. Dad's strong. I'm surprised our old man didn't drive himself to the hospital."

"Sue, he wanted to drive until Sunny told him how much long-term parking cost, then he let her drive." Annie panicked again, "Sue, I can't drive to Atlanta: I don't even drive the Northway."

"Make a coffee, sit by the phone, and, Annie, if the hospital calls, give them my number. We also need to get brother Peter involved right away."

"I'm so worried, Sue." Annie was inept at managing money, making decisions, or handling a crisis, but everyone loved her. "Dad's going to die just like mom."

"A month ago, you said mom died of cancer, not a heart problem."

"Well, what's the difference. It's similar, Sue."

"We can talk it out later, but right now I'm calling Peter." Annie was still crying, when Sue hung up.

Peter John Stevens was not pleased at being disturbed from an investment conference, and he answered his forced interruption coldly, until he understood their dad was seriously ill. "Sue, you were right to interrupt. I could leave work now and sort this out, but I'm in the middle of one bad situation of a meeting. Will you start making calls while I take an hour to wrap this up? Can you manage for an hour, Sue?"

"Sure bro. Leave John Peter Stevens and the hospital to me."

"Sue, I'm just as worried as you are."

"I know you are Peter," but thinking - you still act like a cold fish. "Get back to me early afternoon before Allan's home. He's not happy with the cops, tests, or phone calls."

"What?"

"Nothing. Only my DNA indicates I was adopted."

"No. We always wanted to give Annie away, not you. You could be different cause you were born in Canada, sis."

"Peter. You know I don't like that kidding." One 4th of July, when she was nine, they watched the fireworks over Lake Champlain, and Peter yelled for all to hear, "Sue shouldn't be here; she's a Canadian." And everyone laughed.

"Anyway," he continued, "get dad sorted out. I'll call before Allan gets home so as not to rile your good old boy. Bye sis."

The news from Atlanta was cautiously encouraging. Yes, John's condition was serious, yet after talking with nurses and his doctors, it was clear they were pleased with her dad's medical prognosis. So far a negative outcome wasn't mentioned. Even Annie calmed down when told this news, and cold fish Peter gave a sigh of relief. By early afternoon, Sue let herself relax and tried again, unsuccessfully, to contact her dad's friend, Sonny. The initial panic of the heart attack had become easier to accept, a realization that John's condition had stabilized. But not everyone was pleased.

Allan was furious, "Who's going to pay for calls to Atlanta? Sue, money doesn't grow on trees, and don't you even think of spending time in Atlanta to look after your dad. What's your family ever done for us?" The rant continued all evening. Allie closed her bedroom door and cranked up the TV volume. Some time, late in the evening, a beer bottle smashed into the door frame near where Sue had just been standing.

In the morning, Allan said little, until, with a last outburst of anger before leaving for work, he shouted, "You'll stay home, stay off the phone, no long distance charges, and get this god-damned house cleaned." He flung his bowl of half-eaten milk and cereal toward the sink. It caught the lip, smashed, and scattered bits of bowl, and slush, over the counter.

"Allan, stop it... be reasonable."

"Who's reasonable with me? Not you, not at work, paid nothing and given garbage work every day. So I drink a little, so what. You would drink to if your job could go any day. We can't manage if the job goes, so don't waste money on phone calls." The front door slammed and his truck crunched gravel racing out of the driveway.

Sue stared at the mess of concealing milk and cereal, while Allie asked in a quivering voice, "What will we do, mommy?"

"Allie, come and give mom a nice cuddle. This is going to be a good day. We're going to start a new day, and it's going to be just fine. You and I are going on a trip. No school today."

"No school. Where are we going?"

Sue pulled her daughter closer for another long hard hug. "Let's go pack some clothes dear, we're going to see your granddad." As a clump of soggy cereal dribbled from the sink counter to plop on the floor she added, "Your daddy made the decision for us. Pack quickly Allie, and a taxi will come soon to take us to the bus."

Days later, Allan Charter finished work and drove slowly home to his empty house. Sitting in his new truck, parked in his own drive, he wonders how his wife could treat him so badly. "How could she leave? My job hanging by a thread, life closing in, money problems, and now she takes off with Allie. I don't deserve this shit. Why does it happen to me?"

After a while he backs out, furiously spinning tires throwing gravel, driving down the main road to the Food Mart, where he buys his usual six pack of Bud. "Buying one six pack at a time before going back to buy another, proves I don't have a drinking problem." But Allan does the unexpected tonight. Leaving the beer untouched on the passenger seat, he drives through deepening dusk, turns into an empty church parking lot, and waits as the evening grows cold. Just waiting, eyeing the untouched six pack a number of times, and just waiting. Eventually, a second car parks nearby and the well-dressed driver walks over to Allan.

"Smart truck, Allan. Nice to see you, again. Coming inside while I get the coffee going?"

"Well, I was just driving by Stu, and I can only stay for a few minutes. Maybe, you got a little time and some words of wisdom for me before the meeting gets busy?"

"Hell, yes, Allan." Stu laughs, "Always good at words, just never had much wisdom." Walking beside Allan he said, "Simple as it seems, my making coffee and talking to all kinds of people, that was the start of a good life for me. I don't have troubles these days. You stay in touch with any of your old contacts?"

"No, I never bothered, Stu. You know me. Do things my way, never stay around long enough to keep friends. But this time could be different. I need to be sober for a while."

"Need to get sober, Allan? Why?"

"For me, of course, but being sober might also help cool things out at work."

"I heard something about you and problems at the plant."

"Whatever you heard just isn't true. Management. Backstabbing bastards trying to make my life difficult. My buddies get fired for cheating on the time clock and now other plant jerks are trying to drag me into that mess. Sure I knew about it, many of the guys did, but management can't prove I took part. Nothing to do with me."

"Of course, Allan. I understand. You're just an innocent bystander."

"Always been misunderstood Stu, but a meeting can't hurt, right? Get me in the good books with the world." Then, as with all drunks, he reveals far more than he intends too, adding, "Besides, not much else to do these evenings."

"Oh? Where are your wife and kid? Aren't you still married?" Stewart asks.

"The wife is visiting her dad in Atlanta for a few weeks. He's had heart problems and I told her to go help out. My getting sober now will surprise her. Can't hurt right? Staying sober for myself, of course."

"Right. Allan, coffee soon be ready so, will you set out the cups?"

"Anything stronger than coffee, Stu?" Allan asked, then smiled, and he could be charming when he smiled, "Hey, I was just kidding."

In his Atlanta condo, John Stevens is frustrated and unhappy with his nursing staff. Just an hour ago he had shouted, "I'm well enough to start going out on my own. I don't need you hanging over me all the time." His complaint didn't change the demanding attitude of his live-in nurse or her ten-year-old daughter. They were so inflexible with his care that it was getting him down. He heard the front door of his condo open, with Sue returning, and she called out, "Dad, you all right? I'm back with the medication and your bananas. Tomorrow I could make you a better breakfast than cereal and bananas."

"I like cereal and bananas. For god's sake, you've only been gone a while and come back asking if I'm all right. If I had died, I wouldn't be talking now. Sue, you need something more to do than just look after me. Go find a part-time job in Atlanta. Must be places that would love your management skills? Better still, don't you need to get things in order back home? Take my car and drive north for a few days."

"Dad, going to Clearville is a two-day drive, costs money, and I'll go when you're well."

"I'll give you travelling money, if you go now. I'll even pay you to go. I'm well. Stitches are itchy and healing. Sonny can check on me, and you need a few days to settle things back home. Sue, take a break, drive north. Just go."

"Yeah, I should see Annie, Peter, and my buddy Hank, but Allan isn't on my list of people to see. I could go. You do have Sonny in the building who will check up on you. She's a nice lady, but I'm not leaving you to go see my dumb husband."

"I don't care who you see." John stood up and handed Sue his car keys. "I had a heart attack, and recovering, like a million others. So go, clean up your affairs back home, get Annie's school records transferred here, and give us both a few day's rest. Sonny will check on me every day and you can call every night. I can't break a single rule with you here."

"You're okay with me leaving you, dad?"

"Are you hard of hearing? Sue, you're a lovely, caring daughter, but listen carefully, if you don't go, there's going to be a dead body in this room and I'll be charged with murder. Now, take Allie, head north, and I'll be just fine."

"Well, maybe, in a few days."

Her dad quickly interrupted, shouting toward the other room, "Allie, get your mom's suitcase. You're both going on a trip tomorrow."

* * * * *

"Are we almost there, mom?" Ten-year-old Allie was tired of the two-day drive from Atlanta to Plattsburgh, "I'm bored."

"Almost there, Allie. The lake on the right is Champlain and the green hills on the other side is Vermont, where you live."

"That's where my toys and good stuff is. Can we go and get them?"

"Afraid not sweetie, not today."

"Oh mom, I need them."

"And we need to find your uncle Peter's home before dark." Sue left interstate 87 at the exit south of Plattsburgh, and soon found Peter and his second wife Margaret, sitting on their wide verandah, waiting for their arrival. "What took you so long, sis, Maggie and I make Atlanta in one day, not two. Hi Allie, are you hungry? Ready for dinner?"

"We had a burger, uncle Peter, but I'm still hungry. Mom says I'm a bottomless pit."

"Maggie gave her a hug, "We have enough food here to fill a bottomless pit."

Sue gave her brother a brief hug, and her sister-in-law a longer embrace, "No dinner for me, Peter, all I need is to clean up and stop moving for a while."

"Nonsense, sis, dinner for two is ready."

"Peter, your sister can decide for herself." Maggie spoke softly, yet effectively it seemed, because he didn't object. Maggie continued, "Sue, you make yourself right at home, take a shower, relax, whatever you want. Peter can dish up for Allie, and I'll be on the verandah if you want to talk. Now go inside, kick off your shoes, it's your home."

Half an hour later, Sue fluffed her wet hair, and sat across from Maggie, "God, I might sell my daughter to have a great bathroom like yours; I could have showered in there for hours. Must have cost a fortune?"

"We've been lucky in life Sue, second marriage for both of us, professionals, no kids except for Peter's boy living with his first wife. And your brother is a workaholic. We have to spend the money on something and we both like this home. Now how's your dad? John seems to be recovering from surgery. Least he sounds his old self on the phone."

The screen door gently clicked open and shut as Peter joined them, "He's fine. When I called dad today, Sue, that women, Sonny, said they had just come back from a walk, and then put him on. Annie figures Sonny's moved in. How do you find her, Sue?"

"I like her and she hasn't moved in. She's good for dad. Hey, if Sonny answers the phone then we know dad's not alone, and that's a good thing. She's a nice lady."

The screen door squeaked open again, as Allie poked her head out, "Uncle Peter, can I turn on the big TV."

"Allie, you can watch whatever your mom lets you. But that's a special TV and you only get a good picture if you first get chips and soda from the kitchen. And Allie, did you see the round metal case on the TV stand?"

"Yep, I looked. It's a plastic ribbon. What is it uncle Peter?"

"Thirty years ago, Allie, that plastic ribbon was the latest technology. It's an 8mm film your grandfather took of our family, when your mom was the age you are now. We can watch it a little later with Maggie and your mom. I had it converted to digital display." As Allie went back inside, he asked, "Can she still be hungry after the dinner she had?"

"It's a symptom, Peter," Sue continued, "At home, with Allan ranting, Allie hardly ate anything, then, away from home she stuffs herself. She was fine, after a few days in Atlanta, then the drive here cranked her tension on again and she's stuffing again. I watch her carefully." But do I really? How long do kids remember the bad times?

"You've got problems on every side, Sue." Maggie said. "Marriage, your dad's heart, and Allie; you can't be as calm as you look. How can we help?"

"I've done a lot of thinking while watching dad get better in the Atlanta hospital, and seeing patients struggle. The hospital helped me get a different perspective on life, one of having the courage to follow my convictions. On the practical side I need stability, and that means getting away from Allan. But, I'm still married to the drunk, with a ten-year-old to raise, so I need a job. However, my honest conviction is - I should find out why my DNA doesn't make sense." Sue could see disagreement on her brother's face, so she continued, "So, stability, a job, and most important - a birth search. In spite of all the problems going on, the question of being adopted bugs me the most. It might not be logical... but I need answers as to how I fit into this world."

Peter continued, "Surely, your DNA tests can wait. You should be thinking of legally getting rid of Allan. Long as you're tied to him he's going to be trouble."

"I agree, Peter, but there's no money to get a divorce today or tomorrow, so what does it matter if I wait till next month or next year to split up. Besides, that will be my choice. But sitting by dad's bed in Atlanta, watching him sleep, breathe, get well, I realized that if dad died, we have lost a major link with the past. Mom died twenty years ago and, once dad goes, there's no one to ask about our childhood, or family facts, or why my DNA doesn't match."

"Sis, you're getting morbid. What's your point?"

"It's important to me." Don't you hear me?

"Listen to your sister, Peter." Maggie told him, and then turned to Sue, "You really fear being unable to solve the identity issues the cops are raising. Do I have that right?"

"Well, it was so long ago. Can it even be solved now?

Maggie, I feel set apart, fearful every day. I look in the mirror, and wonder who the hell that woman is. I feel disconnected, that time is slipping away. So, if I don't look for answers now, then when?"

" Dad's been no help and Peter you're being the same. When I start to ask questions, dad tells me the same as Peter, forget the past and get on with life. Maybe a man can forget it, sluff it off, get this adoption problem out of my mind. That's the main reason I drove here from Atlanta. I came to ask for help."

"We do want to help." Maggie returned to the adoption issue, "Sue, what about a baby mix-up? It happens. Hospitals have sent the wrong baby home. Can you check Canadian hospital records? Have you thought of that?"

"I've thought of that. The internet does have stories of baby mix-ups in the States and in Canada. But that moves me right back to square one, no job, no money, and no stability. How can I start a serious search of records?"

"Then settle here with us, Sue." Peter was speaking, "We'd love you and Allie to live with us - least for a while. Maggie and I have contacts to help get you established and find employment. Later, you can spend whatever time and money you want on tracing family stuff. Personally, for myself, I don't look back at the time we were kids. Don't even remember much of living in Georgia and can't see myself sitting down with dad now and asking questions of the past?"

"See how different we are: I need to look back. So far, I've had been fighting science, saying the DNA test must be wrong, but I can turn that around, and use science and records to figure out where this error could have happened in my life. Look, I read how the 911 sites in New York used fast and efficient tests for large numbers of people. Airplane crash sites like Harry's, or disasters, or digging up bodies from war - science asks questions but it also gives answers."

"Sue, air plane crash sites like Harry's, start with evidence and then make a match. It's not the same with you. When the lab says there is a family mismatch, they don't look any further."

"Peter, who knows what may show up. I need to start. Right now, in Argentina, more than 4000 relatives have given DNA samples, hoping to make a future match to any of the 30,000 people who disappeared during their country's dictatorship. Those relatives, today, are setting up a DNA data base to link with those killed over twenty-five years ago, and they are doing it because they need to understand themselves and their relatives. They started by asking questions. So I want to start asking questions now, to figure out how come my two tests say I'm not me. Or would you have me live in the dark?" Come on, smart boy, answer that.

The screen door squeaked open, Allie put her head out, asking, "You want a drink, mom?"

She must have heard my voice rising. "No thanks, Allie. How's uncle Peter's big TV?"

"Awesome. Can we get one?" The screen door squeaked closed, as Allie went back to the living room.

"She still checks on me every now and then." She continued talking, almost to herself, "I can't focus on jobs and things today, until I develop confidence. Never have been strong, but now, Allie needs to rely on me and that's why knowing who I am is just so important."

"I'll do my best to help, sis. Whatever you need." Peter answered his own question, "Let's watch the old movie dad made. It's the summer we vacationed in Panama City Beach. Florida was just great back then."

As the movie flickered, thirty-year-old images of the family came and went on the screen. Peter did the talking as usual. He talked of the cars on the beach, the endless white sand and what a fun weekend it had been. And the pictures didn't lie. It had been fun. Her dad must have taken most of the film as Peter, Harry, Sue and Annie ran in and out of scenes, clowning around on the beach, and splashing in the waves. Her mom seemed fine, not well nor ill, just sitting in the shade of an umbrella for sun protection. Peter pointed out empty stretches of dunes, "It's all changed to condo central now, and most of them for sale. And Sue, look, that's you and Harry, trying to build a sand castle. Remember that weekend Sue?"

"I remember building the sand castle with Harry, and you stomping all over it when I went swimming. Remind me to get even with you for wrecking our stuff."

Then an image from the film caught Sue's eye and she stopped thinking of wrecked sand castles. It was hard to explain the insight exploding in her mind. Her family was caught on film, all of them, waving from thirty years ago, and she realized just how different she looked from her siblings and parents. God, like a kid from a different family. A different child, one that had been dropped down to play with strangers, for a day on the beach.

The last frame had ended and Peter was asking. "Who wants to see this again?"

Sue shook her head. "Once is enough for me, Peter. Can I use your phone? If Annie can watch Allie for an hour tomorrow, there are school papers and business issues that need to be looked after in Clearville."

Maggie stood up, stretched, "Anyone tired? Another glass of wine?" Movie night was over. As Peter put the disk away, Maggie touched Sue's arm to delay her a moment, "You and I need to talk, and sooner the better. Perhaps tomorrow." Maggie paused a few moments, and added, "You're not the only one that has problems with this family."

Chapter 5

In the morning, with a sulking daughter scrunched down into the passenger seat, complaining of the injustices done to ten-year-olds, Sue drove the dozen miles south of Plattsburgh to Annie's home. Allison had one refrain from Peter's house till well past the airbase, "Mom, I'm not staying with old aunt Annie. I want to go with you to Clearville... please."

"Not a chance. My trip is doing grown-up business, Allie. Do you want to wait for hours, while I transfer your school files down to Atlanta?" There were no school files to be transferred on this trip, but if that excuse was good enough to tell her brother Peter, then it was good enough for her daughter. Sue said, "I won't be going near our house or your toys. So, sit up Allie, we're here, and hopefully your aunt Annie is home."

She wasn't home and her car wasn't in sight, so they waited. "Your grandmother used to say Annie was born a day late and that's why she's never on time." Sue parked her dad's car outside Annie's rented house, just past the empty drive. "Your aunt seems to be running a little late as usual." But that's what we always say about Annie.

Between beeps on the GameBoy, Allie asked. "Mom, how long do I have to stay with aunt Annie?"

"No more than a couple of years."

"Mom."

"A couple of hours, dear. Just long enough to see people over in Burlington."

"Could Annie drive me home while you're gone?" Allie

brightened at her own suggestion.

"No way. You don't go near our house without me, Allie. Remember that. I'll be here after lunch; we stay at uncle Peter's tonight, and tomorrow start driving back to Atlanta. Your granddad needs our help for the next weeks."

"Mom, what about my friends and school? Dad wants us home. He told me so. All my things are at home."

"Oh, don't keep going on, Allie. We'll get your stuff when I know where we are going to settle. And remember, when your dad tells you things, he means well, yet he can't always do as he says." How many times did he promise to change? "But you keep talking to dad, it's good for both of you."

"Yeah, well dad's getting a new bike for me, mom. It could be at our house now."

"I'd take you back home in a heart beat if I thought it would work, but you remember the fights and arguments? We can't live like that."

"But mom."

"Enough, get your game stuff ready, your aunt just pulled into her drive." Only half an hour late.

Annie Stevens was shorter than Sue, blonder, and moved with an easy confidence. As usual, she said the first thing on her mind, "Sue, that's not your car is it? Are you driving dad's car?"

"Like I can afford a Lexus, Annie. Of course it's dad's."

"He's never let me drive his car, not once. How do you rate?" Annie waved her niece from the car saying, "Hi Allie. Ready to do neat stuff, when your mom's gone?" She shook a little bag, "Pink nail polish for our toe nails and red polish for our fingers. Should we do that?"

Ten-year-olds are usually beyond pink toe nails. "If I have a choice, I'd like to go to the mall instead."

"Shopping. Now you're talking, Allie... there's a place in the mall, and we can see shoppers getting nose rings." She smiled at Sue. "Allie and I will be just fine. You want to come with us Sue, or is your hot date waiting in Burlington."

Will it always be sparring like this between us? "Annie one quick question. Do you have any phone numbers for mom's Canadian relatives? Why don't they ever contact us?"

"That's funny, asking me for old phone numbers when I have a hard time remembering my own. No, not one. We lost touch because we never contacted them. Mom set them all aside."

"Well I'd like to get in touch. I'm looking for anything to fill in the past."

"Sue, concentrate on Allan and get that part of your life sorted."

No comment. "Thanks for looking after Allie. Be back in a couple of hours, three at most." As Sue pulled away from the curb, Annie smiled, and shouted to her, asking if it were all right to get Allie a tattoo at the mall. "Just a little one."

Sue had no plans to transfer her daughter's school files to Atlanta, that pretense had only been so Peter wouldn't worry about her being on Allan's side of the lake. She crossed Lake Champlain on the southern car ferry, landing directly into Burlington, Vermont, parked near the restaurant and found her friend. Henry Mantes was not smiling. He waved her over to his table, and spoke without any greeting," You must know I'm still pissed at you. You disappeared while I worried that Allan could have gone nuts and bashed your head in. You were going to call me, remember, then, bang - no more Sue in Clearville. You don't act that way to a friend."

"Hank, my life exploded that week. I did call you from Atlanta to stay in touch and, now, I've come to you for help."

"That's just using me? Leaving without a word, now you're back asking for help, and, what makes it worse is I'm listening."

"Hank, after my dad's heart attack, Allan turned violent. I closed the bedroom door seconds before his beer bottle smashed into it." Sue, shivered in recall, then continued, "The next day, it was his breakfast scattered over the kitchen for me to clean up, and as I watched the milk and cereal drip, two things were absolutely clear. First, it was getting dangerous for me to leave Allan, and second, it was far more dangerous to stay. Simple as that. Time to leave. So, after he went to work, me and Allie caught a bus for Atlanta and I deliberately didn't call you that morning because I didn't want to involve you. But now I need help."

Hank leaned forward, moving his body just in from the edge of the table. "Everyone who knew you realized you were living in a mess. So let me ask point blank - is your marriage over, Sue?"

"Hanging by a thread, but, it needs to be clear, today is not about my marriage. Maybe it will end, but right now I don't have energy or money to make a break legal. Besides, there's Allie; Allan is her father and ten-year-old girls need a father in their life, even if he is a bastard. I'm not whining over the past, nor trying to get another man in my life. What I need is a good friend, someone to help balance my fears and wrong thinking. Hank, I desperately need someone on my side. Someone to trust."

"Someone who could become more than just a friend?"

"We've already been there, haven't we? Years ago, when I finished high school, somehow fate pushed us apart then, and I'm not sure it's pulling us back together now." Susan sat back from the table, folded her arms and looked directly at Henry Mantes, saying, "We lost touch with each other and then both made bad marriages. You had the sense to get out of yours, quick, but it's harder for a girl to leave." Sue knew she had to make Hank feel her honesty, "I'm asking your help Hank to sort questions about my birth. No hidden benefits attached. No old romance, no heading for bed, no future expectations, just your help to assist me." She went off on a tangent, asking, "Hank, why did you never marry again?"

"Just didn't happen for me. While it's hard for a girl to get out of a bad marriage it's also hard for a guy to find a good one. Sort of once burned twice shy feelings." Also, why remarry when my number one girl is still married to a mean drunk. "I never stopped being your friend, Sue, so how can I help? Where do you want to start? What are you looking for Sue?"

"I've decided to accept the science that says there is no biological connection to my family. I won't fight the fact but now I still want to know why or how it happened? And I need you because you understand police work, you know how to look and where to look and, as a friend, you can help me unravel just who I am because I don't have a clue where to start searching."

Henry Mantes showed exasperation. "Sue, you have my support, but I know nothing of genealogy."

For the first time since sitting down with Hank, she relaxed. "So I have your support? Dad and the family are there for me, but they don't feel my need to find an answer - for they don't see my birth as a problem. Dad swears all my birth happenings are in order and he keeps saying if these new tests are getting me upset then just forget them."

Hank feigned a slow southern drawl, saying, "Leaving problems alone can be good advice, little lady."

"For god's' sake Hank, whose life do I get on with if I don't know who I am? Where do I start looking? You're a detective."

"A Sheriff. I find bad guys, Sue, not solve family history. Remember, the police resources available to me have little bearing on birth and medical records you might need. And I'm no expert in searching out old families. But given those minor limitations, and understanding that any help I give you is on my own time, then I suggest you start your search by looking at actual records."

"What do you mean by actual records?"

"Don't rely on family memories or hearsay. Check everyone's birth certificate, yours, your mom, dad, brother. Everyone in the family who was alive around the time of your birth. Then if possible, marriage certificates, even driver's licence, and keep notes, making sure of your facts. Even contact distant relatives. All of this will take time and some of the certificates may be hard to get. But right now, start your search in Atlanta."

"Atlanta? Because my dad is there."

"Exactly. Who better understands your birth?"

"Hank, dad's never talked of the past. He's always been a quiet guy." In fact, he seldom talks of mom or the times they were raising us kids. "When I start talking of the old days, dad gets me off track. I can't do this by myself? Is it possible, just possible, that you could take a few days off and be in Atlanta when I talk to dad. You could get a feel for what he wants to talk about and what he wants to avoid. Now, don't start shaking your head no. I talked to dad, and he's well aware I'm going to ask you for help. And coming to Atlanta."

Hank leaned forward, and interrupted Sue, "He'll just love me. Families just love it, when a stranger digs into their past." Hank stopped for a minute, then continued, "Sue, you don't want me to be actively involved in your search at the family level. Poking into the past is sensitive."

"You won't be involved - only listening. Coach me on asking questions while you check the answers. No spy stuff. It's all in the open and dad has agreed. I need you in Atlanta for a few days. Even just a long weekend. Dad's okay with it all."

"Sue, what happens if I tick your family off and then, later, you and I get closer? Could be hard feelings develop with my future relatives."

"Not going to happen. I've cleared everything with him."

"Did he truly say he wants me in Atlanta, to sniff around his families past?"

Sue smiled, toyed with her food for a moment while she thought, then said, "Dad's first choice was getting Indiana Jones, but you came second."

Hank didn't say yes or no. He consulted a well-worn note book before replying, "My best advice is for you to drop the quest. Head back to Atlanta, set all the family searching aside, and just take it easy till you get over Allan. You've had constant pressure since Christmas with Harry being killed, problems at home and being on your own now. You need a rest, not chasing family stuff."

Sue hadn't expected a refusal, "You're flatly turning me down?"

Hank talked past her interruption, "But I know you won't give up on this DNA problem. If your dad will cooperate as you say, then I'll come to Atlanta. Give me a few days to swing vacation time and expect me down south in a couple of weeks." Spending time with you in Atlanta might lead somewhere. "Now, you may not solve your birth issues for a long time if ever. But, on the other hand, it will be a vacation for me and perhaps, just perhaps, you and I will click again, rekindle something between us. It could happen."

"Hank," Susan was smiling, "you're marvellous. Dad will take you to a Braves game. God I can't stay calm. This can work. I'm sure of it. Hank, there's no romance intended, but I'll hug you tight when you arrive."

Hank wanted to touch her hands but instead reached out with words, "You'll be busy getting certificates, documents, anything helpful. And don't forget the photos."

"What photos?"

"Family photos view the past and if you were adopted then..."

"There's no adoption. Dad has a picture of mom carrying me out of the hospital in Milton, Canada, and a picture of mom pregnant just a few months before in California. Hank, I'm not trying to prove an adoption, I'm trying to nail down my birth. Once I have all my birth facts, it could explain why my DNA is a problem."

"Well I can't explain it, and I stayed at a Holiday Inn Express last night." His joke made Sue smile. "Here's the plan: return to Atlanta, look after your dad, and start sorting through any childhood facts you can uncover. See what makes sense and what doesn't. If you get stuck, or run into brick walls, e-mail me. Then, I'll join you soon to see what we can accomplish together."

Sue wiped tears from her eyes, "I'm not going to cry, but I was afraid you would refuse to help."

The phony drawl was back. "Okay little lady. We've got us a deal, to find the varmint who messed with your DNA. Tell your dad the posse is riding to Atlanta."

"God it's a relief getting you on my side. You're my hero today, Hank. Now I must go and get Allie from my sister before she thinks I've abandoned her. When's the next ferry?"

Hank watched her drive on the car ferry and stood at the pier until the ship was a spec on the lake. Shaking his head and thinking at the same time, "That lady is something else. I just can't seem to say 'no' to her."

When Sue arrived in Plattsburgh, she realized there was no need to have rushed back: Annie and Allie were seriously into a video game and didn't even say hello. Finally, Sue asked, "Annie, do you know where your birth certificate is? I need a copy."

"Damn, Sue, don't mess up my game like that. You've always spoiled my concentration, since we were kids. We had better stop Allie, cause I can't beat you. Now what did you want, Sue? My important papers are in the junk drawer in the kitchen. Help yourself."

Sue only found junk in the junk drawer, but a folder on the counter behind the coffee maker was marked important in a black marker. That's what she wanted. "Annie, it's dangerous to leave personal information out like that."

"Why?"

"Someone could snatch it. Cause problems."

"How tragically tragic." Annie laughed, "Someone could steal my bad credit rating and pile of debts. Does that mean I wouldn't have to pay any bills? Get real sis, who wants my identity?"

We're from different planets, Annie. "I'll go to a copy centre now and be back with the originals. Allie, round up your games and thank your aunt for minding you."

"Mom, I want to stay longer."

Ten minutes later, Sue returned Annie's papers with thanks, "Why don't you come to Peter's and make it a family dinner tonight?"

"Can't sister. Macho date tonight, but say 'hi' to Peter and Maggie. I'll see them soon. Today was fun, Allie. We'll do it next time you're here. Bye now, and take care of dad in Atlanta."

After dinner, when Sue repeated Annie's promise of visiting, Peter said, "Never. She won't drop by and we all know it. Only says it to please people. She sees how we live, compares it to herself, and feels uncomfortable. She means well, but our Annie's a very nice, kind, flake."

"Our Annie isn't the jealous kind, Peter."

"Peter has it wrong as usual." Maggie spoke in an even tone. "Annie doesn't come here often, because my husband can be very boring. Now I'm not being critical Peter, and boring can be good. But can you imagine a world where everyone counted their change each night?"

Allie spoke up. "Annie and me - we had a good time today. She said we might get a tattoo next time."

Sue continued her praise, "Annie can be my official babysitter any time." Sue turned to Peter saying, "Can you give me a copy of your birth certificate tonight to save mailing it to me in Atlanta."

"My birth certificate? Why? What possible use do you want it for?"

"Background information for my birth search. I know you were born five years and one month before me, but I'd just like to have a copy. Is there a problem?"

"Yes, there's a problem. Can't be too careful in protecting my identity these days. You don't need a copy."

"I do. What a difference between you and Annie. She's not worried over identity and you're paranoid. Peter, can I have your precious certificate or not?" Why are you making such an issue over nothing? "I promise not to give the information to the Russians. Promise!"

"Peter, I wouldn't trust your sister; she may be a national threat." Maggie told him.

"You two are not very funny. It's just the right principle to be careful. Oh, all right, I'll scan you a copy. And will you two stop ganging up on me." He went to his office to make a copy.

Maggie said, "What you just witnessed a big part of my problems. Sue, he is extremely distrustful of everyone and everything. And, in the few weeks since your dad became ill, Peter is acting worse. At first I figured it was my imagination, but it's not. He's so irritable most of the time now that I don't think he even likes himself anymore. He's getting harder to live with."

"That's just Peter. My brother has always been an uptight guy, Maggie."

"Uptight, yeah, I knew that when we got together, but now

he's a weird, uptight guy. Emphasis on weird. Wait. He's coming back now." She raised her voice a notch, "For a dessert its ice cream and peaches. And for a second choice you can have peaches and ice cream." Maggie shouted over the TV in the family room, "Come and help with dessert, Allie."

The opportunity to continue the private talk between Sue and Maggie never happened, neither then nor the next morning; Peter was always inconveniently nearby. Talking in confidence with Maggie would have to wait. So, with the car packed, Allie hugged Peter and Maggie in the morning, and Sue started south toward Albany, on her return drive to Atlanta.

Weeks later, John Peter Stevens heard Sue and Allie giggling in the living room over a GameBoy game, and counted himself lucky to have his daughter looking after his health. He may not mention it, but he was glad to have her. "Sue, what time do you expect Hank tomorrow? And do you need Sonny to watch Allie? The thing is I've got bridge on tomorrow night."

"Dad, I don't need to have your condo empty. He's just a friend who isn't staying here and I'm not sleeping at his motel. You'll like the man Hank has become. He's no longer the skinny kid, hanging round our place in Plattsburgh, so often, mom would always invite him to dinner."

"I remember Hank having a tough home life. Mom would have him to dinner, cause he didn't get much to eat at home." John continued, "I have no problem with Hank coming here to talk, but I still question his going through our family history. You sprang that on me when you returned from Plattsburgh. I won't cause a fuss, but I don't like strangers looking at family stuff."

A while later he went to his bedroom, closed the door, and

from his closet hauled an old cardboard box just chock full of pictures and family memorabilia. First, he removed an envelope of papers, squirreled it away in his sock drawer, and then took the tattered old box into the living room. "Is this what you're looking for, Sue?"

"That's it. Where did you find mom's box of pictures?"

"Bottom of my closet. Now you and Hank handle this with care, copy what you want but don't keep my originals. You can go through it, but put everything back just the way mom left it."

"Great. Must be years of memories here? Wow, everything's here! Allie, Allie, come see your aunt Annie's picture, when she was your age. I blindfolded her."

Sue turned to her dad, "Thanks. And remember, Hank won't be snooping into family stuff for himself. It's for me. He's only trying to help me, dad."

Chapter 6

Spring arrived early in Atlanta, and spring brings warm weather and the start of baseball. Fans were already talking of winning their division this year and, of course, the World Series. Hank figured taking John to a game might help them to bond a little. So they were sitting in the afternoon sun, watching the Braves trying to come from behind. John was saying, "This is a treat for me. Thanks for getting the tickets."

"Sue figured you'd like an afternoon ball game. A little appreciation for all the photos we scattered around your place in the last few days."

"My daughter says you're heading back to Vermont soon. I figured you'd be staying a second week, Hank."

"I did too, but the Vermont Sheriff's Department wants the staff back in Clearville - something big is happening back home."

They watched the game for a while longer and Hank then asked, "You want a beer?"

"Not in this hot sun. After the game, burgers and beer will be good."

Braves fans were grumbling, restless for action going their way. With Philly leading five to three in the seventh, the Atlanta crowd yelled at Alfasca to pitch a third out - but Philly's Thome on first, wouldn't cooperate: interfering, inching off the bag, he taunted Alfasca, slowly increasing his lead toward second. Thome rocked forward and back, moving just enough to break Alfasca's concentration on Wolf at bat. Everyone waited. Alfasca's throws to first, Thome stepped back on base and mockingly brushes off imaginary dust. Alfasca finally settles down, ignores Thom, throws to the batter, pops up to third, batter out, side retired. Alfasca spits toward first and walks off the field. Typical baseball. Waiting, waiting, then bing, action, a third out to start the seventh inning stretch. Everyone stood up.

Knowing the Braves aren't going to place this one in the win column, the crowd starts to thin out, and John turned to Hank, "Good getting out, but this afternoon is almost over so, perhaps, you had better tell me what's really on your mind. Have you found anything to help Sue get the adoption issue out of her mind?"

Hank laughed, replying, "Am I that transparent? John, I wanted to see a game with you, but, it's true, today is more than baseball. There are a few loose ends in your marriage I don't quite understand. Can we go for a burger now and talk of some hiccups I see in your story?"

"Just you and I, without Susan?" John voiced surprise.

"That's just the point. Without Susan, it might make our talk easier."

"So far you've been a nice guy today, Hank, so don't disappoint me and turn into a bad cop."

"John, my questions are the ones Sue wants to ask. This is for her."

After ordering their burgers, beer for John and coffee for Hank, John could wait no longer and asked, "Well, get on with it, Hank, start your prying. What discrepancies in my life story bother you?"

"You remember the past easily, and nothing stands out as contradictory - except the few events that you don't mention. To start with your memory is vague on Sue's birth and that stands in contrast to the detailed memories of the birth of your other three kids. They you recall well, but almost nothing on Sue. I've listened to you and Sue talk of early family days for a week, and your one blank spot seems to be on Sue. It stands out like a sore thumb. Second, you're equally fuzzy on facts and dates during the early years after Sue's birth. I know the Air Force had you stationed in California, while your wife and kids were in Georgia, but you must have some memories from those years. And as for the present, why do you continually say there is no problem with her birth and also downplay any need for Sue to search her birth records?"

Despite Hanks criticism, John still managed a smile, "You're testing my memory back 30 and 40 years. Do you think your recall will be sharp when you reach my age?"

"I'll grant you memories fade, but this is more. Some facts from her birth don't add up. They can't possibly all be true. Let me explain."

The atmosphere at their table suddenly turned cold. "You know how to spoil the day, Hank. It's normal for memory to fade. When you get to be my age, your memory won't be sharp either." A typical cop, trying to push people around. "And saying facts don't add up is accusing me of lying. You've wrapped it up in nice neat words but say it - you and Sue think I'm lying."

John sighed, "Hank, you're looking into my family details as if it were just a puzzle to be solved but, for me, this is my life and it's both personal and family. For thirty-five years, my daughter never questioned her birth, until a DNA test shows up, and now her respected dad becomes a suspected liar. That hurts. I understand the science mismatch and, her concern, but I can't explain it. I'd tell Sue if I could explain, but I can't. However, there are no birth details being hidden." John stopped, made direct, unwavering eye contact with Hank, and continued, "I don't like where this conversation is going, and if you have more questions then get them on the table quick cause I'm leaving soon. What specifically is bothering you?"

Hank continued, "It's only understood in context, so bear with me. All right, you met your future wife, Joanna Court, in Oakville, Ontario, in '61 and married the next year, in June of '62, at her folk's place. Then joined the Air Force and lived off-base in Plattsburgh, New York, where your first child, Peter, was born. Right, so far?"

John had calmed down and continued now to tell his own story in detail, "Exactly. Peter came in the summer of '63 and that day is clear. We were at Carvers Restaurant, when Joanna announced the baby was coming. The restaurant servers got in a flap, and we made the hospital just in time. My mom came from Georgia to help, because Joanna became ill in the hospital after Peter's birth. Other than that, we were a happy young couple starting a family life. I must have told you that Carvers named a special sandwich 'The Peter' after us: baby onions, baby dills, and little stuff. Plattsburgh was good to us. That's why Peter and Annie choose to live there today."

Hank asked, "And Harry and Annie, where were they born?"

"Annie, my Georgia Peach, was conceived in Georgia and born in the fall of '64, in Plattsburgh, New York. Joanna was ill after Annie's birth, and stayed in the hospital for a while, but we coped with help from my mom again. Then Harry, the true family redneck, was born in Georgia two years later if I recall rightly, while we were visiting my folks."

John needed no prompting to rerun his old memories now, "Back then in December '66, with Vietnam heating up, the Air Force posted me to Point Mugu, California. Joanna and the kids joined me briefly around spring of '67, and we were billeted in Oxnard and later in Ventura. A funny thing back then, I used to complain of gas at thirty cents a gallon, that I couldn't afford to keep the family on the beach and commute to the base. But Joanna and the kids loved

Ventura so we stayed. I bought expensive gas and commuted to Mugu."

Hank interrupted, "In all the photos, you seemed a happy bunch. You have so many good family pictures, stretching from your Oakville wedding till the summer of '67."

"That was Joanna. She had a thing for family stuff. Queen of mementoes. Even saved rocks from the beaches."

Without changing tone, Hank asked, "Why did they stop, John?"

"Why does what stop?"

"You have no pictures between the summer of '68 to fall of '72. Boxes of photos before and after, but in the years spanning Sue's birth, no pictures at all. What's the reason? Did the camera get lost? You see John, there must be a good reason to have the family tradition of taking photos change just when Sue comes into the family."

"Very observant Hank, but there's no sinister meaning. While I was in California, Joanna eventually had four kids to look after and I guess money was tight. Besides, Joanna and I weren't always getting along. Every marriage has problems and the summer of '67 started a bad stretch. Joanna worried I would be killed, when the Air Force pegged me for a 'Nam transfer. Also, Joanna and our kids were staying with my folks in Georgia, and I didn't realize the friction that had developed between her and my father. They were just an oil and water thing that didn't mix. As for the photos, I guess she stopped taking pictures. Perhaps, she misplaced the camera or anything; I just don't know. She was depressed. Hated the war and hated thinking of me going to 'Nam. The pictures stopped because she stopped taking pictures. No big deal."

"All right, leave the camera question. Did you ship out?"

"No. The Air Force decided to handle my systems work State's side, so I stayed at Mugu while the family remained in Georgia with my parents."

"And Joanna's pregnancy with Sue?"

"It wasn't divine intervention, Hank." John laughed, then turned serious, "Actually, it's none of your god-damned business Hank, however, I'll tell you. Joanna got pregnant with Sue the usual way, some time after Christmas of '67 when I was on leave with the family in Georgia. Then, in spring of '68, Joanna came to Mugu and told me she was expecting."

"Had you planned a fourth child?" When John didn't answer, Hank waited.

John brought his hand down on the table, hard, causing the bartender to glance their way. "For god's sake, Hank. Some family issues are private. What's the point of asking? "

Hank struck back, "Hey, don't yell at me, when these questions are from Sue."

"Then you and Sue are asking too much." John could feel his pulse racing. He didn't want these family questions.

Hank waited a moment, then added, "John, humour me, I'm almost finished. You were talking of Joanna being pregnant with Sue,"

Eventually John continued, "We didn't plan Sue, we love her dearly and would have it no other way, but she was coming at a bad time, all mixed with a troubled war and me being ready to fly out. So we argued bitterly over the war, the pregnancy, everything. Joanna hated Military issues and refused to understand my duty to serve America." John stared into space before continuing, "To be fair, looking back then, I didn't understand either her fear for me or her desperation to get out of staying with my folks. Or the pressure of expecting another kid. That spring, when Joanna visited me in California, she was afraid I would be upset when she told me of expecting another kid. And that is just what happened. When she told me of the new baby, I confirmed her fears, got mad, and we argued for weeks. The pictures of her being pregnant on the beach, posing with the family, we look happy, but we argued all the while she was there."

John thought of those days before continuing, "So I said an angry good-bye to Joanna in Mugu, and she took our three kids back to my folks in Georgia, endured a few months longer there, and then her life exploded." John hesitated and then continued emphatically, saying, "I've already told you of Joanna's monster fight with my dad. You know the kind of fight, where anything festering in your craw for the last zillion years is all spit out in anger. Dad was right-wing American military, stubborn, inflexible and always right. Pit him against free-thinking Joanna who had an iron streak down her spine that no one could break, and you can understand the tension. He was obstinate, but she was smart and could always win in a battle of words. They fought hammer and tong, until Joanna just stopped arguing that summer of '68, leaves our three kids with my folks, and goes to visit her folks in Canada. She was telling my dad, 'listen you old red neck, I'll do whatever the hell I want. That's how Joanna came to be in Canada, when Sue was born."

Hank had a question from that past. "Wait a second, Joanna just walked out and left her three kids? Just walked out on babies. Does that make sense?"

John shook his head, "No, no, no, you don't get it, Hank. The youngest was a toddler by then and none were abandoned. My parents looked after them, and then Sue was born in Canada far sooner than we expected. She delivered prematurely in August of '68. The Air Force flew me to Toronto, and I drove the three of us back to Georgia. Thank god my wife and dad scaled down the war between them. They never argued again, nor were they friendly, although, years later, not long before he died, my dad called Joanna for a comforting talk. She never told me what they talked about, just said it was comforting." John opened his hands wide. "That's it. No mystery involved with Susan's birth. No more questions."

Hank replied, "Just one more fact to understand, John. The day after Joanna delivers Sue, you fly to Canada, and a few days later, you drive the new baby back to Georgia. Is that how it happened?"

John nodded, "It did. The Air Force arranged an immediate flight from California to Toronto. I rented a car and drove Joanna and little Sue to Atlanta. That's how it happened."

Hank continued, "It all makes sense except for Sue's birth being more than a month premature. How could the hospital quickly release a premature baby? Does that timing make sense to you?"

"Hank, this was the '60's, when you didn't question doctors. They gave us our Sue; we left the hospital, and if I remember correctly, my biggest worry then was keeping the future peace between my wife and dad. So, what does a few weeks premature matter?"

"Premature birth is always critical. You must know that even today, a few weeks premature is serious, but in the '60's, no hospital would release Sue because, just by your calculation alone, she was over a month premature. Back then, those tiny babies stayed in the hospital. Always. No exception."

John stood, ready to leave, "There's nothing I can say now to have you believe me, Hank. So, Susan was tiny and we took her home. Now leave it alone. I'm finished."

Hank handed John a small hospital baby photo, and continued, "Fine. But it's still a mystery. How can Susan be premature, when her hospital baby picture shows a chubby little baby?"

John stared at the card, then crossed his arms and glared at Hank, "You know, Hank, the way you cherry-pick facts, I imagine you could say the South won the Civil War and Grant surrendered to Lee. That thinking would make many folks in Georgia very happy. Let's pay the bill and get home. I'm finished talking," But he continued to stare at the photo. "It happened like I'm telling you Hank, ergo, premature birth." John stood and threw more than enough money on the table to cover their food. "Ready."

Hank stayed seated, insistent, "Look at the back of the photo. Susan's baby picture has a hospital stamp - a notation of seven pounds four ounces. That's a full term child."

Silence. John remained standing and a minute passed before he said, "Susan is my daughter, Joanna is her mother, and you are an outsider who is butting into our family affairs. Just leave it all alone."

"Okay. Consider it finished." Hank shrugged, and gave a half smile to let the tension ebb. Finally saying, "You don't have to listen to me again. It's your daughter you will need to talk with."

"I'll handle Sue and if you don't say another word, there's a chance we can part on a friendly note." God, you're one persistent bugger, Hank, to get up my nose like you do.

Only later, within sight of Hank's motel, did John say more, "When my wife died years ago, I never felt so alone. It all came back with Harry's death, and now there's a chance that Sue is drifting away. I can't have her leave. But now, she stays in my condo and I see her looking, wondering all the time, if I'm her real dad. Hank, families get torn apart over misunderstandings like this, and I don't want to lose Sue."

Hank nodded and remained quiet as John continued, "Sue's our baby. Peter doesn't need me and, for years, we were at odds. Annie, she's special, but only calls when she needs something. But Sue and Allie are drifting away from me and that's so unfair when I've been telling you the truth all this time. There is no mystery of her birth."

Hank turned toward him in the car, "John, for what it's worth, I don't think you're lying, and Sue doesn't question your word. From all you have said over the last week, it would seem you have no more idea of why Sue has different DNA than she does. But she is different. So, the issue is not your lying, but the unexplained facts of DNA.

John replied, "Then if you believe me, help me out with Susan's baby picture. Slip it back into our photo box without saying anything to Sue. Why upset her? Can you do that? For Sue's peace of mind."

Hank shook his head, "I didn't find the photo. Sue spotted the weight on the back of her baby picture and was stunned. She realized it couldn't fit a premature birth. She arranged our baseball tickets today - thinking you might talk to me easier than to her. Our getting together, today, was her idea."

John took his eyes from the road and concentrated on Hank, "Why didn't Sue show me the baby picture?" He pounded down on the steering wheel and the horn blasted. A few other drivers gave him a brief glance and wrote him off as an angry driver.

Hank opened wide his hands, "I think she was afraid of what you might say. How does a kid approach a parent over a birth issue like this? Sue believes you, but still feels something is being covered up. Remember, for months you have said she should ignore her identity problem. So she figured there must be something you know and that, perhaps, you could tell me. A man to man talk."

Johns felt tired. "Some family dynamics - Susan is frightened of losing me, and I'm frightened of losing her. There has to be a way to repair our trust, but I won't lie to suit your wrong-headed facts. Hank, you may be a great guy, but I'm sorry you ever came to Atlanta. Now here's your motel, and I hope you get an early start to Vermont. Good night."

It was late when Sue had finished washing the dinner dishes, stacking them on the drain board to dry, and still her dad had not come home. Hank had called hours ago, telling her that, "He's upset at the baby photo and angry, because we keep questioning his word. So, take it easy with your dad, because he thinks we're calling him a liar. He will be an unhappy man, when he comes home."

But he didn't come home for dinner. Sue thought, perhaps, this is a fitting kind of revenge for my teenage years. Now it's dad out late, while I stay home and worry. I'll get Allie in bed and e-mail Peter and Annie. See if they have any suggestions to keep dad happy.

Sue was writing her e-mail to Peter when her dad phoned, a little put out. "I've been trying to get you for hours. Your line has been busy."

"I was talking with Maggie, dad, and Allie was on the phone a bit. Are you okay? You're not upset I've shared all this family stuff with Hank? You want a late dinner when you get home?"

"No supper needed, Sue. I visited mom for a talk tonight, then I left the cemetery and drove to Macon for a fish dinner at Barbies. You know the place, just south of the 75 bypass."

"You drove all that time, dad, while I sat at home and worried?"

"I tried calling. Driving to Barbies gave me time to think. And listen. On the way there and back I could hear mom saying - 'listen to your kids, you old fool, just listen' and she's right. I haven't been listening very much, but I'm changing and I'm going to help. There are always ways to solve problems and I've come up with a plan. Now, I'll be late tonight, so don't wait up. We can talk it over in the morning."

"Talk what over?"

"Tell you the details tomorrow. I'll be back too late tonight for talking."

"Okay, dad, and watch your night driving."

"What night driving? I'm calling from Sonny's condo, and we want to chat for a while so don't wait up for me."

Later, snug in his own bed, John had a restless dream, where neither time nor geography made sense. Atlanta had moved north, smack against the Ontario border, and John's front door opened onto a bridge to Canada. When he tried to walk forward, he couldn't move past a line in the sand. He struggled in vain. He turned to some woman with long black hair who lifted one finger and stopped him. "No military here. No uniforms allowed."

John's dream faded as the lady smiled, "We are not a uniform land, you have to go." In the morning, he felt surprisingly refreshed. His decision of last night and his dream were now a plan of action that made sense.

Atlanta sunshine spilled across their breakfast table, highlighting crumbs of toast into sparking jewels, as John laid out his idea, "Sue, I want to act decisively to end any doubt in your mind that I may know of a hidden meaning to your birth misunderstanding. I know you're my daughter and I don't think you really question it either, but since the DNA tests, a cloud of doubt needs to be dispelled. And we won't get past this cloud by looking in Atlanta. This city had nothing to do with your birth, right? We need to look elsewhere. Second, our living space in this condo gets cramped. It's small and we get on top of each other so, I figure, we all need a break for a little while."

"How can you want Allie and me gone from the condo? Dad, I've no money to go anywhere else."

"Calm down. I'm saying we need a break now, to just get away for a while. As for later, when we come back, Sonny wants you to have her spare room for sleeping. Allie can stay here at night, and you can use Sonny's spare room. Give us more living space when we get back."

"Back from where, dad?"

"Canada. See your relatives. My plan is we drive there. You think there might be a baby mix-up in your past so, all right, let's go and find out. I called Hank last night at his motel, and he thinks my plan is good. I also called Peter last night, and he'll be glad to have you back. When Hank leaves today or tomorrow, you go north with him to Plattsburgh."

"Dad, I've just come back from Peter's."

"This is different." John felt Sue becoming receptive, so he went on, "We're going to visit your mom's relatives in Canada. You drive north to Peter's place first, then I talk to my doctors here and follow with Allie in a couple of days. We spend a day at Peter's, then drive to Oakville, Ontario, where you can ask all the birth questions you want."

"Canada. It could work. Can we find the hospital where I was born?"

"Absolutely."

"I'd love it. People would remember my birth. What a great idea."

"Bound to be some relatives still alive who knew you as a baby. Perhaps, find details of your birth to ease your fears. Now, I haven't contacted our Canadian cousins yet, but I'll get it done today. Must be some of your mom's relatives still alive up there?"

" I'll have to call Allie's school before leaving with Hank, but there is nothing else to hold us back. A Canadian vacation is a wonderful idea. Can I take some of mom's old letters to show our cousins?"

"Old letters? What, old letters of Joanna's?"

"Her old love letters. They were in the photo box, and I'd like to read them on the trip. Please, dad."

John couldn't think of a good reason to refuse, so he simply nodded 'yes.'

"I'll call Hank now and then get packing. We could leave tomorrow morning."

When Sue told Allie, her daughter whispered, "Are we going home, mom?"

Sue hugged her daughter, "Sweetie, I know you miss your friends, but we can't go home now." Seeing disappointment in her daughter's eyes, added, "There's one thing we can try. Maybe your dad can bring a box of toys to uncle Peter's house. I'll ask him. Now, do you think you and grampy will be all right driving for a few days." When Allie nodded, Sue continued, "Hank and I drive first and after you and grampy arrive, we'll go and meet your Canadian cousins." And from the back of her mind she added to herself, and I take charge of my life.

Later, with Allie asleep and Sue packed, John asked her directly, "It's none of my business Sue, but Hank likes you a lot. You two planning a future?"

"Our timing is not good. Right now my crystal ball shows a dark future. For a number of reasons I can't reach for Hank, although he wants me. I'm in a bind with my marriage and can't afford another bad choice in men. It was a regretful marriage, and Allie is the only good result."

John was direct. "Then get a divorce and move on."

"Easy to say, dad, but it's not as simple from a woman's perspective." Sue took a few moments to get her thoughts in order. Thinking, you may as well know the worst, dad, she continued talking, "It's complicated dad, really, really complicated." A minute passed before she added, " There's no easy way to tell you but I'm expecting, and Allan is the father."

John had sense to know, that when you don't know what to say, it's best to say nothing. He remained quiet as Sue continued in a strong voice, "It happened one night before your heart attack. I wasn't sure till just a few weeks ago, and I've only told you."

Sue continued, "There are choices, dad. Hank being one, but I won't try to snare him or hurt him. Hank has had a tough life. His family fell apart after his dad died..."

John had known Hank's dad, knew he had been an amputee from Vietnam. "Hank's dad died with a lot of good men, because our politicians didn't have the guts to fight the war the way we could have." John calmed down, and added, "Now you get an early night. I'll stay up a while."

With Sue in the shower and Allie asleep John, finally, had the privacy he needed. He retrieved an old address book from the back of his dresser drawer and then phoned long distance.
"Hello, Fred? It's John Stevens calling. I'm in Atlanta now. Fred, reason for calling is we're going to be in Canada in a few days, and if it's all right, can we come and see you? Is your wife, Maria, there?"

"John." Maria had a strong, distinctly sexual voice, "Fred says you're, finally, making a trip to see us? I'm surprised, very pleased, but surprised. How many are coming?"

"Three of us - me, Sue, and her daughter Allie. Think it's time for a little family reunion. Let the cousins know of each other."

"Be tickled pink to see you all. Any of Joanna's family is welcome with us. Don't make it a short visit - plan on staying a while."

"I'll call again when I get to my son's home in Plattsburgh, and if you arrange a two-bedroom motel close by, then we can visit without camping in your living room."

"Lands sakes, finally getting to see Sue and - what's her daughter's name - Allison. I'm just tingling to see my niece and grandniece. What does Allison like to eat?" In the back of Maria's mind, behind her excitement the wheels were spinning. John, you've ignored us for all these years. Why come north now? I bet you want something. Maria only said, "Glad you're coming."

"Maria, one thing to mention - my daughter Sue is a little fragile just now, working out a marriage separation, so she might go off on tangents asking questions in her delicate frame of mind. So do me a favour Maria, if Joanna's problems come up, make light of it. please. No point in opening that can of worms. So just be tactful, please."

Same old John, trying to control everyone. "I won't lie but I agree, why dwell on bad times. Reunions are celebrations. Is Sue depressive, did that cause problems in her marriage?"

"Not at all. But you two can talk a blue streak over her interest in family history. I'm hoping this visit perks her up."

"Lands sakes, then come as soon as you can, John."

"Counting on you to welcome us, Maria."

"Just come up, leave today, or now, and come up. Tell Sue I'll give her a big hug when you get here." All the while Maria was thinking, what a two-faced devil you are John. You ignore us for years and now call out of the blue. The main trouble with family relations is having people like you around. But she only said, "Glad you're finally heading up here. Remember, Joanna, was special; we were all lucky to have her. Have a safe trip."

As she hung up, her husband Fred said, "Quite a surprise. When will they be coming?"

Maria answered thoughtfully, "He's going to let us know but around four days from now. Question is Fred, why the hell are they coming back up here now?" Maria walked around the kitchen for a moment, then stopped, "Fred, where are those old picture albums? I need to remember what that bastard looks like."

Chapter 7

Hank's idea of travelling was simple - get up and go - but this novel concept was lost on Sue. She was stuck in the molasses of saying good-bye to family. She dawdled, hugged Allie and told her dad one more time, "I don't like leaving you alone. Now, I've laid out your medication for a week. I know the doctor said you can drive but let Allie call us on the cell, when you're on the road."

"Sue, you're worse than your mother used to be. Stop fussing, and go. Hank has been cooling his jets for an hour. Leave for god's sakes."

"Allie, you be good with grampy, and I'll see you in two days. You okay? Now give mom another big hug."

"Mom, we've done the hugging thing. Do they have TV in Canada?"

"Ask grampy?" Sue gave her daughter and dad a last hug, allowed Hank to push her in his car and start north. Clear skies and slightly cool, an ideal day for travelling. Taking I-75, through a land of red earth and rolling hills, Hank made good time to Knoxville, turned east on the I-81 into the Appalachians and, eventually, quit for the night just past Roanoke. Their drive from Atlanta had seen mixed emotions between them. Hank looked at Sue as they pulled up to the Comfort Inn, and she made a decision for them, "One room is fine Hank, long as it has separate beds." As he looked at her, Sue added, "It's just not the right time."

The next day, long before sunset, Hank parked outside Peter's home in Plattsburgh, plonked Sue's bags down on Peter's verandah, and declined her offer to come in for a while. As they walked back to his car he turned serious, "Do you see a future for us, Sue? I'm sure of me, but I'm not sure of you. Look, there's no rush to act but, think it over, think of giving me some indication of moving together or apart. Another level or we stop."

"Hard for us to be just friends, Hank." Sue was standing very close.

"It's impossible. Just can't deny my feelings, Sue."

"I feel the same Hank, but . . . " god, I'm full of so many fears. Who wants me when they find I'm pregnant? Endless complications. "... but I need you to trust me for a week or two."

"Sue, it's simple, make a choice to be free, damn it. We've had two days on the road for talking and nothing much was said. Now I'm leaving and we still say nothing. There's a good life ahead for us - if you break with Allan. What's holding you back?"

"Hank, wait till I come back from Canada, and I promise to have my head sorted out by then." Sue gave him a kiss - a kiss of more than friends, but less than lovers, "I'll call you tomorrow, Hank."

Peter, tall and slim as their dad, had been sitting on the veranda, and he bent a little to give Sue a gentle squeeze. He was such a contrast against her shorter frame. "So, little sister, good trip from Atlanta? I was listening to you and Hank talk. He didn't leave happy."

"Nothing is wrong, Peter. just tired from the drive and needing a long shower." She looked around and asked, "Where's Maggie?"

"My darling wife figures you and I need family bonding time, so she arranged some girls' night out to leave us alone. Which means she is going to get smashed!"

"Hey bro, Maggie's my buddy. Don't knock her - or I could reminisce of how your first wife managed money. You'd appreciate

Maggie then, wouldn't you?" She gave him a smile. "God, it's nice to see you, Peter."

He gave her a light hug, "Your email's were sounding a little gritty from Atlanta. How was it living with dad? Tough time down there?" He's still too military for my liking.

"Dad was fine and he's back to normal health with his heart. My birth questions have annoyed him most. He would be happy if I drop it all." But I'm not quitting. "How can I drop a puzzle connected with my birth?"

Peter nodded, "Sue, I'm the oldest, and anything like you not being part of the family is silly. It's just not an issue. But, from what Maggie explained about your baby picture and the birth weight, then follow it up."

Sue was nodding, "That's one reason to go to Canada. The baby photo, and birth weight, and my being premature, doesn't make sense, but dad insists there is no problem. I feel terrible doubting dad, but what else can I do but keep looking?"

"What does Hank think? Does he see a baby switch of some kind?"

Sue hesitated for a moment, then pointed her finger at Peter, "Hank's smart enough to stay out of guessing. He's told me there are likely more facts to appear, and we should wait to see them before jumping to conclusions. He supports my searching but also says there could be a simple answer like perhaps the baby picture is that of another kid and it was wrongly marked with my name. However, that wouldn't explain my wrong DNA." Sue then asked Peter how he would feel if a baby switch was proven.

"Well, sis, would be one less Christmas present to buy."

"Seriously."

"You shouldn't even have to ask. You're my kid sister now, and tomorrow and long after we're dead and gone. Perhaps, dad will get his nose out of joint, but he'll come around. Our family is solid.

Asking questions won't break this family. One exception, if you discover a link to Bill Gates, I would dump dad in a flash and adopt the Gates clan."

"Nicely said Peter, thanks." You big jerk, picking the right time to say what I need to hear. Sue spread a small packet of letters on the table, "While I shower, read these, mom's old love letters. Did you know mom asked dad out? I can't see him as a shy teenager in the '60's but, apparently, he was. Pretty cool for the '60's."

Peter poked through the bundle of letters and photos Sue had opened, and when she came back from her shower said. "Surprised dad let you have these, Sue?"

"With reluctance. Take a look at what mom wrote in this one, Peter."

Looking at the old letters they didn't realize a car had parked in the drive, until there was a knock at the front door. Peter, looking through a side window, realized this could be trouble, and told his sister, "Allan is outside. Did you tell him to come over?"

"No. No, I haven't talked to him for weeks. How does he know I'm here?" If I'm safe, why do my hands shake? "I don't want to see him."

"Easy. It's my house, so I'll just tell him to go."

"Wait, Peter." God, my legs are trembling. "See what he wants? Better I find out now, with you here."

"Allan's a bully, sis, and you confront bullies." Allan knocked again and Peter called out, "One moment, Allan." Looking calmer than his own sweaty palms revealed, Peter first phoned his next door neighbour, "Paul, I've got an uninvited relative come a-calling. He shouldn't be a problem but, just in case, slip in my back kitchen door and quietly make your presence known. No, I don't think he has a weapon, but you never know. Thanks, Paul."

Peter reached into the hall closet, grabbed a baseball bat,

opened the front door and without any niceties said, "Want someone, Allan?"

"My wife. Want to talk to Sue." He rubbed his clean-shaven face, and shifted his flabby weight, "She's still my wife. Not looking for trouble, Peter. Just a talk with Sue."

Peter tapped the bat into his palm. Wack. Then said, "Allan, you've got five minutes in my house... then you're out of here. No problem buddy and you earn a gold star. Any silly moves and I start batting practice. Understand?"

"Very subtle, Peter." He entered the room and faced his wife, "We need time to talk, Sue. Just you and me. I've missed you and Allie. How is she?"

"How did you know I was here?" God, can he hear my pounding heart? "And please, please don't start by saying you're sorry. I've heard your lies too many times."

"I have changed, Sue, a lot. Just want you back. I'm different now."

Peter couldn't resist saying, "He may have changed... drinking bottle beer now instead of cans?"

"This is between Sue and me, so stay out of it, Peter. I haven't drank in a while. Not a drop." Peter's neighbour picked that moment to step into the living room, silently looking at Allan for a moment, and quietly stepping back to the kitchen and out of sight. He was a big boy; the guy could have played for the Packers as a linebacker. His bulk made the implication clear, keep your cool Allan and don't even think of causing problems. Allan first tried bravado in reply, "What was the big guy for Sue, just another sign your family regards me as zero?" But Allan's courage was ebbing away and his voice became a whine, "Some family I married into... none of you ever liked me. Sue, I'm lost without you; no friends, everyone despising me, I'm all alone. Even my job is breaking apart. All we need is time to talk."

Sue's fury with Allan spilled out, "The last time we talked, you were throwing beer bottles at my head. I don't believe you're sorry, and we aren't talking. Not this time."

"I've changed. Just give me a chance to prove I've changed. Come back home." He opened his hands to Sue, in surrender.

Anger made Sue yell, "Why would I ever go home? It took years to escaped from your abuse. Why should I go back?"

"For our family. Trust me. Sue, come out now, even for an hour. Or come home for any stuff you need. I won't bother you. I'll stay out of the house between noon and five tomorrow. "

"Sure, Allan. Step into your web again. Like hell you won't bother me."

"Sue, listen, come home tomorrow, and between noon and five I'll be out of the house when you come. Promise. Will that build some trust between us? For Allie's sake."

"How dumb do you think I am? Why would I believe a liar?"

"It's your choice, and, if you show up tomorrow or not, I'll keep my word and be out of the house. Sue, we're still married, and I still love you and Allie."

Sue still wondered how he had tracked her to Peter's. "Time you left. And don't come back but how the hell did you know I was here?"

Peter motioned toward the door as Allan made a last plea, courage had returned. "Okay. I'm going. And you can come tomorrow and get any stuff you want." At the door he turned, and smiled, "Allie told me you would arrive today. We send text messages all the time." He stopped at the front door with a parting remark, "I need you, Sue."

Sue was still shaky when the front door closed. "Well, I had to confront him sometime. And I'd love to get some clothes from home, but I'm not going to believe him."

Peter agreed. "Allan would say anything to get his way. You can't trust him. Do you need a drink to calm down?" When Sue shook her head no, Peter continued, "Okay, then show me that baby picture problem and tell me of mom's old letters to get your mind off Allan."

"Peter, you start reading them while I try and relax. And don't rip the page or dad will yell at me." Handing her brother an old envelope whose tattered edges spoke of being handled many times, she was thinking of Allan until Peter asked a question that brought her back to reality.

"Sue, are you sure mom wrote these? Mom never had clear handwriting. She scrawled everything. It's not mom's handwriting."

"She wrote those letters to dad before they married."

"Well, it doesn't seem like mom's writing." Peter read the old note his mom had penned years ago.

June 24, 62
Hi John the very wet rower,

Remember me, Joanna, the girl at the rowing meet who cheered for Oakville. Today is Saint John Baptist day, and, in Canada, a girl can ask a boy out today. Or write a letter asking him out. Been months since we beat you at the Oakville Rowing Club. I think of you often, especially when I'm canoeing on the Credit River by myself. Our Saturday paper said your Atlanta Rowing Club had a first place finish. Yes, I've followed your club since meeting you in Oakville.

With the rowing season winding down, what are your plans for the winter? My folks will drive to Florida in January, which means we travel through Georgia, and I might persuade them to stop near your town. Just for an hour. Maybe, if you still don't have a steady girl friend, we can see your rowing club together. Or hitchhike to Florida and we can swim or just get tanned.

Is any of this appealing? Write. I would love to hear from you.

Your friend,   *Joanna Court*

Peter waved the letter in puzzlement, as Sue returned to the living room, "I can't believe mom wrote this? For one thing, it's not mom's scrawling handwriting and, the girl who wrote this seems logical, but mom was as flighty as our sister Annie. Can you imagine Annie writing a letter like this?"

"Peter. You can't seriously think mom and Annie are alike? Annie can't stay focused long enough to answer my email for god's sakes, while mom was like you and I. Mom was always stronger than dad."

"Mom, certainly, wasn't like me. I remember when I was a kid, mom scrawled stuff. My grade three teacher couldn't read her note once and made a big deal of her unreadable scrawl. Embarrassing. Kids don't forget those things. Mom's writing was so hard to read that dad kidded her about being a doctor. You must remember."

"You have it so wrong. We called her Dr. Mom cause she looked after us. That's typical of you, remembering her nick name and forgetting the reason." By this time, Sue is raising her voice, "I don't know what mom you remember, Peter, but it, certainly, wasn't mine."

Margaret chose that moment to come in, red-faced and full of friendly warmth, just as Sue finished yelling at Peter. Margaret smiled, leaned against the door, "See, I knew you two needed some bonding time. Now can one of you angels help me to bed?"

Morning sunlight glinted on Maggie's blond hair, as she sat at the kitchen table holding her head. Peter was on one side and Sue on the other. An untouched cup of coffee sat steaming in front of her as she said, "Peter, I'm ill. Must have been bad seafood last night?" Without lifting her head she asked, "Where's Sue?"

"Sitting next to you, Maggie. Want a big fry-up with bacon, eggs and toast?"

"I'll pass, thank you." Margaret opened one eye a crack. "Sue, were you here, when I walked in last night?"

Peter glared at his wife a moment, "You don't remember coming in, do you? You were hammered."

"Peter, go pick on a well person. I'm dying."

In disgust, Peter ignored his wife and spoke to his sister. "Dad called while you were showering... he figures on arriving tonight and leaving for our cousins in Oakville tomorrow. And Allie said she's having a good time reading the map for him."

"Why didn't you call? I need to talk with him?"

"I knocked on the bathroom door, but you were so busy using up all my hot water you didn't hear me."

Maggie spoke quietly with her head on the kitchen table. "Children, no bickering. Mommy's head hurts. Could someone get me a cold glass of water? I promise, no more seafood." She turned to Sue, a little gleam returning to her eyes, "When Peter leaves for work Sue, we can have a girl talk over all the family stuff Peter never mentions."

Peter brought his wife a cold glass of water without sympathy, "I'm running late. Sue, if you need to get around then take Maggie's car. I don't think she will be sober to drive for hours."

"Peter, but I've been thinking of Allan's offer to let me pick up some clothes. But I won't go alone. If I have Maggie's car, why don't I pick you up after lunch, and we can drive to Clearville. You could stand guard, while I get my clothes and things. There and back in less than two hours. Allan did promise to be out, and it is my home."

"You've got to be kidding. Go to his house when I threatened him with a baseball bat last night? That's asking for trouble." He turned toward his wife, "Margaret, Sue doesn't get your car if she driving to Clearville. I mean it."

Margaret said nothing. Head down, eyes closed against the sunlight, she gave her husband a straight arm salute.

Sue downplayed the trip."It was just an idea. But I do want my old camera to take pictures on the trip north."

"Sis, stay on this side of Lake Champlain and leave Allan alone."

Sue figured Peter still guarded his toys, but she had to ask, "Well, can I take your camera to Canada?"

"Not a chance. It's my good camera."

Margaret backed Sue. "Peter, think that over. Lend Sue our old camera. If she breaks it, you have a reason to get that new one you keep looking at. Sue, I'll get his camera out later."

Peter knew he had lost the argument. "I'm not happy. She better take good care of it." He touched Maggie on the cheek, and set off for work.

Not long after Peter had left, Sue noticed Maggie, on a second cup of coffee, seemed much improved, and said, "You recover quickly?"

"As soon as Peter leaves, I recover quickly. It's a little game, my exaggerated hangover. I'm always bright and bubbly, and girls like me, can be a threat for any guy to live with. It's a man thing, easily threatened by a girl who can drink them under the table, and Peter is no different. So, occasionally, mornings like this, Peter can natter on at me for getting sloshed. Makes him feel superior so what's the harm? My head did hurt, and Peter now has something to brood over."

"Peter is convinced you have a drinking problem. He told me so."

Maggie nodded and laughed, "Which proves my point. Your worry-wart brother needs to be uptight about something. So, occasionally, I give him reasons - like hiding wine in odd places at home, just so he can find it. He needs a reminder to worry about me, so I give him one. Sue, if I did everything right, all the time, he might worry about some other woman. You know that men like to be in charge, to feel superior of the person they are helping. It's totally a man's thing."

"Well, if we're sharing secrets, then you may as well know I'm dealing with a woman thing, Maggie... I'm expecting."

"Oh... Hank? Do I say congratulations?"

"I only wish." Sue shook her head. "Allan's the daddy. Happened in one of our last tangos, when he was drunk. Not wise or pleasant, but it happened." Sue continued, "So far, only you and my dad know, and I need to keep it quiet till I can think it through. I want to speak to my doctor at the Clearville Clinic, and today would be an ideal time. If you come along I can then stop at my place and pick up clothes, toys and my camera. Want an afternoon drive?"

"I'll be at work this afternoon. Sue, you're a big girl, just go. Never mind Peter, just take my car and go to Clearville." Maggie dangled car keys in front of Sue. "Well! Do you want the keys or not?"

Sue reached out for the keys, "Peter will have a fit if I stop at my place."

"Then don't tell him. Get control of your life. Allan's at work, so there's no problem? You can be in and out in minutes, if you make it fast."

"And if Allan is drunk... what then?"

"Then he's sitting in the kitchen drinking, with his new truck parked in the driveway, and you just cruise on by. Your things are there and buying new ones isn't the same as having your own stuff, is it?"

"I don't want to go alone. That would be stupid."

"Then call your sister and have her meet you there after you see the doctor."

Yes. It could work. Annie meets me near the house, we make sure the coast is clear, and then a quick in and out. "My old shoes are the first thing to grab, then my house coat, blue slippers, and my blue sweater. And Allie keeps whining for her GameCube: and her clothes. Also, my little case of make-up. Ten minutes would be enough time for everything. Let me call, Annie."

Sue was back in ten minutes, "Annie agreed. She will be at the house after I do the clinic thing, so we can get my stuff and be back here before Peter even knows I went. Thanks, Maggie. You're a good friend."

"Sue, it's almost ten. Would you consider this too early for a glass of wine? My head is still killing me."

* * * * *

Driving Maggie's car north, past the University of Plattsburgh, gave Sue a tinge of regret. She remembered her resolve not to go further than a high school education. "It's not fair expecting teens to understand an adult world and make good decisions. At eighteen, I wanted to be on my own, making my own life, and that didn't fit in with taking money from dad for university. So while Peter and Harry both graduated from Suny, I didn't. Harry almost persuaded me to register, after convincing me we could pretend to be students for an afternoon. That was fun. We wandered everywhere through campus, the library, and spent time at the student union. The social life seemed wonderful, but I couldn't see myself reading books for another two years. Besides, what can anyone tell teenagers who won't listen. Choices. University would have meant no marriage to Allan and, therefore, Allie wouldn't have been born."

"Sue stopped talking to herself and drove past large Plattsburgh residential lots running to Champlain's shore, past beer bars on strippers' row, and soon entered Vermont at Rouses Point. A drive south on Interstate 89 went right past her home, and there was no sign of Allan's truck.

She arrived at the clinic in Clearville with little time to spare. Dr. Mark Wearing beckoned her to an empty office, and Sue appreciated the way he came right to the point, "Well Sue, you already know what the tests confirm - your second child is coming along just fine. No complication at this point, and nature is proceeding on nature's agenda. Now, shall I set up another appointment, or do we transfer your records to an Atlanta clinic. Have you decided?" On her way out of the office, the reception desk asked if she needed anything and Sue shook her head, "No thanks, I'm doing just fine."

Now for the next step - get in and get out. No use hesitating. Heading back north, she parked under a clump of trees, watched her house from a distance, and waited for Annie. Sue could see an expanse of Lake Champlain in the distance, her home a half mile away and, this time, Allan's truck was in their drive. "All right," she said aloud, "it's not quite noon, so let's see if he keeps his word." At noon sharp, Allan was backing out their drive and heading to work. Still Sue waited, finally saying aloud, "Annie, it's twelve-thirty, you're late and I can't count on you coming. God, I should know better than to ask for your help. My house is empty, and I can be in and out in five minutes. Just run in and do it."

Parking in the drive, she entered her home with caution

calling, "Hello. Anyone home. It's me. Anyone here?" Sue could see a mess everywhere: from dirty dishes in the sink, to piles of clothes, and even tools on the kitchen table. This was no longer a home. She just shook her head knowing his mess wasn't her problem anymore. Time to fill garbage bags and get out of here.

It didn't take long to bag what she wanted, and she was placing them in her trunk, when she heard the sound of crunching gravel behind her. Allan's truck was returning, coming down the single lane drive to block her in. Fear can make anyone act fast. Slamming her trunk, she got in the car, and locked the doors. As Allan walked over, she moved the window down an inch and shouted, "Liar," through the almost closed driver's window. "Damned liar. You promised not to be home."

"And I wasn't home. Wouldn't be in the house or garage is what I said. Never said I wouldn't come back and talk, did I? Sue, we need to get our life figured out. That's all I ask, come on, just sit in the truck with me to sort things out. I won't get mad."

"You're always mad." Not to mention nuts.

"Don't get me started, Sue. Saying I'm mad only makes me mad. If you won't talk, then just come and listen, Sue."

"Do I have any choice?" Think, dad says there is always another choice, another way to see a problem. "I have to return the car, it's Maggie's. Just move your truck." Think Sue. Think.

"Just talk for ten minutes. That's all."

"Ten minutes? Okay, Allan, I'll compromise." Her hands had turned ice cold, and she knew exactly what to do. "I'm not getting in your truck, and you're not sitting in this car. You want to talk. You get a lawn chair from the garage and sit beside my car window. That's all I'll start with for now." Allan smirked, and walked in front of the car toward the garage, just as Sue, yelled, "Big mistake, Allan."

Sue gunned Maggie's car, propelled it directly toward him, forcing him to jump and sprawl on the drive. Then, she reversed and floored the gas. In anger, he tossed a hand-full of gravel at her open window, but missed, as the car was now backing up fast. With Allan out of the way, there was almost enough space to squeeze past his blocking truck. Almost, but not quite.

Sue acted by instinct - fast into reverse, gas to the floor. Then, while racing backward, her side mirror smashing into his truck, and gravel flying, she felt a stinging sensation near her left eye. She raked his red paint from his front door to rear bumper, but didn't even consider stopping. Not now. Not stopping even for traffic on the main road. Reversing out of the gravel drive onto the main road she heard blaring horns, fast-moving cars, and squealing tires. Sue slammed Maggie's car into drive and raced toward town.

She only slowed when near Clearville, then, reached to her stinging face and removed a blood-covered hand. "My god Allan, what the hell have you caused now? Damn you." She continued to Main and First Avenue, her second visit of the day to Cedar Medical Clinic. One little thing Maggie had said was bouncing around her mind, "You said going to my place would be easy, Maggie, but it wasn't. And Peter will be some ticked, when he sees your damaged car."

Chapter 8

Cedar Clinic's receptionist ignored the blood around her eye only asking, "Insurance? Do you have your insurance cards, please?"

"It's under my husband, Allan Charter. His company plan. I was in earlier today. I can't see with my eye bleeding."

"Ma'am, after you left a while ago, we realized your insurance had been cancelled. It's a work policy and no longer valid."

"You accepted me here an hour ago."

"Yes, we did. However, we found the insurance for Allan Charter has been cancelled on our system. So, there will be a charge for your previous visit and this one. Do you have a credit card? Ma'am, getting upset won't help. We need proper paperwork before treating your eye."

"If I can't see, I can't fill in paperwork. Can I use your phone to call Plattsburgh? And, yes, I'll reverse the charges." Even dialling was a problem, but Sue reached Maggie's phone service and left a message. "I've got a problem with a cut eye, Maggie. I'm at the Cedar Clinic in Clearville, and I don't know how I can drive to your place. Your car will be fine after a dab of paint."

Sue waited untreated and, within half an hour, her good eye focused on Hank coming toward her. "Thank god Maggie reached you."

"I don't know about Maggie, Sue. Allan is at our station now, wanting to press hit and run charges against you. Leaving the scene of an accident is serious."

"He caused it. He was the problem, Hank."

"His story is different. Did you run him down and smash his truck just now? Did your brother menace him with a baseball bat yesterday? If Allan's claims hold up and your traffic offences today go against you, you're in hot water. Sue, being on the wrong side of the law is serious."

"Hank, he blocked me in; I was lucky to escape."

"Right. First, I'll find someone to fix your eye. Then I'll call the station to see if Allan has come to his senses. But if you did what he's saying, he has every right to lay a charge."

"This can't be happening, Hank."

He returned, "Sue, the doctor is ready to stitch up the cut, while I see what your ex-husband has to say."

The doctor had almost finished treating her facial cuts, "You are one lucky lady."

"A smashed car, a cut eye, and facing arrest isn't my idea of luck."

"Now hold still while the topical is in effect." He continued picking small shards of glass from above her left eye. "You're lucky. A dozen glass fragments cut your face and not one entered your eye. Remain still while I remove the blood and foreign matter. You could have lost an eye."

Sue nodded, said thanks, then walked with Hank to a quiet area where he explained, "My station reports that Allan spoke loudly to someone on the phone for quite a while but, in the end, he calmed down and said he would only be considering charges. As to your being a menace to highway traffic, well, no witnesses have come forward. But, Sue, what possessed you to confront him alone; you know he's dangerous."

"Annie didn't show up to help me. Then Allan lied about being gone, he came, and blocked me in." Sue tried to explain. But it seemed to make little difference to Hank.

"Unfortunately, your ex has a good chunk of the law on his side."

"My face is cut, not his."

"Sue, but you drove the car as a weapon. What if you had hit Allan? Is that his fault?"

"I could scream at you men. Allan is the problem. I didn't come home stinking drunk, night after night. I didn't spend money till the family was broke."

"Sue, get a grip."

She didn't care. "I go to my house, my place, to get my clothes, and end up cut and lectured by my one friend." I know I'm losing it, but I don't give a damn. "You want a worthwhile job... go help Allan open his next beer." Sue turned, dry-eyed, head held high, and walked to Maggie's car.

Hank followed twenty-feet behind and when he reached the car, she had lost her composure. Sitting in the driver's seat, she sobbed on the steering wheel while he sat as a passenger. The tears seemed unstoppable, soaking the eye bandage and falling on Hank's shoulder, so all he could do was hold her tight. Eventually, she gained some control and started talking. "God, what a mess. My life is in shambles and now I'm pushing you away - the one person who helps me. Hank, I can't seem to calm down."

"You're in no condition to drive. Give me the keys and trade places." They both got out of the car, met half-way round and Hank first smiled and then laughed, "Your tears have soaked the bandage. I'm going to ask the clinic for a new one. But first, I'll call Peter." Sue looked at Hank and started to laugh. Then she was crying again.

* * * * *

While Hank tried reaching Peter, her husband, Allan, paced in front of a coffee-perk bubbling away, bitterly complaining of his nutty wife. "Stu, she could have killed me; she could have killed me. She drove with the intent to kill. I'm lucky to be alive, Stu. Have you been listening to me? My wife deliberately tried to run me down and then smashed my truck's side mirror and scraped it from ass to tea kettle. It's her fault. I should charge her. I should go back to the station and charge her. Even the cops know she could be charged. She's to blame."

"Allan, check the coffee for me. Think there is enough for tonight? Good. Now as to your wife, well my memory is not the best, so tell me again, what were the arrangements for meeting your wife today?"

"I told you all this, when I called you from the cop shop. She's my wife. I want her back. My plan was to get her talking."

"You wanted to talk to her?"

"Hell, yes. It's my right isn't it?"

"And she got mad when you blocked her in the drive?"

"Okay, so that part didn't work like I planned."

"No, I can see it didn't. Allan, almost everything you say is easily understood, except I can't quite realize how blocking a wife in the drive till she's riled is the way to get her talking? I can understand her yelling at being blocked in, but not talking. If you think about it, there is a subtle difference? And now, seeing she didn't kill you, how will charging Sue with causing a few bucks damage to your truck, bring you together? Am I missing some great point in your plan? How will getting the cops involved make her want to talk with you?" Stu stopped for a moment, and then continued, "Allan, while your mind is reviewing today's comedy, can you give me a hand with setting a few things up?"

Allan stopped pacing and looked at Stu, "I don't believe you. With everything that's happened to me today, you're saying I should just count out paper cups and pour coffee. You're saying I should leave Sue alone. Is that it? Is that what you're saying? That's what you're saying isn't it, Stu Baily?" Allan started counting cups. Lost count and started over, only to stop and shake his head, "You know people lose a lot being sober. Can't even stay angry like I used to. Stu, its one damn hell of a world being sober. No wonder that's why people drink."

Stu laughed. Laughed for a few minutes.

* * * * *

By the time Hank reached the Lake Champlain Ferry crossing, Sue's emotions were raw from tears one moment and anger the next. But she had made a decision. "It's only a man's world, Hank, only men win. Allan won today. While I'm homeless and broke because of him, he's slopping beer in my kitchen right now, and thinking of how he can send me to jail. All my troubles, including Maggie's smashed car, are his fault." Then she added money problems. "I didn't know he cancelled our medical coverage. The hospital bills drained my credit card, and I'm broker than broke. Which is funny, because I was going to ask Peter for a loan before I smashed up Maggie's car. He'll be some pissed off at me now." But, at least, I've made a decision he will like.

"Try contacting him again, Sue. His meeting should be finished by now." When she didn't answer he continued, "He needs to hear you're okay." Hank handed Sue his cell phone, "Stop thinking the worst... talk to your brother."

Peter answered Sue on the first ring, "Are you all right? I called the clinic Sue, but missed you. Have Hank drive straight to my place and don't worry about the car. Okay, see you in less than an hour." But it was so avoidable. I, specifically, told you not to bother with Allan. "Now if dad and Allie arrive before you, I'll play down the accident and say Hank is bringing you home. Nothing else Just stay well."

"Peter, listen to me. The trip to Canada is not going to happen. I'm going back to Atlanta and settle down to a job. If the trip were free I couldn't afford to go. So, I want you on my side, when I tell dad to cancel our plans." Sure I do want to go, if your smart, you will know this is my way of asking for a loan. But you won't twig to this will you? "Just support me in talking dad out of the trip. See you soon."

Hank had heard Sue say the trip was off and looked at her now. She knew he was against it. "Hank, I'm tired of unravelling the past, running out of strength to continue, and no money to even buy small things. Aren't you pleased? In Atlanta, you told me to forget the birth stuff for a while. You said that."

"If I said forget it, then I was wrong. Look, if you honestly want to stop, then stop, but quitting cause you had a bad time with Allan is something you will regret. Aren't your relatives expecting you?"

"It was an idea that didn't work. Truth is, Hank, I'm drained."

"And you should be exhausted." Hank smiled and said, "It's very draining trying to run over a husband." Hank gently touched her shoulder. "Now, don't start crying again. God, forget I said that. Have a good cry, and then a good night's sleep. Going on the trip will look different in the morning. Don't cancel now. Wait a few hours more."

"How? I'm broke, in credit card debt up to my eye balls and dad alone can't keep supporting me. So Peter is right. Looking for work and a place to live is first priority for me. For Allie's sake, we should live in Clearville, near her school and friends, but Allan's there and he will bother me at every step." Visiting Canada was only a thought and dad only arranged the trip to appease me. Besides, I can still question my baby's photo by email and phone calls. That would work. "Living in Atlanta is my best option. So I give up." I'm not going to get emotional. "Wouldn't you quit?" Sue fell quiet as tears flowed hot on her cheeks.

"You need to eat." Hank squeezed her hand, pulled into a McDonald's drive thru, and drove off with her fries and a drink. "Tomorrow, make any decision you like but, right now, stop feeling sorry for yourself." By now, he was driving through the old section of Plattsburgh, large homes and spacious lots, "You know, since the housing crash, the banks give you nothing on money sitting with them so like a lot of folks, I've just stockpiled cash hoping for better times. It's just sitting there doing nothing. You'd do me a big favour, if you borrow some cash I have sitting at the bank and give it a little workout in Canada. Go on the trip. The money is no problem."

Sue figured he was joking. "Money's a problem with everyone, Hank. Even the clinic ripped me off, billing me twenty bucks for calling Plattsburgh. Everyone's pushing me around."

Hank laughed, "Twenty bucks for a call?"

"It's not funny, Hank."

"Seriously, Sue. Accept the money, see your relatives and cover today's medical. No strings attached."

She shook her head no, "Thanks for offering but... if Peter or dad help me, the trip could still happen, but being in debt to you might spoil things between us. Just let me be quiet for a while." But something has to give against the debit that's killing me.

Hank continued, "Just don't quit searching. You'd regret it."

Sue turned toward him. "Oh shut up, Hank, you're all talk. You're babbling on worse than a woman and stopping me from having a good sulk. I deserve to feel sorry for myself for a while." She smiled at him an open smile that covered more than saying thanks.

The drive continued in comfortable silence till they arrived at Peter's home, where a Plattsburgh police car waited. Hank reassured Sue, "That's just the New York cops giving me a courtesy ride back to the Ferry Terminal. Go inside to your folks while I talk to these boys."

Maggie flung open the front door, hugged Sue welcome, held her tight, and almost carried her over to a comfortable arm chair. She was going to be pampered, "Oh poor baby. Bandages and scrapes... like you've been through a war. Sue, are you hungry? Do you want anything?"

Peter remained practical, "How's the car? Much damage?"

"Maggie, I'd love a cold drink and, Peter, the worst damage is to my face and ego."

"I realize Maggie's car can be fixed, but I did warn you not to go. You knew it was dangerous going alone." Dumb move by a dumb sister.

"For the third time - Annie promised to be there. She just didn't show up."

Peter was starting to continue years of sibling bickering, "Since when can you rely on Annie? Since when? She called here an hour ago, saying today was your fault, and you owe her an explanation. So one of you has it wrong." Damn it, Sue, I can't keep looking after you two girls.

"Peter," Maggie spoke sharply, "your sister needs rest. Besides, in all your perfect years, have you never made a wrong decision? Now, go check my car like you want to."

Hank interrupted their family squabble, "New York's finest are ready to drive me to the Ferry dock." Looking toward Peter, he continued, "I know you're all thinking of Sue. Get mad at her tomorrow if you like but, not tonight. Now I have to leave."

"Wait, Hank." Sue pushed her tired muscles and stood up, "Walk you to the car." She linked her arm in his, thinking, will we still walk this way when you know I'm pregnant with Allan's kid. Sue squeezed his arm, "Hank, when driving here, remember the crazy crying woman who gave you a hard time... well, that wasn't me. I'm the grateful girl standing here now, grateful for all your help. Remember that." After kissing him lightly, she watched the cop car vanish into the evening and then walked back inside.

Maggie mothered her. Blanket, pillow, propped in Peter's favourite chair, Sue was comfortably drowsy, "Maggie, wake me when dad and Allie arrive. And where's Peter?"

Maggie rolled her eyes, "Probably checking the car and thinking of scamming the insurance for repairs. Sue, was the old penny pincher always this tight with money, as a kid?"

"He was always careful with money. Just his nature."

Maggie nodded and answered, "Well, Peter is more than careful. He's in the misers' category now. But we are glad you're all right and that Hank looked after you. Looks like he's becoming a regular at our house."

"Maggie, Hank has no idea of my condition. And also, after ten years of a bad marriage, I don't know my emotions anymore. Could be Hank is the right move, or it could be entirely wrong? Ever had a great guy chase after you, someone who would care... but the feelings were wrong? Know what I mean?"

"Sure, that's my everyday shopping experience. While I try to pick up the broccoli, men try and pick me up. Guys chase me all the time."

"Maggie, no joke. I'm talking about a guy wanting passion, while I love him like a relative. Love on different vibes."

"Sue, no joke, that's my everyday trip to the supermarket. Really. Guys give me phone numbers. Got a drawer full. Peter thinks they're lottery numbers, so don't tell him differently."

Sue laughed,. "You're a gem, Maggie. How did my glum

brother ever find you? How?"

You don't really want to know, Sue, not in detail. "Truth is Peter rescued me from a life of crime." She laughed, more than necessary, and easily changed the conversation, "And Annie called again while you were outside with Hank. Still, mad. Wants you to call her back."

"Then, she can just hold her breath till I'm ready." Sue yawned, made herself comfortable and easily drifted into a deep sleep. She awoke to Allie's hug and her questions, "Is your eye sore mom? Does it hurt much?"

"My eye is going to be just fine, Allie. How was the trip? Oh I've missed you so much, give mom another hug."

"Oh mom. It's only been three days, and grampy took me to a ball game the day you went, and we almost ran out of gas on the trip north. I read the map all the way here and grampy says I can be a navigator on the trip to Canada. And I missed you, too."

"Where's grampy now?"

"He's outside yelling at uncle Peter. I don't think they like each other."

Sue focused on her dad's loud voice and heard him say, "But you knew Allan was a loose cannon. When he called us at the condo, he was angry. Peter. You knew that."

Her brother's response was too muffled to hear.

John continued, "Only an idiot would let Sue go alone. You have a duty to protect her."

This time Peter stood up for himself, "I leave for work and come back to all hell breaking loose. Why blame me? Sue's stupidity isn't my fault." Get off my back, dad. I'm not a kid anymore. "I sure as hell hope you start your trip early tomorrow. I don't need to be lectured."

"It depends on Sue being able to travel. Peter, I won't stay here longer than I have to."

Sue yelled toward the open front door. "I can hear you two."

Father and son drifted into the living room. John saying, "We were just wondering how you were feeling, Sue?"

She pointed toward her bandaged eye, "This isn't Peter's fault, dad. He warned me. So you blame me and I'll blame Annie. Anyway, the doctor said I should be fine to travel, but I'm having second thoughts. The trip will cost too much, stop me from looking for work, and I can't keep sponging on you." Peter, if you're going to offer a loan, now would be a good time.

Her dad sat beside her, "Money is not a problem. It's all covered. Besides, your relatives are expecting us. You still want to go, don't you?"

"Absolutely yes, dad, but... "

"No but about it." Her dad was pleased, "Good. I'll call Fred and Maria tonight."

Peter spoke up. Either he was trying to help or just wanted them to go. "Leave early and you'll make Oakville by seven tomorrow night. It's a full day's drive." And enjoy the hassle of Toronto's rush hour - which you richly deserve for yelling at me.

Sleeping arrangements were sorted; Maggie and Peter in their room, John on the living room couch, and Sue and Allie on twin beds in the spare room. Before turning in, Sue talked to Peter alone in the kitchen, "Is there any way you can give me a loan? Credit card interest was already killing me and, today, the clinic in Clearville made it worse."

"Can't Allan help?"

"He sends me nothing. Credit cards are at their limit."

"How much do you need, Sue?"

"The credit cards are maxed out at five grand and will take at least two thousand minimum just to get the balance inline. You know how paying the interest cripples me. But I'll pay you back once I get working."

"Sue, I don't have a lot of cash. I can spare hundreds, but not thousands." Besides, your debts are Allan's debts, not mine. "Just find a job when you return from the trip. Everything will work out."

"Even if I got work today, it's not an answer. The credit card debts are due now."

"I can give you a few hundred against the debt. Or be practical, sis, take a loan from dad or cancel the trip."

"Peter, thanks for the advice but forget I asked for a loan. Sleep well."

Sue was ready for bed, when she decided to make a late phone call. "Hank? Did I wake you? You must know why I'm calling."

"If you're proposing marriage... the answer is yes, anywhere, anytime."

"Hank don't joke. My credit cards are maxed out, over the five grand limit and I can use the loan you offered. If it's still available?"

"Sure." No hesitation at all, "Consider it done. Give your credit card numbers in the morning and they will be paid within a few hours."

"Just a loan, Hank, a loan to be paid back." No strings attached, Hank, no expectations.

"Clearly understood, Sue." He paused a moment and added, "I'd suggest you keep all this in the open, let the family know... so if Allan finds out, we won't have to lie about it."

"I understand. Sounds good." You crafty bugger, no strings attached, yet, you want Allan to know so he gets upset. Is that it? "Okay Hank, but loan only. Sue relaxed and slept well.

But Peter tossed in bed. Maggie poked him in the side saying, "You either settle down or sleep on the floor. Why so restless?"

"A lot on my mind. Worried about dad and Sue."

"Try counting those little white fluffy things that jump over a fence in the middle of green grass. Try that."

Peter switched on a bed lamp and sat up, "You won't believe this, but dad told me why he changed his mind to help Sue find birth answers in Canada. Apparently, Sunny, his Atlanta girlfriend, said she wants dad to be closer to us kids, and I figure she intends to get closer to him."

"Did John say that? He didn't say that."

"It makes sense. Sunny wants to look after him, and his money. The old hypochondriac was counting out his medication tonight while telling me, it wasn't good to live alone. So, dad's taking Sue to Canada as a grand gesture of help, before he links up with Sunny as his next best friend."

"Nonsense. You worry far too much. Now go to sleep."

"Maggie, Sue asked me for a loan." Money is money, and I won't pay Allan's debt.

"Now I understand you being restless." Maggie didn't seem surprised, "You're upset about lending Sue money."

"There is no loan. I turned her down."

"Oh." Maggie stared at the ceiling with wide-open eyes, "But why? We can afford it?"

"Bailing out relatives is trouble, so, I refused the loan and that's the end of it."

Maggie sat up, "Peter, why didn't you talk to me before turning her down? Bet she hardly said a word. That's because asking you for money was my idea, not hers. I told her to ask you rather than accept Hank's money, because Hank's money will certainly complicate their relations. Peter, I assured her, you might stall for a bit but, in the end ,you'd agree to a loan. I told her we had the cash."

Chapter 9

At Peter's home, the exhilaration of a trip to Canada had everyone awake with the sun. Ready to travel. No obvious problems appeared to linger from the loan refusal of last night, and the routines of coffee, breakfast for some, and getting ready for the drive all seemed to easily unfold. John busied himself with car-packing arrangements and Peter helped his dad. He carried a heavy box past Sue, "Dad's doctor specifically said the old man doesn't have diabetes... but he's taking books and a blood-testing kit anyway." They smiled at each other, knowing their dad's health obsession. Peter didn't mention the loan again and Sue didn't ask. Only Maggie seemed uncomfortable with the sibling's unfinished business.

Sue waited, patiently, for her brother to have his breakfast. Eventfully, he sat at the kitchen table to eat the same brand of cereal he had eaten since his teen years, and that's exactly when she phoned Hank. Speaking in a low voice, as if Peter couldn't hear every word, she gave the banking information he asked for and finished with, "Hank, I'll call in a few days, and thanks for everything." Peter heard every word, but never missed a beat crunching his cereal.

While getting ready to travel, Allie called out, "Mom, aunt Annie's on the phone. Wants to speak to you." Sue was ready to tear a strip off her sister, but Annie yelled first, "Where the hell were you yesterday. Sue, I waited outside for two hours and you never came, and you haven't called to explain being a no-show. Next time, ask someone else for help."

"Annie, you were the no-show, not me."

"Like hell. You told me to meet you at the house at noon.

That's what I did. Waited till two o'clock cooling my heels, then I went to the mall and spent money I don't have. Now all this stuff is going back today and that upsets me. You really caused me problems, sister."

"Annie. You didn't park outside the house at noon. You weren't anywhere in sight."

"Sue, I was outside Peter's house at noon, and you never came. I sat on Peter's verandah swing and you were the no-show, not me."

"I don't believe this. You waited in Plattsburgh, while I waited in Clearville? How could you forget my home is in Vermont?" Annie, you could get a one-car funeral mixed up.

"You're living at Peter's place. That was clear to me." Annie was calming down.

Annie, did you truly hear wrong... or were you just spinning another lie? "Look, we're leaving soon, and I'm not going to get into this now. Good-bye." She turned to her dad and said in frustration, "The nut-bar stuck me again. I could wring her pretty little blond head."

Then, Maggie came into the kitchen, while Peter was finishing his breakfast, sat near Sue, and came right to the point. "Sue, I didn't expect Peter to refuse your loan last night. To turn down family is just not right, and I've told him so."

"That's okay, Maggie. Other arrangements are in the works."

"That would be Hank? But you know, taking a loan from Hank is complicated."

"I'm aware, Maggie, yet the bills need to be taken care of today. And Hank offered."

"So will I." Maggie had a checkbook in her hand. "Peter's not the only one who understands money." Signing the check she handed it to Sue, "Look, you need more than just a loan. Hank is taking care of your credit cards now, so just let that stand. Then, when you return from Canada, cash this, repay Hank for covering your credit cards, and put the rest in your account. You need to have some money just to get started on your new life."

"Maggie, I can't take money to cause problems between you and Peter. I love you both and won't start a family fight."

Sue spoke to her husband. "We won't fight over this. Will we dear?" Then, facing Sue again, "The money is for you. But listen, you also need a positive direction and I know you write well. So, since the explosion of online print, there is a constant need to proofread books and I have contacts to get you started. Just a stepping stone into the work market."

Peter spoke up, "Sue, please accept the offer. The only way Maggie and I are going to fight over this is if you turn us down. It's the right thing to do. Deposit the money when you get back from the trip. Please."

Maggie persisted, "Sue, you worked for a few years between high school and marriage. Was it in property management?"

"A real estate firm in Clearview, and I was good."

"Then, it's time you produce a good CV, and start knocking on doors. The world still needs people who are willing to work. So, enjoy the trip and we can think of future work when you return."

Sue thought of all the years she had lived across the lake from Maggie, lived less than an hour away, and she hadn't taken the time to know her sister-in-law at all. It was obvious Maggie was offering more than a loan. She was offering support as a friend.

"Maggie, thanks." Hell, if I don't keep this light, I'll start to cry, "You and I can talk when I get back. Have some girl-time together. Just us." Maggie squeezed Sue's hand, as Allie came in the kitchen, "mom, grampy says I'm the navigator. Come on, Mom. We have to start now."

Sue drove, while John studied the map. He flipped the map

a number of times and finally said, "This part of New York State is so isolated, there just isn't a direct way from here to Toronto." They snaked up and down hills, changing roads, and past small towns, heading toward the International Bridge at Cornwall, Ontario. Once across the St. Lawrence River, Sue found the 401 highway and headed west. Now, it was almost a straight line journey to Toronto.

Allie was serious on directions, "Remember, mom, keep going west." Delighted with her position of authority and gave directions often, "Mom, I followed the map from Atlanta to uncle Peter's. And grampy only got lost once... when he didn't listen to me." Eventually, observant Allie looking out the window asking, "Grampy, where are the mile markers?"

"They use kilometres here, Allie... little miles."

"How do I find where we are without mile markers?"

"Just look for the next big town we pass and then find it on the map."

"Okay, grampy."

Allie was delighted when they finally stopped at a food plaza and said she wanted to order her own lunch. "I've been practising with a girl in Atlanta." When they resumed driving, some of Allie's trip excitement had morphed to disappointment. "Mom, Ontario might be bigger than Texas, but they aren't very polite here. I tried to order in French, and said, 'Est que je peut avoir un bil Mac, s'il vous plait? All the lady could say was, 'fine, kid, now what do you want.' Mom, I've been practising that French for weeks, and they didn't understand me."

"Well, your grandmother spoke French, and many people do, but not everyone. Come to think, dad, I don't remember mom speaking French, but Peter remembers mom singing in French while working in the kitchen. But I have no memory of it."

"Your mom had a pretty voice, but I have no idea when she sang and when she didn't. In my Air Force years, Sue, when you were small, I missed a lot of the family times. Is her singing important?"

"No, but my having a memory that differs from Peter's, could be. It is odd that mom never taught me a single word of French. Not one."

"I would guess our Georgia put mom off speaking French. An incident happened soon after I settled our family at my dad's place. This poor Louisiana family, buying groceries in our little town store, and the store people couldn't understand the poor folks, so your mom tried talking to them in her French. The Georgia folk were laughing, so my dad made the mistake of calling your mom the 'French Lady.' It stuck, and some folks called her that from then on. Seems funny now but, at the time, it upset Joanna that people laughed at her for knowing another language. And she never shopped at that place again."

"Well, mom was sensitive."

"I told her, in rural Georgia, anything not apple pie American, can cause problems." John fell silent, driving for miles, before adding, "Even today, those old town folks probably still remember Joanna as the French Lady." And he fell silent as more miles passed.

"Mom," Allie was restless, "where will I sleep in Oakville?"

Is that a worry of being safe, Allie? "Your uncle Fred is arranging a nearby motel... so don't worry about sleeping or eating. They have just as much food in Canada as we have back home. Might even find a friend your age to play with?"

"Is my uncle Fred related to my uncle Peter?"

"Yes. Of course. Peter is my brother, while Fred is my mother's brother. Fred and Maria are your great-aunt and uncle. Do you get it now?"

Family relations are often mysterious to children. "Is he very old, mom?"

Sue shrugged her shoulders, "I don't recall him sweetie. How old is Fred, dad?" John laughed at this, "Fred's a year younger than me, Allie, and your mother hasn't seen him since she wore diapers."

Allie found that remark hilarious, "Mom was in diapers. Is that true mom? You were in diapers?"

John switched topic, "Allie, what's the next big town?" She answered, straight away, "Kingston, grampy. Twenty kilometres away. That's ten minutes." So John replied, "Are you hungry, Allie?"

"Sure, stop, dad. Kids are always hungry, and it's time for your medication."

John continued educating Allie, "Did you see the strange colours of all the Canadian money. Be less hassle if they just used our money?"

After eating, Sue took the wheel, checked her reflection in the mirror. Only scratches with bits of dried blood showing. And it's getting better. "Sunglasses will cover the worst part so tell Fred and Maria, it was only a bad fall." My relatives don't need to know about my marriage problems.

The trip moved through a flat-farming landscape. Sue commented, "Doesn't this drive remind you of Southern Georgia - the boring part - from Atlanta to Valdosta. Only no billboard signs here. Don't they advertise in this country?"

Allison piped up, "Mom, I need to go."

"Why didn't you go half an hour ago when I asked you?"

"I didn't have to go then, mom. "

"Then, check the map. Where's the next stop?"

Later, with Allie asleep on the back seat, Sue figured it was a good time to talk of her troubles with Allan yesterday. "Dad, I cried on Hank's shoulder yesterday, cried over so many problems hitting me at the same time. I figured it was just bad luck, but Hank has a different view. He says trying to do something different, swimming against the current, makes all my choices much harder. And that has me thinking of our trip. How come it's happening now, when my life is falling apart? Why have we never stayed in touch with our relatives in Canada?"

"That's not simple to answer, Sue." John let moments slip by before continuing, "I figured to get your past straight, then it makes sense to check out your birthplace. I wouldn't go to Canada by choice. They were your mom's kin, not mine. However, I've come to realize we should follow questions raised by science - as long as we remember, that if a hospital baby switch did take place, then it doesn't matter a pinch of coon shit now. You're my daughter. Period." Looking directly at Sue, John added, "I know you feel exactly the same."

"I do, dad. Still, what if we find a baby switch. That means there's another adult, just like me, who has the wrong parents. That could be turmoil for another family. And I don't want to cause that."

"I don't follow. Where are you going with this idea, Sue?"

"I only need an answer for my birth, and not for a second person. Before you arrived yesterday, Peter and I talked of mom, and almost got into a fight. It's true dad, he remembers a different mom than I do... so if my search is stirring up a conflict now, then I need to be careful. Once we know of a baby switch, then I stop searching. I'm content to leave it all alone. This search is to unite the family, not separate us."

"Sue, I'm on your side. As a family we love and support each other; that's all there is to it."

"Wish I could say that for Peter, dad. He argues with anger, and remembers mom so differently, that it worries me. Why does Peter see mom as weak, when I remember strength?"

John hesitated, then continued thoughtfully, "When kids are growing up, they get a wrong idea in their mind and just won't let go. Your brother was mad at your mom for a long, long time. I still don't understand his old grievance, but it was festering for years and surfaced when Joanna died. He was unreasonable. Making snide remarks and saying he was determined to skip her funeral. So we had some harsh words that day, words we both regret."

"Peter didn't skip mom's funeral, dad, and I don't remember any fuss."

"He stayed, reluctantly, only to appease me, and left immediately afterwards. We hardly spoke for two years and he still avoids talking of your mom. I never found out why he made a stink about skipping her funeral. To this day, I don't know what's eating his craw.'

"Could just be losing mom and how death affects people differently."

Her father again was thoughtful before answering. "It didn't seem to be mom's death that got Peter upset, but more like her death released old anger. I lost my cool when Peter said something like, *'Why go to mom's funeral when she didn't help me in life.'* It was out of line, so we argued."

Miles passed before Sue added, "I asked Hank why Peter's feelings for mom should be different from mine. Hank sees it as the oldest child pressure. Peter is a hard worker and responsible, so perhaps, he resented the way mom relied on him?"

"Perhaps, perhaps, perhaps. You can analyse life forever and not figure it out. Peter might skip my funeral one day and say I'm not significant either."

Sue laughed, and lightened the conversation, "Well, if he misses your funeral dad, I'll get even for you, and not attend his funeral."

John turned in the passenger seat to look directly at his

daughter's profile, "Sue, while we're talking of problems, tell me what was happening to you last year Why were you so out of it then? Did you overdose on medication?"

"What do you mean?" God he shouldn't have asked. What can of worms will this open?

"Little things like Harry's visit. He told me he saw you after Christmas but you say he didn't. So either you are keeping his visit a secret, or you don't honestly remember. Now don't get on your high horse. You've changed in the last few months, and I'm proud of that. But what was happening before Christmas?"

"Dad, you don't know what you're saying." Sue gripped the wheel hard. "Harry didn't see me after Christmas, and Allan was the biggest problem last year. Besides, it's not something I need to keep looking at."

"Sue, every time I called from Atlanta, you couldn't remember things. Something zonked you out most every time I called."

"Dad, I didn't realize it was obvious... and it had happened so gradually... I was hooked on prescription drugs before I knew what was happening." Sounds believable, "Codeine mainly. Taking pain killers for my shoulder. Couldn't stop? I hit a brick wall. A short version is... arrested for shoplifting and when the cops finished with me that afternoon, it was late to pick up Allie. The teacher looked after her, and threatened me with welfare. But that woke me up and started the change, while every day Allan stayed drunk and knows nothing of my problems at all. And I couldn't call you. Ashamed. Had no idea you even twigged to it?"

"Everyone was aware. Even your sister, Annie, was willing to take you into her home... willing to look after you."

"The flake would do that?" She never said a word.

"You're much loved, Sue, by all of us."

Sue wiped her eyes while driving a few miles in silence

before saying, "Just so grateful to be free of pills, dad. You're the best dad in the world. Thanks."

As usual, when praised, John gave his practised nod of being cool, his unconscious signal of accepting thanks and saying, let's move on. "You know that it was quite smart of me to think of taking this trip. It should bring our family closer. Fred's wife, Maria, was Joanna's best friend, and if anyone alive knows your mom, besides me, then it's Maria. Oakville should be good for you."

"Dad, I'm counting on them having a good memory and talking till the cows come home. They knew mom as a little girl and have memories of mom that no one else has. Who knows, my Canadian relatives just might understand, or know, something to make sense of my past and clean up this damn DNA difference." This has to work, because where else can I look for answers to my birth?

Chapter 10

Clearville's Methodist church hall was quiet. It's atmosphere only disturbed by the click of paper cups Allan was trying to count and the frustration in his voice, "Can you believe it? Three times I've counted these cups and got a different number each time. Can you understand why my count goes off, Stu?" Stewart Bailey, looked up, nodded yes at Allan, and continued fussing at the coffee urn. "Oh, sure, you understand in a pig's eye. Stu, you're twenty feet away. How can you possibly see where I'm counting wrong? You're clever Stu, but I don't think you're that clever."

"Allan, did you call your wife yet to apologize?"

"Me apologize? Hey buddy, my truck was damaged, my truck, by my wife. By her. She did it. Any apology coming will be coming my way."

Stu ignored Allan for a while, then spoke as if to himself. "This reminds me of my toenail problem. Did I ever mention my toenail problem?"

"What problem you talking of? Did I miss something? You never mentioned toenails."

"Well, my toenails are sort of similar to your truck problem, Allan." He waited, and then continued, "Years back, when I was a big shot, some mornings I'd feel my toenails needed cutting. They bothered me, but I was a busy man back then and didn't have time to cut toenails. An important person. Cutting nails, hell, not a five minute job, but couldn't spare the time while rushing off in the morning. Then at night, being tired, wouldn't take the time to do it. Next morning, same thing, needed to trim my toenails, but I'd rush off to work. A busy man doesn't have time to do little things. It also bugged me getting holes in the toes of my socks and needing new ones."

"Stu, where is this going? What's the point?"

"The point is the hidden cost of things, Allan. There's open cost like when you buy a car - the price and associated costs for insurance and repairs, and there's hidden costs you don't easily see... like being put off your new car, when a neighbour goes and buys the same car for less money. Ever have that happen? Or bragging of a shirt you pick up for nine bucks only to find out it's on sale the next week for six bucks. That bugs the life out of people and if you get right down to it, most costs in life are hidden. Anyway, my toe nails. I go for a job interview, and my big toe slips out of my sock, while I'm talking to the president of the company. Now the president can't see it, and I know he can't see it, but I can feel it. Just enough to bug me. So I try moving my foot inside the shoe, trying to force the toe back into the sock while I'm being interviewed by this head honcho. Did such a good deal of wriggling, lost concentration, and missed a question or two. Turns out they didn't hire me. Maybe thought I fidgeted too much? Who knows? Whatever, the job went to someone else and, at the time, I didn't think much of it. Years later, after no longer being a big shot and waking up to hidden things, like the cost of putting off the obvious, I've always kept my toenails trimmed. Since then, I've never lost another job interview. Now, where were we, Allan?"

"I've no idea Stu. You have a unique way of confusing my mind."

"Oh yes, cups. Your problem of counting cups more than once. Your mind's not clear, Allan, is why you keep getting different results. So do the simple thing and clear your mind. Apologize for blocking your wife in the drive, do it mentally, now, and when you get the chance, to do it in person, too. You'll feel better now and, next time, the cups might count right."

"Stu, is that the truth? Lose a job because of a hole in your sock?" Allan kept counting cups. "Well. What do you know, they came out right this time. And Stu, I don't believe you even have toenails. Rightly, I don't believe you have any."

* * * * *

While Allan counted coffee cups for his afternoon meeting in Clearville, Vermont, Sue continued her Ontario drive in comfortable silence. Her dad had sat quietly in the passenger seat, sitting still in his thinking mode. He looked at the back seat to make sure Allie was still asleep, then asked Sue, "Are you off the pills for good?"

"Who knows? You're asking me a question that can't be answered. No, that's not true. I'm off them, not going back, and don't ever want to get my brain that fuzzy. But will I stay off them forever - who knows?"

"Fair enough. I'm proud of you, Sue. You're a grown woman not some teenager making mistakes with drugs. You're beyond that."

"Am I? I hope so, dad." My physical addiction was gone in a day or two, but my mind had an insidious desire to go back and start again. That pull lingered for months. Still there, at times, even now.

John checked on Allie still sleeping on the back seat, then said, "You can beat drugs with strong willpower. The mind can figure things out and willpower is the answer."

"Willpower, works perhaps, for some. Dad, for me, I couldn't explain why I started, and when I stopped, couldn't say why it happened. It's odd, but a lady who served me in a coffee shop helped me. She never talked of pills or my being ill but, somehow, she knew I was a sad case, and she would touch my shoulder, when she gave me a cup of coffee. Small little touch, impossible to explain, but it worked magic. That simple touch from a stranger pushed me past some terribly difficult days. Now I've had it with introspection. Let's get happy." Sue pointed to the map and said, "Find out where the hell we are and enough with the questions."

John unfolded the map, "Close to Toronto. One more stop. Then drive through the big city and find the little town of Oakville." Let's get there, see the relatives, and get me back home. "Sue, the map shows a shorter way back to Atlanta. We could skip returning to Peter's and go back to Atlanta through Niagara Falls."

"How? My clothes are at Peter's. He's expecting us, and I need to see Hank." She called to her daughter, "Wake Allie, dad, there's a rest stop ahead." Allie had the sleeping gift many kids possess - out like a light one moment - then wide awake the next.

She awoke, "Are we stopping for something to eat, mom?"

John made the decision, "Stopping for dinner, Allie. It just wouldn't do to arrive at our relatives and expect to be fed." He asked Allie, "Are you looking forward to meeting your aunt Maria? Bet you didn't realize you had so many relatives in Canada?"

"Did you always know they lived up north, grampy?"

"I certainly did Allie."

"Then, why didn't we visit them before? Why wait till I'm almost eleven?"

"I've already explained that sweetheart," her mother answered. "There were four kids in our family after I came along, and mom said it was just getting too hard to travel north with that many kids. Your grampy was still based in California for a while, weren't you dad? So we didn't visit Canada anymore. It happens sweetie, families, sometimes, go in different ways. But, your aunt Maria said on the phone, they will be delighted to see us all."

"And there will be a bed for me, right mom. And a TV."

"Yes sweetie, I'll make sure there's a bed for you and a TV. Now let's go for dinner and then drive to Oakville."

With a hundred miles to go, Sue encountered the rushing edge of Toronto traffic with drivers scurrying in and out in ever slowing lanes. Their drive had become a superhighway with eight lanes of traffic in each direction. Sue asked, "Dad, where did the Canadian wilderness go? This mess is worse than Atlanta's rush hour." As traffic slowed to a crawl again, she chatted to her dad of odds and ends until she found herself talking of gut feelings, "Dad, isn't it sad mom didn't live to see Allie. How long ago did mom die, over ten years ago? I never realized mom was so ill."

John waited a moment before saying, "Just do what you can in life Sue and leave the regrets for others. But I miss her, too. Your mom was unique. I knew that from the first day I met her that she was extraordinary, and the only girl for me. We clicked, from the moment we met."

"Dad, tell us me how you met mom. Allie, listen to grampy tell how he met your grandmother."

"Mom, he's told me this before."

"Well, listen again. Go ahead, dad."

"Again? Must have told you a hundred times." John smiled at his own memories, "I was a substitute on the Atlanta rowing team, and our coach took us all up to Oakville for training. I was a long skinny kid from Atlanta, when I met your mom for the very first time. Teenagers. And there was a physical spark the instant we talked. Seemed as if the few feet of space between us had gone into some kind of silence, slow motion, and only your mom and I existed. Electric. But also sad. How can a kid from Atlanta dream of having a girlfriend from Oakville. And she was standoffish. When I suggested we write each other, she damn well ignored me. What I didn't realize is Joanna was thinking, concentrating hard and at the end of the day, with absolutely perfect timing, she caught me off balance and pushed me into the Oakville river.

"Now that got my attention, but it also meant she had to take me home to her place to dry me out and, that gave us something to talk about. Joanna never admitted she pushed me deliberately, but every time she talked of it, her eyes were alight with smiles."

"Did my grandmother really push you in the river, grampy?" Allie asked, with a ten-year-old's delight.

"I was shivering, Allie, soaking wet from head to toe and when she took me home, her parents just laughed and dried me out. That's how we got to know each other. But your mom knows this story backwards."

"Well, dad, mom mentions that story in one of her letters I brought to show our relatives. And mom's letters have some of her poetry. It was a surprise to find she wrote poems."

A voice piped up from the back seat, "Neat. I write poetry. Does grandma take after me, mom?"

Sue grimaced, "Allie, you have big ears. Just find that envelope in my purse and give it to grampy." As John opened the old papers, Sue pointed to one page, "Have you seen it before? Read it, dad."

While Sue drove, and John read,   Allie listened to her grandmother's words from half a century ago.

Warmth of Tea

I would like a cup of tea, a hand to hand it onto me
to sit and talk, while loving lips, softly whisper a future plan
on life, on love and dreams unfolding, on years that span
bonding us, over brimming cups, I with he and he with me

lightly brimmed toward a promised child, a golden life
design of warmth, touching, soaring, starting spark
as if drinking tea will somehow change a lonely strife
of raining pain, again, spreading on, to gloomy dark

as coming night reducing me
to begging for a cup of tea.
not me, not you, but all of thee

Joanna

Sue was touched to hear her dad's voice reading her
mother's thoughts, "Wonderful isn't it, dad? It's open prose, like
Whitman wrote, except he used stuffy old man's words. Look at the
date - mom was only sixteen, when she wrote that dark poem."

"Sue, but I've never seen this page before." John looked
closely at the handwritten page. "It's Joanna's writing, Sue, but I
don't remember your mom ever showing me this. Where did you
find it?"

"In an envelope at the bottom of mom's photo box. This
poem and a dozen more like it were in an envelope in a larger
envelope. Hank found the pages. I wanted Peter to read it - except
he wasn't in the mood to talk of the past. Dad, what was mom like
when she was writing these poems?"

"I have no idea." John turned the poem over and looked at
the blank side of the page, as if the empty page would provide an
answer. "My school years were wrapped up in sports. Joanna was
different; complex, talented, and extremely private. She wrote poems
often, but showed very few to me, and I think she destroyed most of
them. I guess this is one she forgot to burn." John held up the poem,
"But, this is her. Always thinking, talking, examining everything - an
extravert. I sat in the background just plodding along in life, while

Joanna was the take charge intellectual."

"Dad, you did well in university."

"College. Joanna always embellished my academic mind, saying I went to university, but college was all I graduated from. She pursued the university as education, while my Air Force studies were job-related. Poetry didn't matter much, when we had a war to win in Vietnam. I liked everything your mom did, just didn't have her level of understanding. Joanna knew my simple philosophy began and ended with the Pledge of Allegiance."

"But, it's good to be patriotic."

John shook his head, "I believe so, Sue, but your mom would differ. She once said 'patriotic and parasitic are similar - living on someone else.' Where I saw waving the flag as supporting our country, your mom saw that same patriotism, as narrow, preventing me seeing a greater world. And I understood that, understood her view was larger than mine, yet she could be so damn infuriating with it. I've never forgotten one time, when we were arguing, she stopped talking in the middle of a sentence. Dead stop. And simply spoke above our conversation, saying, 'John, there's no point in our debating this, because as an American you won't comprehend a world view.' She wasn't angry or meaning to insult me. It's as if she realized a child was dealing with an issue it couldn't understand. Then she walked away. Maddening. She had this different way of thinking. Her education, antiwar views, being a Canadian, French heritage; it set her up to see life different from my eyes."

Big ears from the back piped up. "My mom's Canadian. Aren't you, mom?"

"American, Allie, I'm American."

"Your mom's American, Allie. She doesn't like to be teased on this." John said.

But Sue had become angry, looking toward her daughter on the back seat and loudly saying, "How many times do I need to tell everyone - an American, born in Canada - but an American. Allie, I didn't mean to yell, but this still gets to me. Your uncle Peter never missed a chance to rub it in, that I was the one born in Canada. As if it were my fault. And when I complain, no one listens, no one."

Sue, pre-occupied by the teasing, missed seeing the signs for a road split, and that turned instantly dangerous. An eighteen-wheeler veered in front of her car, forcing Sue to break hard and move again to her right lane. "I must be in his blind spot, dad. He can't see me." Again, the truck headed for Sue's lane, forcing another jog to the right. Now, on a road split she didn't want, she was channelled onto the main highway split, moved into a feeder lane and, in an instant heading south on another massive eight-lane monster. "Dad, where the hell am I going. I'm driving south and Oakville is west."

Ten-year-old Allie, oblivious to traffic speeding by, just read the map, "You're okay, mom. Can't go too far south. A big lake will stop you."

"Great sweetie. Just tell me how to get to Oakville?"

John waited a moment before asking, "Sue, want me to drive?"

"No. No, it's not the driving or being tired, dad, it's the teasing. I want the teasing to end. Yesterday, stupid Peter tells Allie I was born in Canada and encourages her to needle me. You know he's done it for years, knows it bothers me, and now Allie's started doing it. And you and mom never stopped him, did you? Well, I don't like my stupid brother. Sorry Allie. I was yelling at my brother, not you. But don't you tease me again."

John looked at Allie, and then shrugged. She grinned back.

Chapter 11

The drive continued west to Oakville, exiting at Trafalgar Road south and, from there, Allie read aloud the detailed directions to Fred and Maria's home. When Sue pulled into the bungalow's drive in the old part of town, there was, no doubt, Fred and Maria Court were expecting them; the outside lights were on, the front door was open, and two people sat outside waiting. Joanna's brother and sister-in- law embraced their American cousins with an unmistakable warm welcome. From the first hug, Sue was comfortable with her aunt Maria. And Maria couldn't stop her chatter, "Come in, come in, we've been waiting. Hope you're all hungry? In the kitchen, everyone. You will be sitting in the dining room tomorrow, when the rest of the cousins get here. Sit, please... Fred, get them something to drink and don't forget the ice, they must be hot from travelling. Please, eat, start with what's on the table while I serve the rest. And Fred, where are those drinks? Are you comfortable, Allie? Come on Fred, you're slow as molasses in January." Everyone was talking, often at the same time, talking through dinner, over dessert and coffee, with Maria making sure Sue and Allie always felt at home. Endless, comfortable jabbering, from relatives reunited after years out of touch.

"Allie, you get the guest bedroom with your mom. Then, Maria whispered to the young girl, "Pick the bed by the window and you'll see our pesky squirrels attacking the bird feeder in the morning. You won't need an alarm clock with them squirrels around. Do you want to go check your room now?" Turning to John, Maria added, "For you granddad, we've arranged a motel a few blocks away - much more comfortable than our old sofa. So it's all set then. Fred and I are just so glad you came to visit."

Maria lost a little of her smile as she added, "Your visit is a happy time, happy for all of us, but it's sad to know Harry is gone. We only knew him as a little kid and didn't hear of the airplane crash, until John called the other week. I looked through our old pictures and found one of Harry." She gave Sue a beautifully framed black and white of a little kid - a kid playing on the beach with the lake in the background and smiling at the camera. "It's for you. I think this was taken the last time your mom brought Harry for a visit."

Allie skipped back into the kitchen and lightened the sombre mood, "Mom, aunt Maria is right, I want the bed by the window. You can have the other one."

Later, with Allie asleep and her dad at his motel, Sue easily told Maria of how her DNA test didn't match her family and that's why they decided to make this trip. Finishing with, "... so, my marriage on the rocks, and the family confused over my birth, I figured coming here and just looking at the place I was born might help to settle my mind. Dad suggested it, that we come and see you, hoping to settle this somehow... find some answers."

"Heavens sakes, Sue, I don't know much on science and testing, but I'll take your word on being in turmoil. How can we help? Heavens, I've squirreled away a pile of old pictures and papers, some might help you, and you're welcome to see it all. And Fred and I will gladly give whatever science samples you need. Family testing. Long as I don't give blood. Just hate needles."

"I hadn't considered testing our relatives, Maria. I'm just hoping to reach into your memories of the past and understand my mom better. Perhaps, see the hospital where my mom gave birth to me."

"Then, you're in the exact right place for memories. And old records. I have boxes of them." Maria continued to reminisce, "Your mom was my best friend since grade school. Thick as thieves for years, long before she married your dad. Joanna was a fascinating person and I saved all the letters and stories Joanna left here, when she went to live in the States."

"You have things my mom wrote?"

"Pages and pages. Fred's the pack rat in the family and he stored all Joanna's writings, her journals, and notes... going back to high school years. Hoping one of her kids would value them enough to sort through the lot."

"Can I see them, aunt Maria?"

"See them? Lands sake, Sue, you take them all home. Our basement's so full of junk now, I couldn't find the furnace if I tried. Fred knows where everything is down there. Shall we get him busy bringing your mom's things into the kitchen?" Maria, walking toward her husband's computer den, raised her voice, and called, "Fred, I've got a job for you." Coming back to Sue, she said, "He can look while we talk, because I've a ton of questions to ask... if it's all right to ask. Don't want to be nosey." Maria laughed at her own words, "Oh, may as well tell the truth, people have said I do, at times, ask a few questions too many. It's just a treat for us to have contact again with Joanna's daughter and granddaughter." Seventy-year-old, Maria Alhambra Court, continued to be charming, "Tea and cookies while we talk, dear? If the English are remembered for anything, it's likely for having tea and socializing."

"I have a poem my mom wrote about tea... did you know she wrote poems? It's marvellous, but dark."

"Heavens, Sue, your mom was always jotting down dramatic short stories and poems. Very dark ones. God, it's all coming back after so many years have gone by. I remember our Algebra teacher, Mr. Sims, quietly moved Joanna to the back of the room, where your mom could work on stories and not bother anyone else. He was a hoot. I still remember him, at the end of the year, saying to her 'If you promise never to take another math course, I'll give you a passing grade in Algebra.' Oakley and I laughed for years over that. And we never took another math course."

"Oakley?"

Maria looked surprised, "Sure, we had nicknames. Your mom's went from Joanna to Annie to Oakley. English stuff, Cockney slang. I was Camille. It suited me perfectly. Oh, my teens were so tragic, god, it was awful. Were you that tragic in your teens? I was. Taking forever in the morning on my hair, having to skip breakfast and then, at school, Oakley would put her arms around me, saying, 'Camille, oh poor Camille... you have to eat or you will just die. You will fade away to nothing.' Our troubled teen years were great times. And your mom also used the name Joyanna at times. You should fine that on some of her letters."

"I did see that name in her papers. I had no idea it was a nickname." Keep talking, Maria. I never knew my mom like this. "Are her letters in the basement, too?"

"Enough junk down there to start the Joanna Court Museum. Give me a minute to see what Fred's found." Maria left the room, and returned carrying an old, square, C.C.M. Skate box overflowing with letters and papers, "This is part of them. Hope your dad has room in his car for stacks of musty old papers."

Maria, searching in remnants of Joanna's past, was delighted as memories flooded back to her. "Joanna's teachers marvelled at her intelligence. They all knew she had a gift. I remember these... now if I can find one particular scrap of paper that reveals how bright your mother was... now where is it? Ah, here it is." She held a tattered restaurant table menu with a stylized A&W on it. "Sue, do you remember the old drive-in restaurants?"

"Drive thru ones?"

"Nope. Drive-ins. The car would pull up to the restaurant,

with girls coming out to take your order, and then carrying food to the car. Anyway, just after your mom first met your dad, Joanna and I went to the canoe races, the big war canoes at Port Credit and, afterwards, we went to the A&W. I told Joanna to get a local boy friend, to forget your dad cause Georgia was so far away. Find an Oakville boy friend I told her." Maria paused in remembering, "Well, your mom looked at me as if I had two heads, and right at the A&W, as easy as snapping your fingers, Joanna turned over this very menu and wrote the poem on the back. Joanna didn't stop to think, or take time, she just wrote." Maria handed Sue the old tattered paper.

June in northern place
one gentle hand to hold
your touch becomes so bold
as vibrant passions move my face
no soul so sparkling rushing bright
now reaching for a southern light
and vows in life to hold our place

"Sue, I saw your mom write this out as quickly, as you and I would copy it now. She never corrected a single word. Now, I couldn't do that, could you? That takes a special talent that few people have. Brilliant. Read the stanza carefully. It's her love poem to your dad. And look at the last line... Joanna is saying 'Till death do us part.' Isn't that's a marriage vow?" Maria's eyes were damp.

"Mom wrote this before she married dad?"

Maria nodded yes. "Joanna, then gave me that poem, just casually flipping it across the table, 'I signed it for you.' Can you see a signature, Sue? I couldn't at the time... but look Sue, look again, look at the first letter of each line - Joyanna - your mom's pet name for her poems."

"My mom wrote this on the spur of the moment?"

"Exactly as it is. An instant love letter with her initials starting each line. She was special." Little tears formed under Maria's eyes. "Don't mind me, Sue, just an old aunt remembering a happy past."

Later, with the house settling in sleep, Sue picked up the phone by her bed, used a Bell South calling card, and rang Hank in Clearville, Vermont. He was pleased she called, "Miss you already, Sue. Those Canadian relatives treating you okay? Any help yet, understanding your mom?"

"Hank, aunt Maria is a gem. Fabulous. Remembers everything about mom and, best of all, she has boxes full of mom's letters. She's been waiting years to pass mom's stuff on to any of her kids that want it. It's mine now, if dad will cram his car full and bring it all back."

"Sounds like you found a treasure of memories. What about birth records? Is your aunt cooperating on those?"

"Hank, my aunt and uncle couldn't be better. They're both open with everything. When Fred realized my trip to Canada started over a DNA problem, he said, 'Take a sample from me, I'm the closest relative to my sister that's still alive.' I might take him up on his offer, just to see how uncle Fred's DNA fits our family pattern. So, his sample, plus all mom's old material Maria's going to hand over, just might be the break I need to resolve mom and my testing problem."

"It's funny how your trip has worked out so well. In Atlanta, your dad only reluctantly dug out a few of your mom's letters, and grudgingly released those."

"Hank, dad is the only thing that's out of step. He's helping, yet sort of not helping, dragging his feet just so subtlety, that I'm not even sure he's an issue. Maria has put Allie and me up in her home and they arranged a motel for dad, all of which is logical, because my aunt and uncle have a small place, but I know dad didn't like the arrangements. There seemed a cold chill between dad and Maria, when he realized we were being separated. Since then, while Maria is friendly with me, she covers dad with a reserve or a little too much politeness. And, dad, gives the same vibes back."

"Relatives. Just leave them alone, Sue. Who can understand old family emotions? How long will you be staying there?"

"Three or four days. I'd like to stay weeks to sort mom's old papers and stories. She wrote all kinds of things. One of them is eighty-five pages. Uncle Fred carried up six boxes already and said there's double that still in his basement. They are funny. Maria told me Fred's a pack rat, but when she wasn't listening, Fred says it's Maria that hoards family stuff. Whatever, it's a miracle they saved mom's papers."

"And if you talk to Maggie tell her 'thanks for Peter's camera' cause tomorrow Fred's driving us to a Milton hospital, where I was born. We can get a few pictures. You know Maria remembers visiting mom in that hospital, when I was just a day old. And dad says he remembers that hospital, when he arrived to take us all back to the States."

Hank asked the impossible, "That's years ago, Sue. Would your birth records, like who your doctor was - would that still be at the hospital?"

"I have no idea and Maria just shrugged when I asked her. Hank, it was thirty-five years ago, and thinking they would have my records is expecting too much. But it could be."

Hank persisted, "A long shot but ask them? Just ask. If Canadian hospitals work like ours, then they keep records on everything - and hold them forever. Your records could be sitting in a dust-coated box just waiting for you to find them."

"You're an optimist, Hank. Just going to the hospital tomorrow is great for me. And who knows, I might even get my dad to put on a smile tomorrow. Every time Maria starts to ramble on, he grows silent with cold vibes."

"Well, your life in Clearville is turning positive. Apparently, Allan called our station today, and he won't press charges against you for damage to his truck, or against your brother for menace. He's dropped everything. Just a misunderstanding he says."

" Can you call my brother and tell Peter the news."

"Not necessary. Apparently, Allan called him - had a sociable conversation, and it's resolved as far as our station is concerned. So get busy up there ... and," he paused for effect, then added, "come back to Clearville and marry me next week."

"Hank, it's illegal proposing to a married woman."

"Only if you accept." and Hank's voice then changed from kidding to serious, as he added, "Will you be ready for a long talk when you return?"

"When I get back, take me to Carvers for lunch and, prepare to listen, instead of jumping the gun to rush me." And lighten up, Hank. "Can the Mounties charge you with illegal marriage arrangements across an international border?"

Hank chuckled. "Mounties don't handle cop things in Ontario, so you can't call them. Besides, I'd deny everything."

"Wish me luck tomorrow. I'm tired, so say good-night, Hank."

"You hang up first."

"Hank, don't play childish games."

"All right. But you hang up first."

"Good-night." Sue put down the phone, yawned, and headed for bed.

Hank heard Sue click her line closed and, then, a fraction of a second later, he heard an extra click. He thought to himself, "Odd. Why a second click? Could be a glitch, or the simple explanation - another phone hanging up after Sue hung up? Probably nothing, but I'll mention it to Sue, next time we talk."

In her bedroom, Maria put down the extension, let out a comforting sigh, and drifted into sleep.

As Maria had promised, in the morning, chattering squirrels woke Allie. She watched them try, in vain, to reach the bird feeder, scurry-up a plastic sheet, fall off, chatter in frustration, and then try again to reach the feeder. After a while, she made her way to the kitchen and told Maria, "You were right, they make a lot of noise and kept falling off the plastic."

"That's your uncle Fred's invention, Allie. He'll be pleased his squirrel block still works."

"Should I tell uncle Fred that one squirrel made it to the feeder?"

Maria just laughed, "Here's your mom. You sleep well last night?"

Sue nodded and then hugged her daughter. "Morning, Allie." Allie just nodded in her sleepy morning mode, and was quite content to let the adults chatter on. Maria was saying, "So it's settled. After breakfast, the five of us can drive to Milton in our car, tour the hospital, and return here for lunch. Afterwards, maybe your dad and Fred can have a walk around Oakville, while we gab at home and sort through your mom's papers. Sound okay?"

"Perfect. And why did they all end up here?"

"More chance than anything." Maria laughed, with her infectiously open laugh, "When your mom married and went to the States, her papers stayed at her parents' home for years. Later, when I married Fred, the family house was sold and we stored her boxes."

"Why did she just leave them?" Sue touched her mom's old books tenderly.

"No clue, but anyway, it's your stuff now... if you want the lot?"

"Absolutely yes. Her papers and the old books. I'll take back as much as the car will hold. Did my mom have a favourite book?"

"Your mom's favourite was whatever she was reading at the moment. Always with two or three stories on the go, and still able to start another. Often your grandmother would get fussy, tell Joanna to tidy the house, and Joanna would make a great fuss, talking sadly to each book, 'Marie Cecil is jealous of you Margaret Atwood. Marie Cecil doesn't like you either, Mr. Mitchell.' Oh, your grandmother and Joanna were very close."

Maria handed Sue a worn, dog-eared novel, "Now, this book almost had your mom kicked out of high school. It's Atwood's, *Surfacing*. Joanna insisted that Atwood had created a great antiwar novel and, demanded, the school declare it compulsory reading. Now, Atwood's book is set in Canadian cottage country, but Joanna maintained it was antiwar and should be read by everyone. The principle warned her about stirring up the students, but she didn't care much for warnings. Then, she made her famous speech in the cafeteria and finished by taking off her bra. They sent her home for that."

"Wow... mom must have been a fighter. I was never allowed to stand up for things in my school. And anyone who did, got kicked out."

"They were good kids in school," Maria continued, "but those were the '60's. A different time with rebellion in the air, peace movement, ban the bomb marches, and the anti-Vietnam fight - so, students were both teenagers and superheroes at the same time. We were ready to change the world, Sue. Especially Joanna, she was horrified over your Vietnam escalation and argued passionately against the war. I remember one article in the *Toronto Star*, that sent Joanna into a depression for weeks. A Buddhist monk had burned himself to death in protesting the American involvement. She hated the Vietnam war."

Sue was quiet, thinking, where is this going, Maria?

"Both sides figured they were right." Maria had stated the obvious, and continued, "Good people, both for and against the war years ago, just had different views. Your dad, he was quite proud of his job back in those different times." The ringing phone interrupted her, she said hello, and passed it to Sue, "Speak of the devil, he must have heard us talking about him."

"Hi, dad. Ready for Milton and the hospital I was born in. How did you sleep last night?"

"Not well. In fact, I changed motels late last night and the new one wasn't a great location. Still feel tired. So I'm not going to go to the hospital today."

"Why change motels? What was wrong with the one you were in... too noisy? " Sue told Maria, "Dad's in a different motel."

"Sue, this trip is getting me down and only getting back to the States is the only cure. I checked out because Maria had arranged that room and I won't be indebted to her in any way. Perhaps, we made a mistake in coming here. So, go see your hospital, I'll get a good rest, and we can get back to the States soon. Leave after lunch."

"After lunch today? You can't be serious, dad? We need to stay longer even to just look around?"

"No, we don't need to stay longer. It's just my being uncomfortable here. I want to return to Atlanta."

"Well, I suppose. I could see where I was born, sort mom's stuff, and we could leave tomorrow morning."

"Damn it, Sue, you're not listening. Go take a picture of where you were born, say good-bye to Maria and Fred, then start packing. We can leave right after lunch."

"Dad, Maria has other relatives coming to a special dinner for us tonight. I don't want to rush back. You stay in that motel for a nap and come over here for lunch. Rushing back doesn't make sense." Am I missing something? What's going on?

"Sue, the truth is Maria gets my blood pressure up by just being in her company. Make whatever excuse you want, just tell her we're going."

"What about mom's papers?" Sue turned to her aunt, "Maria, can you talk him out of leaving?"

If Sue expected Maria to humour John into staying, she was mistaken. Without taking the phone from Sue's hand, Maria spoke, knowing John could hear her words, "He's running away, Sue. He's done it before with the family, and he's doing it again. We'll have a good morning and your dad can stew in his own way." Maria's hand moved quickly to the phone and broke the connection, "Now dear, we will be here for a good hour if John wants to come over. Don't worry... he won't run off and leave you stranded."

An hour passed and still no call from John. Sue said, "Maria you shouldn't have hung up. He's going to be mad."

Maria wasn't concerned, "Oh bosh! Just carry on as planned. If you're worried, put a note on the back door telling him 'we will be home by lunch,' and leave it at that."

Sue nodded, wrote the note and went to the car. Maria, as the last one to leave the house, closed the back door, pocketed Sue's note, and headed for the car out front. "Everyone ready? Good. Then let's go."

Chapter 12

Fred drove north through rolling countryside, with the road running parallel to a long, low ridge of hills in the western distance. He pointed, "That's part of the Niagara Escarpment, running a hundred miles between Niagara Falls and Toronto. Nature made the area below the escarpment into exceptional farmland with, your birthplace, the old Town of Milton, nestled near a fold of those hills. I could never figure out if the land made the people hardy or if hardy people settled the land. Interesting regions." Fred, knowing he was the only one keeping conversation alive in the car, continued talking of the area he was driving through. Sue kept wondering why her dad was so adamant against Maria. And Maria kept her own silence. Eventually, Sue asked her, "What did you mean telling my dad 'you've done it before.' What did he do before?"

Her aunt gave a long sigh before answering, "I spoke out of turn to your dad and should learn to keep my big mouth shut. Your dad is stuck on a family feud from years ago, happened soon after you were born. But, to be fair, ask your dad what happened. I wasn't part of that incident. Fred and I married years after the fight and, by then, the bitterness was set in place."

Fred said to Sue, "Maria didn't know I existed, when you were born. She was too busy living the high life in Toronto to think of me or settling down in Oakville. She was never partial to small town living."

"That's not true, Fred, I always liked Oakville, just wasn't attracted to you. I didn't have a car back then, and Oakville was like living in the bush." Maria could see that Sue still wanted to know why her dad was upset. Turning to Fred she said, "Tell her, Fred.

Sue wants to know why her dad had a little tantrum. She can hear his side of things later. Tell her what happened."

Fred drove a few miles before saying, "When John called a few days ago we were just tickled pink to know of your visit. Sue, and all of you, including John, are most welcome. As far as we're concerned, any past problems are all water under the bridge of life, Sue." Fred hesitated, scratched his face a little, then continued, "All right. It must have happened on a Wednesday, some 35 years ago, cause Wednesday was my bowling night. We had just finished dinner and everything was fine, when I left the house to go bowling. My parents, your mom, John, and you, a tiny little bundle, were all getting along but when I got home, my mom was in tears and John had taken you and your mom back to the States. Your dad had arrived three days before to see your mom and you in the Milton Hospital. I picked him up at Toronto International, Malton, then, took him to Milton, and he spent two nights there. Then he arranged a car, drove you and Joanna to our family home in Oakville. But while I was bowling, his visit went sour."

"Sue, when I got home from bowling, my mom was crying and my dad was fit to be tied. Apparently, John had argued, shouted at them, apparently shouted like a mad man, grabbed Joanna and you, and headed out to drive to the States. He left that evening vowing never to set foot in Canada again. Just a bad scene." Fred stopped, thought a moment, and added, "That's it."

"Fred, there has to be more. Dad can get his back up at times but not over nothing." Sue said, "If my dad won't discuss it, then how will I ever know what happened?"

"I don't like talking of it cause I wasn't there but, mind you, my mom was badly shaken over it. She was crying, saying John had argued over that stupid Asian war, saying 'Canada   side-stepped that damn Asian war cause you're just a bunch of cowards.' Apparently, my dad told John to mind his manners or leave their house. So John demanded Joanna get you ready and he bolted, then everyone got upset, and the house was in an uproar. But if you want the low-down, then ask my sister. She was there and can tell you exactly what happened."

Sue wondered if her uncle was losing it, "Fred, remember, my mom died years ago."

"Yes, but Cecile is living. Joanna's older sister knows what happened. Ask your aunt Cecile."

"Aunt Cecile... mom has an older sister? And she's still living?"

"Of course, she's alive." Maria interrupted her husband, and continued, "Cecile was a mother hen to Joanna. Older sisters are like that. Heck, Cecile introduced your mom and dad." Her aunt's wide smile was almost a giggle. "And if I remember right, Cecile came to the Milton Hospital the very day you were born. She came from Oakville and I came from Toronto, every day, to be with your mom until your dad arrived. Then, he starts a big brawl with Joanna's folks, and hurries you all back to the States. The sad part of that fight is it doesn't matter anymore. Fred's folks are dead, your mom is dead, you were too young to remember anything, and the war is over. Only your dad wants to continue the fight. Comes a time to let the past alone."

"Maria, forget my dad, tell me of Cecile. My parents never spoke of her. Is she coming to the dinner tonight?"

"Haven't seen her in years. She lives down in Crescent City, California, and sends me a Christmas card every year. I may still have some of them saved. She would be pleased to hear from you, Sue. Old family arguments needn't separate relatives."

"That's exactly why I came, to reconnect with family. Especially, the secret relatives in hiding, like Cecile."

"Hiding?" That made Fred laugh. "Cecile is no secret. Hell,

I've known her all my life."

Maria relaxed in the front seat and turned to look at Sue, "You, and Fred and I, we all feel the same way. We've wanted this family reunion for years." Maria continued, "We should be close. Like the old days. Your mom would bring Peter and Annie for a few weeks, and the family watched baby Harry, and everyone expected this to continue. However, after your birth, after the rift in the family, Joanna never saw her relatives again. Never came here again."

Sue wondered about her dad carrying a grudge and staying angry for thirty years over nothing. "But he wouldn't cut his family off from relatives. Not my dad!"

Maria shrugged, "Well, then talk to him and get his side of things. Let him speak. All I know is Joanna's mom and dad blamed John for the rift. The family was adamant that John caused problems, talked against Cecile, badmouthed the family, and refused to visit here. He was an angry man because we, in Canada, wouldn't join his little killing war in Asia. As a result, John never again allowed Joanna and the kids to see their relatives. Beats me why he even came now?"

"It doesn't make sense, Maria; there has to be more involved to set him off?"

Maria looked both thoughtful and bewildered at the same time, "So, maybe, you can ask your dad another time. Focus on your birth issues. We've arrived at the Milton Hospital."

Fred slowed the car and parked in a large, open lot, facing a four-storey, white stone building. The hospital was nestled into a green area, on the southern edge of the bustling Town of Milton, with the escarpment rising behind it. Maria spoke, "Now just hold it, Sue. Don't get out yet till I get the camera." Maria started a video camera, getting a picture of Sue stepping onto the hospital parking lot, while saying, "This is your life, - and the birthplace of the world famous Susan Stevens, and I remember the day she was born in the little hospital of Milton. God, Sue, your mom was so proud. She was over the moon to have you. I remember everything that hot summer."

* * * * *

Back then, thirty-five years ago, Joanna stood by a window, on the second floor maternity ward, and watched her mom and dad arriving to visit. Then, waving to her parents as they crossed the sweltering hot parking lot. They noticed Joanna right away, and waved back, while her dad held high a gift of flowers struggling to stay fresh against the oppressive heat wave engulfing the region. As her mom and dad walked out of her sight to enter the hospital, Joanna prepared for their visit, combed her hair again and looked in the mirror for the tenth time to see her pale image reflecting back. But pale and drained looking was normal after having a baby. Perhaps, tomorrow, she could ask her mom to bring makeup to add a glow. But for now, she couldn't wait to take her mom and dad to the nursery, anxiously delighted to show off tiny Susan Stevens. These were happy family days with John arriving tomorrow. When released, they would spend a few days with her folks before driving back to Georgia. She missed her kids. Couldn't wait to cuddle her little Peter and Annie and Harry and start a new life with little Susan as the family's newest child.

Now, her mom and dad were in the room, beaming, her mom talking a blue streak, "Oh, you look just fine, Joanna," her mom said, "a tad pale, but my home-cooking will get you perked up. Now, where is little Susan? Are you well enough to show off your daughter? Come on, let's find my granddaughter."

* * * * *

Now, Sue viewed the same Milton Hospital with adult eyes and, truthfully, felt a little disappointed. "Maria, I can't say I feel any great connection to my birthplace. Perhaps, I was expecting too much. But it's a nice hospital." What now? Do I mentally resolve that from this very point I will determine my own life? "Can we go inside?"

"That's what you came for. Mind now. This building is new and big. I vaguely recall the old hospital as tiny." In the main lobby, they looked at pictures of past and future hospital expansions. Maria studied them closely, "Now, the centre part is new, but you were born in a smaller wing. See this picture, if I remember, your baby ward was on floor two. Years since I've been here. Any vibrations from the past, Sue?"

"No tingle effect, no walking over a grave feeling or anything like it, but today could be a new start for me. From here on, I'm in control. Now, my friend, Hank, told me to ask for birth records. But it isn't likely, old records would be kept here, is it?"

Maria smiled at being asked about paperwork, "Don't ask me of medical records. Fred says I can't keep track of my shopping list, while I'm shopping. But information is over there."

The information desk and the young girl behind it were both bright, shiny, and useless. She listened to Sue's questions with an uncomprehending gaze. In the end, she pointed down a hall, saying, 'check with medical records.' At medical records, a girl tried to help, asking Sue, "All right, let's start with your OHIP card?" When Sue, asked, "What's an OHIP card?" The medical records' girl rolled her eyes, "Ontario medical records are linked to an OHIP number. If you don't have a card number, it will take a supervisor to help you."

And by a stroke of luck, supervisor, Renee Tandet, entered the conversation. Sue explained, "I'm from the States but was born at this hospital thirty-five years ago, and I'm trying to find anything on my birth. Do they keep paperwork or birth records from long ago?"

Supervisor Tandet was blunt, "From thirty-five years ago? You're kidding me right? Lady, those records would have been dumped in some landfill site years ago."

"I figured it was a long shot. My home is in Vermont, and I've no clue where to begin finding my birth information in Ontario. You say absolutely no records would be left?"

Renee Tandet shook her head. "Not hospital paper records. Your best bet is billing records, even from that long ago, they might survive. Ask OHIP, Ontario Hospital Insurance Plan. It would be a challenge tracing records that old. But, there's another possibility. Who paid the hospital cost back then? If your parents were American and had you in Canada, who paid the bills for the birth in '68?"

"I don't know. My dad was in the US Air Force... so, I guess they paid."

"Then contact both OHIP and the US Air Force. It's a long shot, will take months, and you will have to do a lot of pushing, but the financial records may very well exist. You can do all this from your home back in Vermont. But the best of luck."

It wasn't information Sue wanted to hear. She turned to Maria, "Frustrating, I can't even find out basic information like who my doctor even was. But I'm not giving up yet."

Renee overheard and spoke. "Why didn't you tell me you needed the birth doctor's name. That's easy. Go to Queen's Park in Toronto and ask for your birth registration."

"I already have a Canadian birth certificate. It doesn't list the information that I need."

"Sue, a birth registration is different from a birth certificate.

If you were born in Ontario, no matter your nationality, you will have a Certificate of Registration of Birth on file at Queen's Park in Toronto. No exceptions. If you're born here, then you're registered here. It's been that way for a hundred years."

"Really? What else would be on the certificate?"

"It's detailed: from your mom's maiden name, dad's occupations, the hospital, doctor who delivered you; it even lists who registered your information. Simply go to Queen's Park, pay ten bucks, and get your birth details."

"Is it that simple? Ten dollars, and they hand me my past."

Supervisor Tandet, concluded the conversation, "Now don't get me wrong cause we like having tourists, but you could have applied by mail or email, and saved a trip to Canada. As long as you can prove who you are, it's relatively simple to get the information. Does that help your search?"

"Help, my god it's made my day." Sue hugged the supervisor and turned toward Maria, "What's this Queen's Park place and how do we get there?"

"It's the Government buildings in downtown Toronto, Sue. Fred won't drive in Toronto traffic, but you can get on the GO Train this afternoon. I'm sure Fred will go with you. perhaps, you can clear the air with your dad."

Allie spoke up, "Mom, what if grampy is still mad? How do we get home?"

"Grampy will be fine - once he gets over his snit. Perhaps, he'll drive me to Queen's Park." Sue and Maria both smiled as Sue continued, "Why not, he might go for it?"

On the drive home, Sue stayed quiet in thought for awhile and finally asked Marie, "This may seem silly, Maria, but how do you know I'm Joanna's daughter? How can you know I'm me?"

"That DNA mistake must bother you. Well, that is a silly

question, Sue. But I can see you're very like your mom. Lot of the same mannerisms. You're just a grown-up person of the little baby I held in my arms decades ago." Maria waited a moment and then continued, "The important question is - what would you like for lunch?"

Later, when they pulled into Maria's drive, Sue could see her note missing from the back door, "Well, Maria, the notes gone, and dad's not here. Why is he doing this to me?" After being home half an hour the phone rang, and Maria looked at Sue, "You want to get it in case it's your dad?"

Sue picked up, and found Peter calling from Plattsburgh. He was ticked off, "Sue? What's going on up there? Why the hell did you fight with dad? You have to get it settled, cause I don't have time to drive there and get you."

"Stop yelling, Peter. I can't talk if you're yelling. Now what's this all about?"

"Dad's in Lewiston, New York, mad as hell at mom's family, and talking of driving back to Atlanta. He's pissed off about something in the past."

"He said he changed motels but driving to the States is ridiculous." Did he come back today, read my note, get mad and leave again? "Peter, he's in a snit and I think this is dad's old need to control everyone. Dad's the problem today, not mom's relatives."

"Sue, dad can be a control freak at times, but something else must be going on. He was fine arranging the trip, and now calling saying I might have to pick you and Allie up."

"What did dad actually say, Peter?"

"He wants to kill Maria. Said, 'in all the years she was mom's friend, she twists stories to suit herself.' Maybe, he's jealous of you and Maria getting along. But whatever the reason, Sue, dad regrets taking you to Oakville."

"Well, it's too late cause I'm here. I'll just call him and

somehow get him calm. Then, we leave as soon as can be arranged. He has to drive us back to your place. Besides, I need him to carry the papers back that Maria is giving me. Boxes of mom's papers and poems, showing mom as a strong, determined ..."

"Sue, our mom was a carbon copy of Annie, and Annie is a flake."

"Open your eye's dear brother. But leave that, Peter. Do you have a phone number for dad? How do I reach the miserable old troublemaker?" I'll use whatever persuasion it takes, dad, to get one more day in Oakville.

John answered his daughter's call at the Lewiston motel, still angry, "Sue, you saw Maria in action, and heard her sly remarks against me. She welcomed you and Allie and arranged a motel for me. She was quiet toward me. It was obvious... underlying hate, bitterness from the past. You saw it."

"Dad, take it easy. You're just out of hospital for heart problems." You stupid old fool. "Are you all right? Have you had lunch?"

"Maria was ignoring me. I don't stand for that nonsense from anyone."

"Hey dad, when in Rome sort of go with the flow. A man of your experience can handle Maria. Is it possible you overreacted?"

"Going with the flow doesn't mean much now. I've taken a stand."

"Okay, but taking a stand can be trouble. Remember Custer. Dad, honestly, what can be done to get our trip back on track. Should I lock Maria in the cellar, when you come back for Allie and me? Besides, I need one piece of paper from Toronto. Remember, we made this trip to get my information and I only need another day. So can we compromise? Now, being practical, when do you want to leave for home?"

John answered, "How does half an hour sound?" But his

voice was less adamant.

Sue stayed with him, "That's quite a compromise you suggest. But, anyway you can give me a little more time here? "

Eventually, John came around, agreeing to stay this one day in Oakville, "All right, we will leave tomorrow. You get your certificate in Toronto this afternoon, while I calm down for tonight." He was quiet a moment before adding, "How is the old battle axe? She wouldn't want me to show up for dinner after all this, would she?"

"Maria's still expecting you."

"Well, depending on traffic, I just might be able to get there. Good luck in Toronto."

"Thanks, dad. Apparently, if I go in person, I get my birth registration the same day. I don't want to leave here without it."

"Okay, one more day. Then we go. But nothing else."

"Do you think there's room in the car for mom's old papers? Lucky for us, they were saved all these years."

Anger underlay John's answer, "Don't give Maria any credit. She kept that stuff for her own purpose. Sue, believe me, Maria is nothing but trouble. Sue, but mark my words, be careful around that queer bitch."

"Hey, dad, one more day and we leave. We don't have to continue the fight."

John lost it then. He was shouting on the phone, "My feud? You're damn right. It's my feud." Once started, his fury increased, and he spat out, "Maria almost ruined your mom's life. Haven't you figured it out? She's a dyke. Maria is a lesbian."

Sue was lost for words as John continued, "Don't believe me? Then ask her. She doesn't just hate me; she hates any man that stands up to her. That's why mom and I stopped visiting. Ask Maria."

"All right, so Maria's the worst human being since Adolph.

If you can stay calm then come for dinner, and we can head back tomorrow. Let Maria be." And something's phony. Your story still doesn't fit together, dad, cause even if Maria were a problem, that does not explain why mom would stop seeing her parents? "Dad, careful. The doctors warned you of getting angry?"

"Sure, but those doctors never met Maria. She would cause anyone to get high blood pressure. But you're right, I'll try and be social for a while at dinner. But keep Maria on her leash. See you tonight." Then he hung up, leaving Sue pondering another question that her dad's rant had brought to light. Even if dad wouldn't come here, why did mom keep her distance. For years, no visit, no letters, no contact. Why? Did mom fear dad as a control freak?

Dad, you're worse than a kid - you open a can of worms, stamp your feet, and then run away. Well, it's time to look under all the carpets. Especially the sexual ones.

Sue joined Maria in the kitchen. "John agreed to be here for dinner - but I can't guarantee how social he will be. He's unpredictable Maria and most of his anger is pointed at you." She waited a while to think her question over, then asked, "Honestly, Maria, my dad made some insinuations that are hard to talk about. Can we be honest with each other?"

Maria sat down next to Sue at the kitchen table and gently clasped her hand, saying, "You say whatever has to be said, Sue, and I'll answer anything you need to know. Remember, family doesn't always go smooth, but it's always family. We're just pleased you're here to talk."

"Right." Then, after a long pause. "Okay, dad's exploded with nutty allegations. He's ranting against you." Sue took a deep breath and continued, "Maria, look, my dad's implying... saying... he's saying your sexual preference is different. He says you like girls." God, how embarrassing to be a guest and talking like this. "Why the hell would dad say you liked Joanna far too much?"

Maria started saying, "He wants to cause problems..." Then she stopped. The ticking of the kitchen clock faded to momentary silence. Maria didn't deny John's accusation, nor confirm it. "Good for you, Susan. Uncovering the past often take's courage and, besides, your dad is partially right, but far off base. I loved your mother, intensely, a teenage mutual respect, but never sexual at any time. What developed between us was normal, like sisters. Our teenage trust was always platonic. Later, boys, and life went its normal course... except, Joanna and I still had this strong, special, bond. Karma." She laughed a little, adding, "He couldn't understand our feelings."

Maria, fussing around the sink, continued talking, "John paints it as dirty, but our feelings were normal. So, the question really is this; 'Why is your dad dredging up red herrings today?' Look closely at why he is saying this, Susan."

Sue realized Maria had called her Susan twice just now. No longer Sue in her aunt's eyes, but a return to her birth name. She felt somehow closer to her mother's generation, "And what would questioning my dad gain?"

"Who knows? It's your search or, perhaps, searches. On more than one level perhaps." Maria sensed Susan's confusion, adding. "Your birth issues are obvious, and Fred will be pleased to take you to Toronto today. Get your certificate settled."

And my other path? Susan, asked, "What else is here?"

"Your mom. She died when you were a child, so this is an opportunity of knowing her. If someone questioned my birth, sure I'd want answers about me, but I'd also want answers from my parents. Want to know what they did back then, what they were thinking. And if your dad won't talk, then stitch facts together from your mom's life. That's what I would do."

"Yes." I hadn't voiced it like that, but yes. "I'd like to find out all I can of my mom. Everything I can. That's a bonus for coming north."

"Good. Tonight, there's a the little dinner party to welcome you and Allie, I've invited a bunch of family just so, you know, you're not alone in this world. One of them, Caroline, stayed with your aunt Cecile for a summer out in California. Have a chat with her. Ask about your California aunt. Now, go ask Allie if she wants to help make dessert, while you spend the afternoon in Toronto talking to Fred. Tonight, after dinner, you ask me all the questions you want. We can have a good little chin wag."

"I'd like that. One more talk before I leave tomorrow. It's just that what dad says and what you say, are worlds apart. And I don't want to get him upset again."

"Susan, I tell no lies and my memory is sharp. Now, where's Allie. I need some apples peeled." Then, she shouted toward the living room, "Fred, time you took Sue into Toronto."

* * * * *

In the dusty bar in Clearview, the bartender asks Allan, "You want both, a Bud Light and a black coffee?" Then he shrugged and served the drinks. What people drank was their business. Allan sipped his coffee and watched little streams of condensation run down the side of the beer. A warm day, the cold beer looked inviting, and he stared at it all the while he drank his coffee. Eventually, he phoned Stu and then promptly, started lying.

"Not doing anything, Stu. Sort of in a coffee shop having a coffee."

"Sort of? What's a sort of a coffee shop? And its past lunch - where are you, Allan?"

"At the bowling alley, having a coffee... well, sort of sitting in the bar next to the bowling alley. Just drinking a coffee... and thinking how tempting a beer seems just now."

Stuart laughed. "Allan are you trying to kid me? Of course, a beer is tempting. Especially on a hot day and, especially, that you drank beer for years; it's natural to think of drinking. But you've been down this path before. You knew this day was coming."

"Wanting a beer on a hot day?"

"No. The point is, you knew you wanted to drink. Get honest with yourself you dumb jackass. The warm day means nothing; you drank on warm days, cold days, in sunshine and in the dark. And you know your record with social drinking. The point is, you heard stories of other drunks talking, saying they would get well, and then trying it on again. Hell, many drinkers, after being sober for a week, convince themselves they never had a problem in the first place. So they start the cycle again. But you know all that... you're well enough to have some clear thinking by now."

"I only came in for a coffee."

"Right. Look around dummy. How many other people are in the bar drinking coffee? Go ahead, look around and count the ones drinking coffee."

"Stu, I haven't been drinking." Not yet. "You want to come here for a talk."

"Oh, you are funny, Allan... why the hell would I want to talk in a bar? It's a bar. Look, kiddo, drop into a barber shop and you'll, eventually, get a hair cut. Now, I don't have time to sit around a bar listening to bull. So make a decision - warm the damn bar stool or leave it. And, one more thing, Allan?"

"What?"

"The beer you say you haven't ordered; the one sitting in front of you - if you resolve to leave the bar, then give it to someone else. No point wasting good beer." Stu hung up.

Chapter 13

Fred and Sue settled into their seats on the double-decker, green and white train travelling east to Toronto. Fred was quite talkative this afternoon, "Allie is wonderful and bright. I bet your girl teaches Maria a thing or two, while we're gone. They were making a great mess of the kitchen."

Sue nodded, "She's the joy of my life. Did you two ever have kids, Fred?"

"We weren't fortunate, Sue. Nieces and nephews galore but no kids. I married late in life, and Maria had been married and lost her husband many years before. So we're a pair of old fogies, comfortable together, and content to quietly grow older."

Sue tried to get her uncle talking of the family rift. "Fred, my aunt, Cecile, in California - why was she involved in the family fight from years ago? Help me understand what happened?"

Fred settled back in his seat, as the train swayed along the tracks. "Me and your aunt Maria, we don't want to spoil your visit here. It's old stuff, and with your dad coming to dinner tonight, I'd rather not remember things he's touchy over. This afternoon is for a day in Toronto. What else can I tell you? Ask me how often I travel this train?"

Sue could take a hint. "Okay. Do you take this GO Train often Fred?"

"The first and third Tuesday of each month. A bunch of old fogies have lunch and talk opera. Music has been my passion since high school days at the choir school in Toronto. Still chum with friends I made back then. The choir school was special and, over the years, I developed a love of opera. Puccini's *Tosca* is coming to

Toronto this fall, and I was able to grab two front row tickets."

"Opera? Maria is an opera fan?"

"Not Maria. Can you imagine that chatterbox staying quiet for a couple of hours? Both tickets are mine - for an afternoon, and an evening performance. Twice in the same day."

He paused a moment and continued, "Sue, I don't say much around the old chatterbox at home, but having your visit is a great occasion for us. You and Allie are like the prodigal son returning." Fred paused again, then indirectly alluded to her dad, "If you have to leave quickly... cause circumstances change, then we understand. You can always come back. Always."

"I feel the same, Fred." Why does dad want to leave so soon? It doesn't add up.

Fred pulled out an MP3 player, "These little inventions are a god-send to music lovers. I mean relatives are important, but... they can't replace music, now can they?" The twinkle in his eyes gave him away. And Sue played along.

"If I get a starring role in *Madam Butterfly*, will you come and see me perform in Atlanta? Combining music and relatives - how could you resist?"

"I'd be there. Anything with music can get me hooked. Your aunt says I'm crazy to think this way... but after your dad called, I got thinking of your mom's funeral in Atlanta and the funeral music."

Sue said, thoughtfully, "I was just a kid, but I don't remember music at my mom's funeral?"

"Your memory is right, there was no music and that's the point. Joanna would have wanted music. In the confusion surrounding a death, the last wishes of the person are often lost. So a week ago, I started planning just the right music for my funeral. Maria says I'm nuts, but I made the CD's with clear instructions in case I pop off tomorrow."

"All because there was no music at my mom's service. So, tell me, what did you pick for your funeral?"

"You can find out at my funeral." The twinkle was back in Fred's eyes.

Sue teased back, "That's not fair. I could die before you and never know. Come on, Uncle Fred, what did you choose?"

"One of the finest. The Mozart vesper - *Laudate Dominum* by Kiri Te Kanawa. To be played once at the start and once at the end of the service. And I don't give a damn what they do in between. It's a perfect choice; two hundred and fifty years old, yet as fresh as if the notes were penned yesterday."

"It's that good? I don't think I've heard it."

"It's that good. It's what my friends will remember after they say good-bye to me." The train was slowing down for Union Station. "Our stop, Sue. Just follow the crowd. Toronto is an easy city to figure out, so I'll give you directions to Queen's Park. After you get the Birth Registration, we meet back here and tour Toronto, if there's still time."

Sue was glowing, "This is a wonderful day. Getting a piece of paper that will put months of uncertainty to rest. Tonight, I'll be able to celebrate and mark the mystery as solved."

Fred chuckled, "You never were a mystery for us, Susan. I met your dad at Toronto airport years ago and drove him straight to the Milton Hospital. And you were as good as gold, never made a peep that day, just snuggled up with Joanna while John sat beaming. But if you need verification, then sure, get the proof you need."

Maria left Allie mixing flour and butter in her kitchen, moved to her bedroom phone and dialled John's motel. When he answered, she said, "Don't hang up, John. We should talk."

"I'm listening, Maria," was his chilly reply.

"John, I don't think this call will warm your cold little heart toward us, but it can help your daughter. This silly feud has Susan conflicted and it should stop now. My niece, deserves love, John, not family discord. And I know you agree. Besides, it can't be fun, alone in a motel, knowing your daughter is getting upset."

He continued to listen, then rasped, "Get to the point, Maria."

"Mercy sake John, what kind of a military man are you? Can't you recognize a truce being proposed?"

Part of his anger faded from his voice, "I didn't hang up yet, Maria."

"Well, then, can we move past being disagreeable and find a middle ground? Look John, a truce. Calm things down, and give Susan a few days of family memories. I'm proposing a peace offering. Come to dinner tonight. Arrive when you want. One condition. Leave the family fight in the past. You don't have to answer me. Just know there will be a place set for you at dinner. I've even made the special potatoes you like. You are family, John."

"Some relative you are. I left to get away from your jabs and remarks. You keep talking around the edges of past problems. Maria, I don't want to bring up the past, or go there, or relive years of problems. Sure I can return, even be jolly over dinner, long as you stop with events long gone."

"It's not meant to hurt you, John. When Susan asks questions, I just give answers. Now I'm ringing off, so don't be an ass and stay away."

Maria hung up, walked to the kitchen window, and looked at the pesky squirrels, vainly trying to get seed from the bird feeder. But her mind didn't focus on the garden disturbance. She remembered last night, when Sue was ready for bed. A man might miss the implication, but Maria was sure. It was clear. Sue's nightdress left no doubt - a tiny bulge was starting to show.

The thought of Sue's pregnancy was on Maria's mind. Just

what was her niece planning. An abortion in Canada is a medical procedure and easier to obtain than in the US. Is this Canadian visit more then reconnecting with relatives? She could be in Toronto now, getting information and checking medical contacts. Life isn't fair to any woman.

* * * * *

Allan, finally caught up with Stu, working on his daily Sudoku challenge, in a coffee shop. "You're a hard man to track down, Stu. This is the third coffee shop I've checked." Stu continued working on his puzzle in silence. Eventually, Allan pushed his puzzle page aside, "Aren't you going to say hello?"

Stu looked up for a moment, "Hello, Allan." Then continued his puzzle.

"Stu, I didn't get drunk. Not even one drink."

"So?" Stu put down his paper in exasperation, "You expecting a medal to be struck or, perhaps, an honourable mention on CNN tonight for doing what most people do? Allan, I don't know if you realize it, but most people stay sober at one in the afternoon... and they don't expect congratulations. What makes you different? Why tell me?"

"Weren't you worried about me?"

"No, I didn't worry, Allan. Did you expect me to worry that you might drink, expect me to track you down and knock a beer from your hand? Drinking is always your choice. Always. And so is staying sober. No one in the universe ever has to convince me to stay sober. I might need help staying sane at times, but not sober."

"Okay. I see that, Stu."

"Do you? No one will need to knock a beer out of my hand to remind me of the value of sobriety. If I forget about being sober, lie to myself and, drink again, there is one prime fact in the universe that happens. One unfailing condition inevitably gets my attention, when I drink. I wake up drunk as a skunk the next day. Never fails."

"But I didn't drink, Stu."

"Marvellous. Glad to hear it. Now go stand outside and wait for the brass band coming to celebrate your amazing choice of not drinking." After a few moments, he continued, "Someone made a mistake on this puzzle. These numbers just don't work." Stu added a little softer comment, "Try and remember the sequence, Allan, it's always the same - you think then you drink. Your feet don't walk you into a bar, but your mind does."

"Right. Want another coffee, Stu?"

"I'm impressed. You offering to buy coffee?"

"Sure. Well uh... truth is, I need to borrow five bucks first."

Stu handed him the money, "Great. And if you're buying this one, on my money, I suppose you want me to buy the next one. Allan, this episode indicates you're ready for another challenge in life."

"Right. To watch my thinking?"

"Wrong. You need a part-time job, so you stop spending my money. Now, tell me about your family. Been in touch yet?"

"I plan to call them. Thinking of Sue and Allie all the time. But haven't called them yet."

"Because... come on Allan - be honest. Still angry? Do you realize a mind full of anger can't see clearly?"

"Maybe, I'm not angry. Don't have any anger left against Sue. I've forgotten she damaged my truck. I haven't said a word about her damaging the truck. Not a word. Do you hear me, Stu? Stu, I'm not bothered that she did damage down the whole side of the truck. "

Stu's attention was back on solving his puzzle, "You getting the coffee?"

* * * * *

Maria's kitchen seemed transformed into a cooking school, as she heaped just the right amount of praise on her star pupil. "Allie, that's good dear; you learn fast. Now the Devon cream - taste it first. See, how delicate and just slightly sweet. Spoon it over the peaches now, and we will add the whipping cream later, just before serving."

"How many do we make, aunt Maria?"

"How many could you eat?"

"A lot of these."

"Then, we need a lot. Make a dozen for tonight and, a few more, so you and I can sample one before dinner. It's our job. We have to sample them Allie, to make sure they're good. Now, your uncle Fred just pulled into the drive, so you can show your mom what you made.

Before Susan was through the back door, Allie asked, "Mom, can I have one very tiny dessert now, before dinner? Very tiny aren't they, aunt Maria?"

"Certainly." Maria answered, "Too small to spoil an appetite." And why aren't you smiling, Susan? "How was the Toronto trip? Get your certificate?"

Sue flopped into a chair. "Not good. I arrived at the office after two and, same day service, is only on applications submitted before 10:00 a.m. I can't pick it up tomorrow, because dad's insistent on leaving. So the best thing was to mail it to Peter's place. Just a frustrating afternoon. So close to getting answers and now it's delayed a few more days."

Maria suggested taking it easy, "Go have a nap before dinner. And your friend Hank called while you were gone. Said he'll call back around six tonight. Now go get a nice rest." An hour later, Susan returned to the kitchen, even more in a funk than when she arrived. "Can't seem to rest, Maria. Is dinner under control or what can I help with?" So they fussed and talked of everything and nothing, talked while Maria gave Allie her good silverware to set the table in the dining room, and then gave Allie her best china for place settings. Susan washed some dishes and talked while trying to find the right place for things to go. Before long, relatives were arriving and Fred was greeting them at the front door. Susan was still chatting, "... and so we found my baby picture's discrepancy, but dad still hasn't talked of that at all."

John, arriving at the open back door, heard Sue's last fragment of the conversation. "What's my fault? What am I being blamed for now?"

"Dad, you're not being blamed for anything."

John faced Maria, saying a little stiffly, "Thank you for this invitation to dinner." Then turning toward his daughter added, "See, I ate crow and did it early. Now, we can all enjoy the evening. What were you on about just now?"

Maria changed the subject, "Come in John, come in. Susan, I called your dad while you were in Toronto and we declared a truce - so it's going to be a good evening. John, can you reach up and get those dessert bowls down for Allie; she needs to place peaches in them." She pushed Susan toward the dining room. "And you make sure the table is set for ten people."

Maria returned to John. "Good. Your granddaughter makes a great dessert." Let's test your sense of humour, Johnny Boy. She shouted toward the dining room. "Susan, seat your dad against the wall, so we can't talk behind his back." Maria smiled at John, adding, "Just kidding, Johnny!"

Dinner guests arrived and scattered in the small house and garden, so Maria gave Allie the task of rounding them up. She rang a tiny silver bell to announce dinner was ready. And the party was off. Excellent food helped the conversation flow and, in spite of his previous trepidation, John relaxed. After a second glass of wine, he could admit to enjoying himself."

Among the dinner noises and conversation, Allie was turning up her nose at a new taste, "I don't eat black olives."

"Well, you don't have to eat them, dear." Her aunt Maria was sitting next to her niece. "They are an acquired taste."

Even Fred was talkative, "Do you know the olive story, Allie." As she shook her head, Fred continued, "Much different from planting corn or tomatoes. It takes both farming and faith in the future to plant a new olive grove. Mediterranean farmers are often middle-aged before owning land to plant a new olive grove. It, then, could take thirty-five years before the grove produces fruit. So the farmers who plant the groves may never see the fruit from trees they nurture. Isn't that an act of faith?"

Allie looked at her uncle Fred for a moment, then said, "I still don't like them."

Maria passed cabbage rolls down to John, followed by sour cream, while saying to her husband, "Fred, why tell us pointless olive grove information? Why?"

Fred chuckled to himself, "Well, if the farmer went to all that trouble to grow the fruit, then Allie might try an olive or two. Make a poor farmer happy." He continued to chuckle.

Allie caught the spirit, "I'll try one to make the farmer happy. Any without stones?"

Maria feigned anger, "Fred Court, let the girl alone. Or I'll serve you black olives with your cereal tomorrow morning."

"Cool," Allie joked. "Mom, I'd try them in my corn flakes."

Dinner talk, the clatter of plates, glasses, and cutlery blended together for a memorable reunion. A fine, relaxing dinner. Then, Maria rang the little silver bell, and announced, "Our very special guest, Allie Charter, will now serve the world famous Peach a la Allie. Go ahead dear, and give your granddad the one you made special."

After dinner, Sue talked with her mom's cousin, Caroline, who had spent a summer at their aunt Cecile's place in California. "They have a nice little place, almost on the beach. You should go visit her, Susan. She's an odd lady but very gracious. Contact her."

Sue asked, "Did Cecile mention why she didn't stay in touch with my mom. Their old fight must have been monumental to cut us off from them. Did Cecile mention that quarrel?"

"No dear. I spent several weeks out west and don't think we talked of a quarrel. Just didn't come up." Caroline added, "I'm just an old busybody gossip, Sue, and if there was anything to mention, I'd be the first to tell you. Truth is, your part of the family, being out of touch for so long, just slipped away. Sorry, but not a word was said about your mom. However, Cecile was not kind in speaking of your dad. You'd need to get it straight from her, but your dad's actions was a tragedy for Cecile. Speak to her."

The guests helped clean-up, said their good-byes and started drifting away. By now, John was mellow and ready to leave. Sue nudged him, asking, "Dad, all of mom's writings - how many boxes can we carry back? Maria says we can take them all."

John wasn't happy driving junk back home, "I don't care. Leave it for tomorrow then take what will fit." He thanked Maria for dinner, told Sue they would leave about eight in the morning, and said, "Good-night, everyone." Friendly, but still reserved.

With Allie in bed and John at his motel, Maria and Susan chatted in her kitchen while sorting Joanna's notes and writings. Sue tugged at one folder, and it spilled out a few children's drawings of boats and water. Sue asked, "Who would have made these?"

"Looks like writing on the back, Sue." Sure enough, big letters in crayon - Annie.

"Oh. My sister. Yet they're in mom's old stuff?"

Maria shrugged her shoulders, "Years before I married Fred.

He might remember them?"

Sue returned to the kitchen in a few minutes, sat down with Maria, saying thoughtfully, "Well, in a way, he does. Apparently, Annie spent a summer here with Joanna's parents, arriving in early spring and staying till late fall. The odd thing is, I've never heard my family mention this visit. And Fred says he remembers because it's the last time my family came to Canada."

Maria shrugged again. "If I can figure out the year's right Sue, then I was married with my first husband and living down in Central America. Perhaps, your dad can understand why the visit was so long."

"Dad doesn't talk of family much. I've understood more over the last two days than dad ever tells me."

"I offered your dad a truce and he accepted. Still angry... but that's his issues." Maria then continued, "Could be the search to understand your mom is touching on a time of life he found difficult. And to complicate his emotions he, somehow, feels that talking of Canada is knocking the States. Our countries are good neighbours, but we have developed in different ways." Maria was speaking with a gentle voice on a divisive subject, "Your war in Vietnam, shaped a generation, for and against that war. Fred figures that when your dad looks back to the '60's he remembers the times, while we look back now, on that part of history, and we only can see facts. Different when you live the times. The facts today, don't show the anger that filled many lives and conversations of yesterday. Read Joanna's letters. She was against the American military. That, alone, would set up bitter arguments over war. While John lived in it, Joanna fought against it."

"How do you know this? How can you know what my dad is thinking?"

"Sue, I lived those times. My first husband died in Central America over the same problems of killing people to get them thinking your way. It's all in your mom's old letters. The summer you were born, Joanna and I talked late into many nights. She told me they argued bitterly. It's not a mythical difference between our countries that still bothers your dad. It's the way he and Joanna were. Look, countries can differ and live apart - but in a marriage, there's no avoiding fundamental differences. Their differing views caused problems in their marriage"

"But dad loved my mom. I know he did. And she loved him."

Oh, for god's sake child, grow up. "Yes, they had a deep love in a very troubled time. Vietnam in the '60's, a divided country, hawks versus doves, and seething underlying anger - read it all in the history from back then."

"Maria, why should I care about that time now?"

"Well, you don't have to care. But it's the fabric behind the family split. John believed distorted lies against Canada. Believed this land was full of communist pinkos, or Cuba lovers and, as a result, he caused the family split. Between the lines, your mom's letters clearly say John's anger at Canada is why their visits stopped. To understand your birth, then understand your parents. Susan, even today, John distorts things. Didn't he accuse me of being a lesbian?"

"Well, he was angry when he said it." But I can't pit him against you, Maria. He's my dad. "Why would dad paint you that way?"

Maria smiled, "Jealousy! Jealous of your mom and me being close and friends for life. Perhaps, John never understood our simple friendship."

Susan wondered what else could explain his accusation, "Dad was wrong to knock you, but I can't fight with him. We support each other." Sue was getting tired and Maria could see it.

"Of course. Forgive an old aunt meddling in family problems. You need to rest for the drive tomorrow. Ready to turn in?" Maria, paused, and added quietly, "Unless anything else is on your mind.

I'm a good listener."

Sue stopped packing her mom's papers and looked at Maria, "You know, don't you?"

Maria smiled, "Your pregnancy? Yes, your nightdress revealed it last night. Otherwise, I would never have known."

"Well, only you, dad and my sister-in-law Maggie are aware. And I needed time to think. Just being here convinced me that family is important, but raising another child on my own is a big step. And I'm tired. It's been an amazing few days but, right now, I want a soft bed and a good night's sleep."

In the morning, Susan found a dozen more boxes in the living room. "Maria, they won't all fit into the car." Her aunt laughed, "Fred did get carried away. Take what you want and we'll store the rest for another trip. Ready for breakfast?"

"Sure am. Good morning, Allie. Any pancakes left?"

"Morning, mom. The pancakes are great. And this is real maple syrup. Know where maple syrup comes from, mom?"

"Of course I do, silly, the maple syrup store."

"Does not. Comes from Maple trees, doesn't it, aunt Maria. And grampy just arrived, mom."

"He'll flip when he sees the boxes I want." Hard to say good-byes when I would dearly like to stay. "Maria, you've been perfect, making us just so comfortable..."

Her aunt had tears in her eyes, "We all win, if the family stays in touch. Allie finding so many new cousins. And, Susan, don't forget you wanted a DNA sample from Fred."

"If it's no trouble?"

"He won't mine. In fact, come in the kitchen with me for a moment. I know this isn't necessary, but it might be needed some time. Hand me the scissors in that drawer, so I can give you a snip of my hair. And reach me a couple of plastic bags from under the counter." Susan bent to get the bags, while Maria snipped with the scissors and placed a tuft of hair on the counter. She, then, dropped the sample in the ziplock bag Susan was holding. "Now, I'm trusting you to keep the results of my hair test secret, Susan. No one else need know I'm not a natural blond. Take the other bag to Fred. Mind you, he doesn't have much hair left."

With the samples bagged, Maria pulled Susan aside to talk quietly. "After you went to bed, I dug out this old poem. Your mom gave me this before you were born."

Sue unfolded the page and found her mom's now familiar handwriting. A note from before she was born made the hair stand up on her arm.

Missing,
a silver edge of laughter, and its brilliant sparkling side
Missing,
love and life and heart, with troubles all outside
Conceive,
a golden mind wanted to shift the world from sadness
Reject,
no love, no hope, no faith with war and all its madness
Trust,
illusion of hope, of children, of bringing such gladness.
Joanna, Point Mugu, Spring, 1968

"Maria, it's dated months before my birth? She wrote this before I was born."

Then, unexpectedly, a smaller paper slid from the folded poem and fluttered toward the floor. Susan picked it up. Three words in Joanna's handwriting - War is Evil. Each letter pushed deep into the paper, written with such passion and emotion that the pencil lines had cut through the paper in places. Only three words. War Is Evil.

Maria placed the papers together and gently handed them to Susan. "Your mom was complex, Susan. Be patient to understand her. Joanna was a wonderful mother."

John sounded the horn. Time to say a last good-bye. Fred gave Allie a folder of pictures of her new found cousins, and one of Allie making dessert with her aunt. There was one special picture of Allie eating her first black olive. From the look on her face, it wasn't sure she would have any more.

The car had started backing out of the drive, when Fred motioned them to stop. He handed Susan a CD. "I almost forgot. Susan, you might find time to listen to this one day." Everyone waved good-byes. Even John.

Chapter 14

Allie automatically resumed her navigators-responsibility guiding them back to the States, reviewing her map seriously, and making pronouncements, "Next city is Belleville grampy, and we stop there."

John figured she was wrong, "We don't stop in Belleville, Allie."

"We do. I have to go to the bathroom."

After Belleville, John decided to rest and handed Sue the car keys. Later, with their navigator asleep to the hum of driving, Sue looked, thoughtfully, at her dad sitting in silence for mile after mile. He was always content just to be quiet, but increasingly more noticeable over the years since mom died. Now, he would sit for hours without saying a word. Eventually, Sue, started the conversation, "Thanks dad, for not causing a fuss with Maria last night. Our relatives up here are important to me, dad."

"Well, I wasn't going to win against the wicked witch of the North, was I?"

He's got it wrong again. Glinda is a good witch. "Maria helped me more than I expected - so thanks for taking me there."

John raised his coffee in a mock toast, "Here's to the witch. May she make her evil brews in bad health." He looked at Sue thoughtfully, "But the visit accomplished what you needed in connecting with family? And, you have boxes full of mom's papers as a bonus."

"Yes, it was all I expected and more." Almost resolved. "When I get my birth registration, I plan on showing it to Hank and his lab buddy from Burlington and telling them where to stick their

DNA tests. I was so uneasy going on this Oakville trip, but it has nailed down my heritage. Plus, a bonus, of getting mom's old papers and letters, made it a memorable trip."

John relaxed, almost mellow, in the warm car as they approached the border to enter the US. Allie, awake by now, and looking out the window said, "Look at all the American flags. Must be a million of them, mom." Sue responded, "Yes pumpkin, at least a million. It's good to be home."

Heading toward Watertown, New York, the flat road changed to gentle hills and endless trees. It was a sparsely settled area, where they made the first stop for gas. Sue spoke with certainty, "I'm going to build a new life... perhaps in Atlanta. And there's mom's old papers to sort. Peter can figure out a way to ship the rest of mom's notes from Maria's basement. And later, in Atlanta, I plan on contacting mom's sister, Cecile."

John asked sharply, "You never mentioned mom's sister before. How do you know, Cecile?" His mellow mood had vanished. "You don't want to contact her. Maria is just an old gossip, but Cecile is a snake in the grass. She's not what she seems."

"Dad, I'm only going to contact the lady. She is my aunt."

"No, no, no, don't even try to contact her. Soon as Cecile knows you're my daughter, she will slam down the phone. It's the truth. Best thing Cecile ever did was stay in Canada. Don't go back and see her."

"Cecile's been in the States for years. She lives in California."

"Not likely. Years ago, I made sure immigration wouldn't let that socialist set foot in the States."

"Well, someone slipped up, dad. Mom's sister, Cecile, lives in Crescent City, California."

Sue pulled over to the side of the road, because John was breathing heavy and getting red with anger. Yelling, "She's a communist. I wrote our government about how that witch applauded our cowardly draft dodgers hiding in Canada. I told them she bragged of sending money to American Veterans against the war. And how she criticized our country as a military monster. That's a fair picture of Cecile."

"Dad, calm down, you're getting Allie upset." Sue was trying to understand the past. "What did you do? What did you say against mom's sister?"

"Your mom supported me in everything I sent the State Department. All the details of her being a Socialist. Everything we knew and suspected. I'm still proud of what I wrote."

Sue could feel a curtain rising to reveal a very ugly scene. This was a new perspective to the family feud. "Oh, dad, did you rat on her?" Maria said you caused a family rift. "Why?"

John went quiet, as Sue resumed driving and miles passed in silence. Finally he said. "Sue, just because you're my daughter doesn't give you the right to either know what I did in the past or judge me on it. The whole sad involvement with Cecile is none of your business, so leave the past alone."

"Great, dad. Just great. You're doing your usual silence to shut me out again. Just talk to me about it."

John closed his eyes, "I'm tired of talking." His meaning was clear - don't, absolutely don't mention Cecile. Over the next two hours, they said very little.

Arriving at her brother's place in Plattsburgh, Peter looked dismayed at the boxes stuffed in the car, asking sarcastically, "Hope all this junk is destined for Atlanta, Sue? There's no room in my garage."

Ever helpful, Allie answered, "More boxes coming from aunt Maria. Right mom?"

"These boxes will have to go in the house to be sorted. Your garage is too damp for mom's papers. Damp would ruin her books."

"Sue, this is a pile of junk, look, yellowed newspaper clippings forty years old."

"Okay, it worthless junk, but keep it safe and dry just for me, brother, till I get a chance to go through it all. And don't even think of throwing it away." She carried one of the smaller boxes.

He gave up, "Fine, you stack them in the living room and you deal with Maggie over the musty smell in the house. You know, Allan isn't the only one in your family with an attitude problem. You can really be bitchy." Her brother just shook his head and picked up a box, "Hold the door for me, Allie, while I get these riches inside. And Sue, your sheriff friend called earlier."

"What did Hank want?"

"Didn't say. The man wants you to call him after you carry in these boxes."

* * * * *

That afternoon in Clearville, Vermont, Allan, unnecessarily, stirred his black coffee for a good minute before answering Stu's question, "Sleep? I sleep okay. Get tired from worry, not lack of sleep. Can't believe my life became so screwed up."

As Stu remained quiet Allan continued, "Not everything is my fault. I didn't set out to cause problems... it's just... people don't understand me, Stu, they give me a hard time and don't listen. So... blocking her in the drive wasn't one of my better ideas. But I had good intentions. To get things straight."

Stu asked, "Did it work? Has she been in touch?"

"She can't be in touch just now. She's in Canada."

"Sounds as if she's getting on with life. What are you doing?"

"Nothing, 'cept wasting hours yakety-yaking with you. Work is all right, most bills paid now, and there's a little money to start helping Sue and Allie. If she would call, I could send it. But I still don't sleep well, Stu. If my family were back, everything would be better."

"Say that again Allan. Did I hear you right?"

"I can fix all my family worries just by getting my wife back home."

"Sounds like you're singing that tired old song, 'Give me another chance mama cause this time will be different.' But what will you do if you don't get another chance? Try and be clear on what you alone need. You want Sue to talk, but unless she's ready, then forcing the issue is asking for trouble. Have you asked her what she wants to do? You do know that might help?"

"I'm not stupid."

"First, ask your wife what she wants to do. Then, wait for an answer. One message, just one, asking a simple request. Send the message and sleep well. And you may, or may not, get the answer you like."

"I know that."

"But, there's a second part. Your wife and daughter can't live on air; they need financial support. Send money on a regular basis and that money should have no connection to your wife's returning to you or not. Just send the money. Plus, let your wife know you want regular contact with Allie. Your daughter needs contact with her dad. Do you understand what I'm saying?"

"Sure, Stu. I hear you. You're saying go softly at first, then I demand contact with Sue. If she doesn't answer the way I want, I track her down and scream all over her face - in a gentle way. Is that the message? Stu, do you want another coffee?"

"Allan, I worry about you. And are you buying?"

"You know I don't get paid till the end of the month. I'm offering to get you a coffee, not buy it. I'm saving money for my daughter." He pocketed the ten dollars Stu handed out. "You want a sandwich or something to go with the coffee? Now, on contacting Sue, any suggestions on what to say?"

"Try the truth, Allan. Perhaps, a catchy phrase, 'Dear Sue, I'm the one who threw the beer bottle at your head.' Or, something like, 'I'm the guy who blocked your car in the drive. Remember me.' Bound to get her attention."

* * * * *

With all the boxes piled in the living room, Sue, still had energy to open another box of her mom's writings. She was looking through papers that had been boxed away forty years ago, when she remembered to call Hank. He answered on the first ring.

"Thing is Sue," he was saying, "one of my mates, Jim Acheson, is living in those flats overlooking Burlington Bay. That old section of Burlington two blocks back from the water. I pointed them out when I was driving you home after you hurt your eye."

"Okay Hank, but I was a wreck that day."

"Thing is, Sue, old Jimmy's girlfriend is moving to New York City, and he's going with her, so I've asked him to hold off a few days before telling his apartment owner of his move. Those flats will get snapped up quick. I can help a little with your rent. Allie can either bus to Clearville and finish school with her friends, or she can register in Burlington. It all seems to fit, Sue."

"Hank, slow down. I can't be rushed, and this is beyond rushing."

Hank persisted, "Just think about it. Once you're living there, it will give us time to be together." Hank repeated himself, "It all seems to fit, Sue. And you'll be near the ferry dock to go see Peter or Annie any time you want. This is a golden opportunity."

"But the timing isn't as good for me as you think. Why don't I come and see you in a few days for lunch in Burlington? Right now, I'm tired from the drive. Love you." God, Hank, are you that transparent? First, I would owe you money, and then I would be under your roof, and then what? I'm trying to gain independence not give it away for flats near the water.

Margaret waltzed into her kitchen, waved a newly arrived letter in front of Susan, and teasingly asked, "So my uptight sister-in-law, do you know anyone interested in a special delivery from the Ontario Registrar General?"

Sue grabbed it, "Oh, Maggie, I've been waiting days for this. I could hug you."

"I'll settle for lunch and that talk we haven't had."

Sue waved the letter, "This comes first - our talk will have to wait." She ripped the letter open, took a moment to scan the page, and started to cry. "My dad was right all the time, Maggie. This copy is a handwritten registration page outlining all my birth details, even to the attending doctor, someone called D.A. Wyks. Everything's in writing, including that my mom was visiting Canada, from Atlanta, Georgia, when she had me in Milton, Ontario, Canada. Plus, it shows the person who declared this birth information. Mom's sister, Cecile Court."

"The aunt in California?"

"Cecile. She sends aunt Maria a Christmas card every year, so she was alive and well last Christmas. Now, I know dad won't like it, but I'm going to contact her, and if Cecile confirms writing this, then it's case closed for me. DNA science be damned. This page is proof of who I am."

Maggie said, "And my husband said your trip north was a waste of money."

"Well, first I call dad and tell him he was right, then Hank gets told he was wrong, and then you and I are going to lunch. My troubles are solved, Maggie, so I can listen to yours."

The call to Hank didn't go quite as anticipated. "Hi, Hank.

My birth registration arrived, confirming all the facts my family has been telling me. Samuels will have to rethink his science. How do you like that for apples?"

"Just fine if it makes you happy, Sue."

"That's a lame apology?"

"It's not an apology. Sue, a birth record doesn't have any bearing on your DNA tests. Something unexplained happened to the baby born in Canada. Somehow, or somewhere, you have ended up with a different DNA than you should have. Nelson Samuels can only tell you the result of your test, but not why or when something happened. I said from the beginning, just stop looking for an answer - be happy with your family."

Sue spoke with emotion, "Hank, that's such a cheesy answer. Now you sidestep the proof I just found without even seeing it. Samuels should see my birth registration - even if you don't care."

"I'll be glad to look at it and even show it to Samuels. But it won't change facts."

"You're being a jerk. You won't apologize; you won't admit a mistake, and you won't show it to Samuels with an open mind."

"Okay, okay, why don't you explain it from your point of view?" Will you bitch like this, when we're together? "Nelson will be in Plattsburgh tomorrow. Meet us for lunch at Carvers Restaurant. You can show him the registration form."

"Hank, you and Samuels started this battle over the DNA."

"I'm not fighting, so don't be angry. God, I haven't even mentioned the money you owe me. Just calm down and see you at lunch tomorrow."

"All right. Carvers, it is Hank." Sue hung up and stayed quiet for a moment before realizing Maggie was still in the room. "Life is a bitch, Maggie. Play a man's game by their rules, then just when you're winning, they change the rules. Hank discounts my birth information."

"I heard." Maggie continued, "Sue, Allie's with your dad, and you need a break - I'm taking you to lunch. We need to talk about your ex contacting me."

"Allan?"

"The very same. Now are you hungry?"

The busy hum in the crowded restaurant was ideal for a private conversation - the buzz of noise meant they didn't have to talk lower. Maggie came straight to the point. "A few days back, he waited outside my work, and approached me going to lunch. I told him bluntly, get lost - his issues are with you."

"And?"

"He didn't argue, just asked me to pass you a note. I told Allan I wouldn't take it, so he thanked me, and walked away. He was polite, not out of line, and not surprised I refused. He was quite normal."

"You could have taken the note. What did he want?"

"No way, I'll not be a messenger. Let him buy a stamp and mail it."

Sue nodded her agreement, "How did Allan seem? Is he looking after himself?"

"He seemed fine. Seemed like the polite guy you married ten years ago. A single girl would jump at having lunch with him."

"Trouble is he doesn't want a single girl. He wants me, Maggie."

The waiter served and left when Maggie asked, "So, tell me, does Allan know you're pregnant?"

Sue shook her head, "No, and neither does Hank. I'm going to have this child but I still won't tell him yet, till I get a sense of stable emotions. And for sure, there won't be a future with Allan."

Sue continued in a soft tone, "Maggie, at aunt Maria's place, I saw just how comfortable a real family can be. Simply the loving way she and Fred and the relatives all acted. As one big family. It convinced me to continue the pregnancy. But neither Allan nor Hank are aware of my situation and, until I know my heart, that's the way it's going to stay." She changed the subject, "But enough from me, we came to talk over your problems. Is it sex and a juicy story?" Sue moved the olives in her salad to the edge of her plate.

"It's Peter's first wife." Maggie confiscated Sue's olives. "Quite by accident, I met Janis a few weeks ago, and we ended up having a frank talk about Peter."

"And how is pudding head these days?"

"Doing well. Never remarried, but very successful in business. You'd like her, Sue. We had a good talk, open, almost as friends, and when saying good-byes Janis made a cryptic remark that brought some issues into focus for me. She said, 'Peter could have been a good husband, except he hated his mom. His obsessive hatred against Joanna spoiled too much of his mind.' Later, I realized Janis was extremely perceptive. Have you noticed how Peter talks of everything, all the time, except, he doesn't talk of his childhood. Ever?"

"That's our Peter. Always been a very private guy."

"Think about it, Sue. Before you left for Oakville, Peter got raving mad arguing with you over Joanna. He was yelling. And yelling is Peter's breakaway tactic whenever I ask about his mom. No discussion on Joanna. Verboten."

"How come I never noticed my brother being that stark."

"I sleep with him, Sue. You've only lived across the lake for the last ten years. For instance, did you know Peter almost boycotted his mom's funeral?"

"Dad mentioned it on the drive to Canada. It was news to me."

"Something else, you may have missed. Peter had great difficulty contacting his only child from his marriage with Janis. When the boy was six and a visit was arranged, Peter was physically ill before seeing him. It was awful."

"Maggie, is this going anywhere? My brother's a good guy. Is this leading to divorce talk?"

"No. I stay with him, because he is a good man. However, for some reason, Sue, his issues of childhood were intensified, when you started your birth search. It upsets him. Especially, at night, when I hear him tossing and turning. Since you started searching, he doesn't sleep well."

"But my family search isn't Peter's problem?"

"Widen your focus in looking at your childhood. Could be there is something hidden that affects all you kids? Sue, you're a catalyst for Peter's issues to surface. Since you started searching, Peter has become weird, almost unhinged at times. He's deeply disturbed." Maggie finally got to the point, "He's in a shell Sue, that's ready to crack, and I don't want to lose him. I can't get through to him, but you can. Will you talk to him?"

Chapter 15

Sue's hesitation was obvious, "Maggie, older brothers never listen to their younger sisters. I care for you both, but I've got a skin full of my own problems to sort out."

"My issues are your concern." Maggie sat back, "You don't get it do you? Peter's problems are childhood related - like your birth search - and they could be connected. Ask yourself why Peter sees your mom radically different than you? It's because your mom is the focus of this mixed up Stevens family yet it's never discussed.. Everyone dancing in denial around Saint Joanna and no one saying a word."

Sue leaned back in her chair, folded her arms to create a distance, and became thoughtful. "Of course us kids are connected to my mom, not in problems, but in her looking after us. Don't knock her - she was ideal. You're implying there's a mutual denial, all of us kids in on it, and that sounds far-fetched. Peter's bag of problems are his and separate from my issues. I don't know if confronting Peter is a good idea, but I will think on it."

Sue leaned forward with her hands flat on the table, and continued talking, "Tomorrow I meet with Hank and his DNA specialist, so Peter and his problems will have to wait for later." Sue dropped her voice a little. "Maggie, I'll talk to Peter, but wait a couple of days. Let me think this through."

"Okay, I can wait till you see the connection. In the meantime, I want to propose a conspiracy between us." Maggie speared the last bits of chicken on her plate, and continued, "You're looking for pieces missing from the past. And I'm trying to make Peter whole. Let's become a team. You can listen in Atlanta and I can to the same here. We can watch and compare notes. We both need a good buddy to watch our backs."

Sue understood. "Spying. You're suggesting I check on dad and you watch Peter? Without them knowing. That's underhanded, Maggie."

"Yes. It's a dirty fight, if you want to find out the truth. Sue, if you want to win, you need to use your wits. You call it spying, while I call it fighting for my husband. Is it a pact?"

Sue toyed with her salad fork and nodded her head a few times before replying, "I help you and you help me? And we can trust each other. Trust is very important to me."

Maggie reached across the table and gently touched Sue's finger tips, "I knew you were a bright girl. Now, what say we have dessert. Then, tomorrow, you can tell me about lunch with Hank and his forensic pal."

* * * * *

The next day, during Carvers' busy lunch hour, it took Sue a minute to spot Hank with Samuels and join their table. Nelson put Sue at ease. In spite of being her opponent, she warmed to the man - late fifties, distinguished looking with a charming and educated manner. "Hank tells me your Canadian documents will revise our DNA science. If so, then I will gladly nominate you for a Nobel Prize."

Sue smiled, "I wish."

Nelson continued, "So do I. Upset the scientific community and you get a bundle in prize money. Plus, I could introduce myself as the one who helped your career."

"The money would be just compensation for trouble the DNA report caused my family."

Nelson became sympathetic, "I'm sorry for any problems you were caused."

Susan thumped her Ontario Birth Registration on the table,

"This proves my mother was Joanna. Absolutely. My aunt Maria remembers my birth, Nelson. This Canadian Birth Registration form lists all the details. Plus, my aunt Cecile, actually filled out my birth registration."

"Yes, I can see it's signed by Cecile Court. And I guess she confirms writing this?"

"My next step will be to contact her. But there's more. Aunt Maria saw my mother in the hospital, hours after I was born. The doctor who delivered me is a D.A. Wyks. His records could be checked and, if he is still living, he just might remember the birth. My birth was paid for by the American Air Force, and I am contacting them for records. Plus, while my mother was giving birth, my dad flew to Canada and that flight may be on his military papers. Later, he drove me and my mom to Georgia, where I stayed with mom till dad was finished with the Vietnam war. We lived in a small town in Georgia, till I was six. A small town where everyone knew everyone, and you couldn't possibly reach through my bedroom window and substitute a different child for me. Everything checks. I'm me."

Nelson Samuels was looking across Carvers, out the window, staring into a distance, yet seeing nothing. Then, his mental focus returned to the conversation, "These Canadian certificates are a wonderful record. Detailed. I've seen them before and often wish we had a similar system down in the States. Very detailed." He paused, smiled, and continued, "You've gone to a lot of trouble to find the truth, Sue, and I dearly wish your effort would leave everyone happy, but it won't." He pointed to her Birth Registration and continued, "This form only proves the birth of a child to Joanna Stevens and, yet, your DNA science still tells us that this isn't your birth. Something is wrong."

"Let me show you." Samuels placed a print-out on the table. "Everyone's DNA is inherited from both parents. Think of the DNA molecule as resembling a large twisted ladder, with each of its rungs holding a base pair of DNA. Billions of DNA. Plus, we humans, have two kinds of DNA. You're familiar with the first kind, the gnomic - 46 chromosomes - determining characteristics as sex and eye colour. Sort of familiar with this concept, Sue?"

"Think so. Taught us in high school."

"Good. But there is a second type of DNA present in everyone in smaller quantities, mitochondrial. Although both male and female have mitochondrial, only the mother's mitochondrial gene is passed on to children: a special code passed only on the mother's side. So, the mitochondrial your siblings have...."

Sue finished his sentence, "Should be the same code for me."

"It should be. But it isn't." Nelson's voice changed from a classroom manner to a quieter tone, as he placed pages on the table. "Now look, these print-outs clearly show your brother and sister have the identical mother and you have a different mother. Plus, your siblings have DNA from one father, and you have DNA from another. You had different parents than your siblings."

Sue, suddenly, felt warm and sluggish and heard herself saying, "Nelson, what if you're wrong? Can I get a second opinion?"

Nelson Samuels looked quickly towards Hank, "Now you see why I prefer lab work." Then he focused on Sue and continued, "Of course, you can. You can do anything you want that's legal, but it's a waste of money repeating the tests at another lab. We already tested them twice. I'm sorry. I can see my talk has made you emotional. Do you need something, a cold drink?"

Hank watched her face go pale. "Easy Sue, you need some fresh air."

"I feel sick. Everywhere I turn, the doors are closing." My god, what the hell is the truth? "I just want to cry." Sue sat very still knowing what she had to face. "So granted the DNA is right, then my dad is damn well lying. Someone is lying." If I'm not related to my family, then I can be sure of one damn absolute fact - someone is lying to me, lying through their teeth.

"Hank, there is no solid ground to stand on. Facing the fact my parents aren't my parents, means I have been lied to for years. This birth registration form is meaningless, and I've been raised in the wrong family. Either I'm sane in a crazy world or crazy in a sane one, and I can't figure out what's true."

Nelson dropped the second shoe, "Sue, don't discount your birth registration. It's valid, for someone's birth, just not yours. Something happened. Perhaps, an accidental switch in a hospital? Whatever, there must be an answer to explain the dilemma." Nelson tried to give some hope, "This registration form contains details that a Cecile Court provided information on your birth. Question her. Be frank, ask Cecile if she remembers any time, or any possibility, when the child born in Milton, Ontario, could have been switched." Nelson smiled, adding, "Sue, there is another avenue to explore. This Canadian registration is for one child and your DNA shows a different child. That means two children, you and someone else. It suggests an initial hospital delivery mix-up. It's even possible that another child is searching the same facts as you are."

"Nelson, I'm a housewife, separated, no money, with a ten-year-old daughter to look after and this search is driving me nuts. I don't have the energy to keep looking."

Nelson continued, "Well, if you do continue the quest, I will help if I can. Start from day one, start with the hospital. Mix-ups are exceptional, but they do happen. A wrong tag, or even setting a newborn in a different place, anything can lead to misidentification. You need access to old medical records, and a doctor buddy of mine from Oakville owes me a rather large golf favour. He might be able to ask questions for you. So don't give up. This Cecil Court may know something. Accept the DNA as fact and question everything else. I'd look for some abnormal circumstance that could explain a baby switch."

Sue was finding her resolve again. "You think an answer could be waiting for me to find? All right, Cecile would be a good place to continue looking." Dad won't be pleased. He will not be thrilled. "I will keep looking."

"Ask about childhood illness, or who looked after you. Ask if you were hospitalized as an infant and where, or left in the care of anyone else?" Nelson looked at his notes and turned to Hank, "Why have we not checked Sue's mother for DNA?"

Sue answered, "Mom died years ago, Nelson."

Nelson, against his practice of staying uninvolved, continued to offer help. "Then get a sample from Cecile. She has the identical mitochondrial DNA to your mother."

"Nelson, I brought a hair sample from mom's brother and his wife. Will you check their DNA before Cecile's swab?

"That's the spirit. Give me the samples now and if Hank covers the paperwork, a STR test is easy to perform. I can't promise a positive answer, but I'm willing to try."

Sue waltzed out of Carvers' restaurant with mixed feelings. Yes, she had lost the certificate battle, but she had the tacit backing of a scientist to keep searching. Nelson would test a few samples.

She paused a moment, then used her cell phone. "Hi Maggie, I've decided to join your spy club, and you can start tonight. Start sorting through my mom's papers. Tell Peter it's your idea to help organize them. This will both involve you in my search and give you a reason to question Peter on old family matters. It's a great place to start our teamwork."

Maggie was intuitive, "Thanks Sue, we need each other. Now, you haven't mentioned the lunch with Hank. How come?"

"They threw a bucket of cold water on my birth registration. Maggie, I've been acting like a beggar, waiting for crumbs of information, and that way of thinking stops today. The birth search goes on. And neither Dad nor Peter will stop me. Tell you my plans tonight, Maggie."

Her second call was to leave a message with Annie, "Hi sis, just me - leaving a message. Annie, you made crayon drawings up in Canada, when you were around four? Can you remember being there? Why were you there for a summer? Call me and I'll spring for lunch. Bye."

Sue, hesitated before making her third call, but knew it was time to contact her husband. "Allan, I need to keep this call simple. Allie and I are all right. However, my birth search is still going nowhere. I know it was part of the tension between us. Yet, I will keep searching. Crazy, but I need an answer " He listened, surprisingly quietly, as Sue explained how the trip to Canada had connected her to family, but didn't produce an answer on her birth. "Plus, I apologize - sorry for messing up your truck."

"Sue, we didn't split over your birth search. Drinking... was the main problem." He paused long enough for Sue to wonder at this new Allan, then he continued, "I went nuts myself the last few weeks we were together. Fact is, I was worse than my dad before he went back to Vietnam. He had to be hammered to get on that plane and that's how low my life had gone. Sue, I miss you and Allie dreadfully. Do you want to meet up?"

"No. Not yet. But you and Allie should stay in touch."

"I'd like that."

"Okay, call Allie tomorrow night, about seven, and, perhaps, ask her out this weekend."

"That works for me." Then he hesitated, and continued, "Now I have a tip for your birth search, if you promise not to laugh. My mom often said you can tell families by the shape of their ear. You ever hear that? She said ears remain the same shape through many generations."

"Allan, is that true or an old wives' tale? Ear Phrenology?"

"Now don't laugh, Sue. My mom used to point it out. Kid's ears were often just like one of the parents. Mom wasn't silly. Check it out for yourself."

Allan your kooky. "Right. Checking on ears is a light note to end an exhausting day. Call tomorrow evening and talk for a while. Right now, I'm tired and going to head back to Peter's."

Stilted good-byes followed with a vague commitment to talk soon - but neither said I love you as they hung up. Besides, Sue had fibbed about going directly home; she had one stop - for research at the local library.

* * * * *

Maggie had started making dinner and Peter was setting the table, so when the phone rang, John answered, figuring it was Sue. He was surprised to hear his other daughter, Annie.

"Well, this is nice, Annie. You calling the old man to wish me a safe trip back to Atlanta?"

"Uh, oh, sure dad, have a safe trip back to Atlanta. Look, is Sue there?" When told Sue wasn't home yet, Annie continued, "Well, her message was asking of the summer I spent in Canada at age seven. For god's sakes, she knows my memory is not the best. I can hardly remember seven weeks ago. I guess her search is still going?"

John replied, "I thought she had finished, Annie. What message should I give her?"

"Say, I remember three things from the Canada visit. It was always hot. We were at the lake every day. And mom wasn't there. That's it. Have Sue call me when she gets in."

"I'll tell her what you said Annie, but we all leave for Atlanta tomorrow. So, she may call you from my condo."

Sue arrived home in time for dinner and noticed three of Joanna's boxes had been opened with contents scattered on the carpet in a sort of organized chaos. Peter spoke, "Now, don't yell at me, Sue - I told Maggie to ask before sorting through mom's stuff. It's your fault for bringing it back."

At the dinner table John reminded Sue of returning to Atlanta, "You have remembered, we are leaving early tomorrow for Atlanta." When Sue looked thoughtful, he continued, "Your brother can't keep us forever and I need to get back to my old routine." He moved a bowl of salad toward Sue, indicating she should serve. "Sooner you get a job in Atlanta, the sooner you can plan for the future. Remember, we agreed on leaving tomorrow."

"I forgot. With everything going on, it skipped my mind. Well, my plans changed today. Hank and Nelson have convinced me there must be an answer." Everyone could sense a pronouncement coming. "I've given this a great deal of thought, and I'm going to take the next few months to search my birth." Sue looked at her dad, and continued, "I know, I know, I need to be practical. So the time limit is to look for six or eight weeks, then, if there is no resolution, I stop. Switch off. Get a job and start paying back the loan I'm now going to ask for." Sue looked around the table and knew she had their attention.

After eating another fork full of salad, she continued, "This search won't be cheap. I'm asking the family for three things - loaning me money, searching their memories for clues to help me and, most important, understanding how important this is to me."

Silence, except for clinking forks and cutting knives. The table was quiet. Sue continued, "Look, either I do this now or I wonder all my life. The money could be as much as a ten thousand dollar loan. But, I'm doing this. Sue ate with relish, "Maggie, you make the best pizza and fries I've had today."

John asked about the money, "So much! Why ten thousand?"

"It could be less dad, but the big cost will be a trip to California to see mom's sister."

John's fist hit the table, "I will not finance a trip for Cecile to rake up garbage. She's a problem."

"I understand your reluctance, dad, but you don't need to deal with Cecile... I will. Don't worry, I promise she won't convert me to communism. And you don't need to finance the trip. This is my journey."

"Don't be a smart ass. Asking for money and joking at the same time... count me out."

Sue turned to her brother, "Peter?"

Peter avoided eye contact as he spoke, "Sue, be practical now, don't go. It's not the money; it's family... your search will only cause problems. Dad knows that."

Even Allie was against it. "Mom, I need you with me in Atlanta. I don't want you to go."

Sue answered that directly. "Allie, most of the time, you and grampy and I will be together. If I travel, it will only be for a few days. But mommy has to do this."

"Dessert anyone?" Maggie interrupted. She came from the kitchen, placing small bowls of peaches and ice cream in front of everyone, except Sue. Maggie handed Allie a crystal wine glass. "Give this one to your mom."

Setting the glass by her mother, Allie asked, "What's the paper inside your glass, mom?"

Maggie spoke. "It's a check for fifteen thousand dollars. Take it, Sue. Pay off Hank's debt first and spend the rest on searching. If my money-bags husband makes any stink of giving you an interest free loan, then tell him to stuff it."

Seemed they moved and talked all at once.

John filled the air with frustration: Peter wasn't pleased, and Allie moved over to be with her mom. Maggie smiled, saying to

Peter, "Have a heart. Your sister needs money. I have it and don't need it right now. Okay Ebenezer."

Only Allie finished her peaches and ice cream at a quiet table. "Mom, I want to go to California with you."

"I'm not going anywhere near Disneyland, sweetie?" As Allie pouted, Sue continued, "Dad, don't be angry, I need your support if I stay in Plattsburgh for a few days longer. You and Allie drive to Atlanta, and I'll be there in less than a week. Plus, I went to the library and spent the afternoon checking out life in the 60's. Can you reminisce on some of your old memories after dinner? Just a chat." Her dad sighed and nodded.

Later, as Sue helped clean dishes in the kitchen, Maggie handed her a newspaper clipping. "I found this tonight in one of the boxes. A 1963 article on Vietnamese monks burning themselves in Saigon, and she stapled her poem to it."

Perceive - our bloody future's secret
look - before war blinds your eyes
touch - the child who cries and dies
hear- their birth becoming death
listen - try to hear my child's last breath

So play, play your old march to war
Play your war as played before
Till children die and are no more

State your beliefs - Stand up soldiers.
Pants on fire - Liars, liars - bunch of liars.
Bunches are rotten - beyond the stink of human fires.
Joanna - '63

Sue read Joanna's poem at the kitchen table and it triggered an internal question - 'Mom, what are you telling me - war, and birth and children - all in one poem?' Then she read the article; Buddhist monks staging a revolt, self immolations, against the American supported Saigon government in 1963.

"I'm not sure I would have liked your mom, Sue." Maggie said. "She had died before Peter and I met so, perhaps, it's not fair to judge her, but she's not my kind of lady. Too intense for me."

Sue reread the short poem. It was intense. "Maggie, could these dates be right? I've always thought Vietnam only turned bad in 1967, but these monks were killing themselves in 1963? And, this article lists our involvement back to the 1950's." Sue recalled Maria's words, 'To understand your mom, understand her time." Does that include the war, and people burning themselves? Dad knows, but he won't talk."

Maggie was sensible, "You're upset, and that's no time to yell at your dad."

Sue stood. "I've waited in silence too long. It's time to make some noise." Dad might stonewall his memories but, it's time, I set the tone for asking the questions.

Chapter 16

John's vision of being the head of his family was rooted in paternalistic cloth. Caring for his family was a duty. He waited patiently in Peter's den, while CNN cast a flickering display of light and shadow over the room. It was time to listen to Sue's questions.

Thinking, 'The Canada trip was a mistake. I know there's nothing too hid in Sue's past, but simply going up north confused her. Besides, Maria's half truths and innuendoes didn't help.' Eventually, Sue came and sat down opposite. He half joked, "Is this going to be a friendly chat or an inquisition?"

Sue laughed, "Friends, dad, all the time. Did you know I talked to Allan today? On the phone he was talkative, rambling on more today than he had in a year. And something he never does... he talked of his dad. That got me thinking of my grandparents, and how little I know of them. It never occurred to me before, but how did you get on with your dad?"

John scratched his head, thinking, "Don't join the CIA: your questions are too transparent. Still, looking for hidden secrets behind your birth?" He went quiet for a moment and then continued, "Let's talk of your DNA difference once more. It's still unexplained. And your baby picture with the hospital weight seems at odds with a premature birth. Right?"

Sue had been nodding her head as her dad was speaking. "Exactly. Those two facts are the main reasons I keep looking. I can't explain them."

"And neither can I. They stand out like a sore thumb." John's voice rose ever so slightly, "However, you are family, you are my daughter and despite the flawed bits of fact that I can't explain, you should trust me."

"I do, dad, I really do. Yet the questions remain..."

"I'm on your side. I'm not fighting you. Do what needs to be done in Plattsburgh, and I'll look after Allie till you return to Atlanta. What else do you want me to talk about?"

Sue moved the conversation back to her agenda, "Just kick back and tell me of your mom and dad. What was it like years before you took mom to live in Georgia, when you were a kid living at home?" When silence fell, Sue continued, "Anything. Just how do you remember your dad. Please."

John got up saying, "Want a beer? No, well I need one." He returned with a drink, made himself comfortable, and started rambling, "My dad, John senior, was of the old school, - a private, quiet, proud patriot. Proud American. He was born John Peter Stevens in 1918, and grew up hearing the old Georgia boys talk of great military victories. Life, now, is so different from the times my dad lived in." John's memories came flowing out. "I still have his little wooden rifle he carried at four. So, true to character, he enlisted in the army on Dec. 10, 1941, and then injured his leg in basic training in 1942. He stayed in the army, training men who went to war. But he hated missing a chance for combat. He went to his grave bitter, truly bitter at being denied the chance of fighting in Europe. He never shirked his duty and was a good soldier."

"Dad tried liking Joanna, if for no other reason than, because she was my wife, but he found it impossible. And she didn't help. He might just be talking, perhaps saying someone needed a horsewhipping, and she would be yelling at him for being a bully." John was smiling by now, adding, "Worst of all, I was caught in the middle of those two. Not pleasant."

Sue remembered her mom's determination in life, "Sounds like two fighting cats, dad."

John laughed, "Polecats... that they were. They didn't feud

at the start of our marriage, when we lived in Plattsburgh, or even when we would visit ma and pa in Georgia. But living under the same roof became a different kettle of fish."

"Was mom always antiwar, like before you married?"

John moved to the edge of his chair. "War was the essence of her conflicts with my dad. Joanna seemed born to be antiwar and her views became explosive as Vietnam heated up. By the time Joanna made a home for our three kids at my dad's place in Georgia, which was before you were even thought of - well, it just didn't work having your mom and my dad under the same roof. Not a fun time for any of us. Some days, your mom living in Georgia, would phone me at five in the morning in California, crying over how my parents were treating her."

"Dad," Sue changed their conversation, asking, "when you were at Mugu and mom was in Georgia, was I ever hospitalized as a baby?"

John took a moment to recollect, "Hospitalized? No. Now you're raising the baby switch theory again, aren't you? And there's not a chance in hell of it happening. Joanna always looked after you kids. We lived in a small town, on the outskirts, and our two dogs wouldn't let anyone near the place without raising a ruckus. And when Joanna was ill, my mom and dad took care of you kids."

"Ill?" Sue asked casually, "Why was mom ill and when?"

And John hesitated, thinking, "As I remember, it was complications from giving birth. It happened at Peter's birth and all the rest of the kids, 'cept for you I think. Joanna often stayed in the hospital for a few days longer than most wives, at times, even after the baby could be released. The doctors prescribed medication, and she became fine. It happened in Plattsburgh for Peter and Annie and, in Georgia after Harry was born and, while I was at Mugu."

"If you were in California, how can you be certain nothing happened in Georgia?"

"For heaven sakes Sue, will you get the idea out of your mind that you were swapped by Gypsies." John laughed to mask his frustration and added, "Forget a baby swap. Your mom and grandmother would never let anything happen, at any time, to any of their children or grandchildren." John continued, "Sue, think what a baby swap would mean. A new born gets bonded quickly. You raised Allie. When could a switch have been made that you wouldn't notice or question?"

"I agree, dad. It seems a dead-end line of thought, but Hank's friend, Nelson Samuels, says it could happen. But leave it for now. Why did mom leave Peter and Annie and go to Oakville for months, before I was born?"

"Because she and my dad had a nuclear war, before you were born. And no point dwelling on it, cause you can't have a baby swap before birth." John looked tenderly at his daughter, "If I could give you any more information... I would. I really would. This back and forth uncertainty isn't good for anyone in the family."

Tears were not far from Sue's eyes, as she touched her dad's hand in support.

John continued, "So do your California trip, clear your mind and then, hopefully, we can put it all behind us. Now, it's getting late. Finished with the questions? Good... and remember Sue, everyone in the family loves you."

"I love you too, dad. Thanks for gabbing with me. Hey, you want another of Peter's beers?" John shook his head no, and gave her hand a little pat.

"Time to turn in. Need a good night's sleep for the drive to Atlanta tomorrow."

Taking his empty beer bottle to the computer, she soon realized directory assistance had no listing for a Cecile Court in Crescent City, California. Next, a call to Maria in Oakville came up empty, with her aunt saying, "Susan, I've never had to call Cecile.

Her Christmas card address is all I have. You could write and ask for her number. Give my love to Allie. We miss you."

Eventually, Sue gave in and called Hank, "I feel a pest, but can a person's address be used to find a phone number?"

"It's called a reverse trace, Sue. What do you need?"

Sue gave Hank Cecile Court's address in California.

"Okay... I'll call you back."

Over an hour later Hank called, "Busy night. Thing is there's no Cecile Court at 17 Bay Street, but the address lists a Bonnie Hunter as paying the phone bills. That makes sense to you?"

"I know almost nothing of my aunt, so Bonnie Hunter is a place to start. Thanks, Hank. And can I see you tomorrow? The Starbucks near Carvers at two? See you then." He won't like getting his loan back, but Maggie is right. It complicates our relationship.

Since it would only be seven in Crescent City, her California call was answered on the third ring.

"Bonnie Hunter." Clearly a young voice had answered.

"Bonnie, I'm Susan Stevens, in Plattsburgh, New York, and I'd like to speak to Cecile Court."

"Bad connection, can you say your name again?"

"It's Sue Stevens calling my aunt on a family matter. Does Cecile Court live there?"

"Yes, she's here, and why are you calling?" Bonnie was obviously screening.

Sue was ready to blurt her story out, "I'm calling from New York on a family matter."

There was a pause before Bonnie said, "One moment," and the phone was set down for a long pause before Bonnie was back on, "Cecile wants to know if you're one of Joanna's kids?"

"Cecile must remember my mom. She would know me as Susan, Joanna's youngest." Moments went by as the phone in California went quiet and then was picked up again. Susan asked,

"Have I passed the test? Can I talk to Cecile now, please?"

"This isn't a good time, Susan. Cecile's almost nodding off with her medication now. Her best time to talk is late morning, even then she may not know you. Old folks get weak and their memory is... spotty at best. Try calling tomorrow about eleven. Bye for now." Bonnie had already hung up. At least it had been a promising start and, tomorrow, Sue would call again.

Morning unfolded with the appearance of normality, yet, later, in future months, Sue could pinpoint this one particular point in time, when the dominos started to fall. And the odd thing about looking back to this day is the way it unfolded, without a ripple.

Allie whined, "Not fair, mom. You get to see California and I don't. I'll be as old as you before I ever see the ocean, and it's your fault."

"That will be a global tragedy, Allie." The problem is you want to be with me. "You swam in the Atlantic, and you didn't like the salt or the cold. The Pacific is just as salty. Probably twice as salty. Now grampy wants to get travelling to Atlanta." Must remember - life can be tough on ten-year-old's. "I'll fly to Atlanta in less than a week, and you can meet me at the airport."

"Mom, a week away is forever."

John shouted from the front door saying, it was time to get on the road. "We're almost packed, dad. Allie come on. I've got calls to make and, things to do. Now, let's go to the car. And remember to call your dad tonight." Sue would long remember their departure, when a few words might have broken the links being forged in a chain of events moving toward disaster. This morning would forever remain in the cross hairs of Susan's memory.

Sue packed Allie's stuff in the car. "Now, dad, I've a seat on a California flight tomorrow. I call Cecile this afternoon, tell her I'm arriving tomorrow, which means I can't meet Hank till three this afternoon. There's just too many arrangements, but it will work. You two get going and drive carefully."

John still fussed, "How will you get to Crescent City?"

"I travel American to San Francisco, a connecter flight to Eureka, and a car from there. All set up. I fly tomorrow. If Cecile is that frail, I want to see her now."

"Mom, you said I could talk to dad tonight."

"Oh, I didn't forget sweetie. Dad, when you stop tonight, can you call Allan. Allie's trying to set up a routine for calling each other."

John gave a wry smile. "Looking forward to it, Sue. Now when you return the loan to Hank, will you need extra money?"

"Well... if you're offering me your credit cards, just kidding... no, I'm fine." Everyone yelled good-byes, the car rolled, and a day unfolded. Even Allie was waving and saying good-bye, and telling her mom 'good luck' in California, "See you in a few days, mom." Sue knew she was a lucky mom with Allie blossoming, since they escaped Allan. Her granddad was happy, too.

Sue called Hank's cell and left a message, "I need to change our meeting to three instead of two. See you then." That's done, so now I just wait nervously to call Cecile. What if she refuses to talk? God, what if she's an old grouch with bad breath and a worse memory?

Half an hour later Hank returned her call, "Sue, three is better timing for me. But I'm calling with information from Nelson. You can rule out any birth switch involving babies born at the Milton Hospital close to your birth."

"You're sure. How do you know?"

"Nelson's doctor friend in Toronto checked the birth records for the Milton Hospital. You were one of five kids born within a ten-day bracket of your birth. Against the odds, the other four were all males."

"That's a definite answer. Can't switch a girl for a boy? Someone might notice." Sue was starting to feel a little giddy. All right, Milton Hospital wasn't the answer, but Cecile might be. "Thank him for me, Hank. We still on for three? I can pay the loan off now."

"Pay it off?" Hank paused, in thoughtful silence, then asked, "You back with Allan?"

"No. Not now or ever, Hank." Not going with anyone. "Tell you of my plans over coffee. See you at three."

Sue could hardly wait to call Cecile midmorning, California time. Thinking, god, my thoughts are scattered. Not hungry for lunch, what's on TV... an episode of the *'Young and the Restless'* sure, why not. Now Victor, with his unlimited wealth, there's a man to solve my problems. He could adopt me.

Eventually, Sue called. Deja vu of yesterday, Bonnie Hunter answered on the third ring. "It's Susan calling back, Bonnie. How is my aunt today?"

"Frail and cranky, as usual, but she can handle a call today. I'll get her phone set-up." Bonnie was gone, then a moment spoke again, "Susan, if she cuts you off, then call me back. Okay, here's Cecile."

A weak voice came through to Sue, "Yes. Hello."

Keep it simple till she knows me. "Aunt Cecile, I'm your niece, Susan Stevens. Joanna's daughter."

The weak voice came back, "Do I know a Susan Stevens? Joanna's daughter married a Charter. Are you that girl?"

"Yes, aunt Cecile." No senile moss on you lady. "I'm Susan Charter, and I'd like to visit you. Would that be okay?"

"All right, I won't be going anywhere today, Susan. Chocolate cookies are ones I like."

"Cookies. I'll bring a bag full of chocolate cookies, when I visit."

"And bring my sister Joanna with you. You tell her to come, Susan. She doesn't visit me."

Oh dear! "Cecile, my mom died a few years back, and..." Her aunt's phone clanked against something, and Bonnie came back on the line, asking, "For god's sake, Susan, what did you say to get her so upset?"

"Cecile asked about my mom and I said she died years ago."

"I should have warned you, Susan, that Cecile cycles from active to comatose just at any mention of death or dying. She should be fine. Eventually. Try calling back in a few days."

"Bonnie, I'll be flying to Crescent City in days. Can you make sure she knows I'll be coming there . . . and tell Cecile how I'm sorry for the upset just now?"

"Oh, Cecile's momentary upsets are soon forgotten. But why come to Crescent City when she might not even be with it? Talking on the phone might be best."

"I have to come. There's family information that doesn't make sense and Cecile may be the last living person who can understand it. Bonnie, I'm already booked for Wednesday, on American, and I'll call you when I get to San Francisco."

"Fine then, we can handle your visit. Besides, I'm curious to meet a relative of Cecile's."

"You know of my mom? Are you Cecile's care-giver, Bonnie?"

After a hesitation, so brief it may not have happened, Bonnie was saying good-byes, "Cecile as always had good care. Be nice to meet you, Susan, and show a New Yorker our west coast hospitality. Call when you're coming. Bye."

Sue set down the phone. "Calling me a New Yorker - she must have traced my number." Bye till Wednesday Cecile, you've just become my favourite maiden aunt. And you, Bonnie Hunter, what is Cecile to you? How do you fit into the family menagerie?

But now, it's time for a well-deserved coffee break with Hank. He never showed. Sue waited, sipped her coffee, while his coffee slowly turned cold. Waiting, she read a discarded paper, reviewed plans to fly west, and still no Hank. Then, checking her cell phone she found two recent text messages. One, as expected, was a brief note from Hank, "Busy, c u later."

The next, an ominous message from Allan, reading, "You're setting me up and I don't like it. Why do it? We need to talk." What are you mad about, Allan? I can't figure you, and there's little point trying. No use calling back if you're angry. Sue left the coffee shop, looked east across Lake Champlain toward Vermont, and shook her head. Then, she drove back to her brother's house to pack for California, blissfully unaware that today the State of Vermont had deducted her first family support money from Allan's paycheck.

* * * * *

On the Vermont side of Lake Champlain, Allan breezed into a Clearville coffee shop and plopped down next to Stu.

Stu greeted him bluntly, "You're late." You said three, it's almost four... you're late. And don't blame it on someone else."

"Stu, life is getting to me. Vermont just deducted child support money from my pay. I got hot for a while, then calmed down and followed what you've been telling me. Think first. You should be proud of me for realizing the money is still mine, cause Sue and I will be getting back together."

"Your wife tell you that?"

"A man can tell. Women don't always say what they mean. It's all in hidden signals with them. Like tonight. I'm calling Allie about seven, then I figure Sue will talk. I'll say my text message today was hasty and invite her over. So it's pizza for me at my place while phoning Allie and starting our new family time."

"Aren't you making the coffee tonight?"

"I was... but someone else can do it. Any ideas on who?"

"Just keep your word and go make the coffee. Talk to your daughter at seven, make the coffee before eight."

"Stu, if I handle tonight right, Sue will talk for a while and soon be back to my place. See what I mean. The coffee is not important."

"It's not the coffee, Allan. It's the commitment of keeping your word. Breaking commitments is just building castles in the air. It's crazy thinking."

"Don't say I'm crazy. Never been crazy... even when drinking - not then, not now."

"Oh, sorry Allan, if it hurts your feelings. But nuts, those who drink and drug through life aren't thinking straight. They might think they are sane, but they aren't. Nut case drunks, get sober and live right for a few months, then they somehow believe their years of craziness inside their mind is magically cured. They expect everyone to forget their nutty past and never mention the insanity lurking beneath their skin. Like the elephant in the room... don't mention the obvious. Does that sound familiar?"

By now, Allan was standing, holding the back of his chair and glaring at Stu, "You don't have a wife, don't even have a chance of a wife, so why pull my chain? It's my life, my rules, not yours. Tonight is pizza for me, family night, and getting back with Sue. Could be a rocking start to my future and I would be nuts giving that up to make coffee."

Stu, realizing he wouldn't reach Allan, at least not tonight, said, "Fine. Forget the coffee, Allan. Call if you need me."

"Won't be calling you, cause Sue will keep me busy." And he stomped out to his truck.

* * * * *

At dinner, Maggie turned to Sue, "Isn't it quiet with just the three of us? I miss Allie? This place is dead without her, like a light went out."

Peter spoke up, "Oh, dad left you a message, Sue. A bad rain storm stopped them early near Petersburg, Virginia. He's tired and won't call again tonight."

"That's halfway. They should make Atlanta tomorrow." It will give Allie time tonight to call Allan. "And Peter, can you run me to the airport, day after tomorrow? Early?"

Peter's answer was stopped by a knock at the front door. He returned with Hank in tow, who apologized, "Sorry folks - don't mean to interrupt dinner."

Maggie smiled, "Just in time for dessert, Hank. Come and sit down with us."

"I'll say thank you... but no, Maggie. Here to apologize. I need a word with Sue for standing her up today. But you could come with us." He looked at her, "Starbucks for a dessert? All four of us could go."

Maggie laughed, "I don't think you want me and Peter to tag along." Pushing them out the front door she quipped to Sue, "I'm going to sort some of your mom's papers tonight, so take your time."

Sue and Hank had been gone an hour, when Allan called Peter's home to speak with his daughter. Peter spoke the truth, "Allie left with my dad for Atlanta this morning, Allan. I thought Sue would have told you?"

"Sue told me to call. Put Sue on then."

"She's out, Allan, but should be back soon. Any message?"

He turned insistent, "I won't yell at her over the money. Put her on, Peter."

"Told you already, Sue's not here. And the loan is hers to do with as she wants."

"Loan? Where is she? I don't want trouble, just need to know where my wife is?"

"She's an adult, and we don't keep tabs on her."

"Right. She's with Hank. Damn it Peter, it's my right to know where my wife is." He was shouting by now.

Peter hung up. The phone soon rang again and, this time, Peter spoke without saying hello. "Grow up, Allan." And hung up a second time.

Allan could feel a madness in his mind. Red hot anger. He grabbed a ferry to Plattsburgh, started looking for his ex, and eventually spotted Hank's car. Parking nearby, he was rewarded with a side view of his wife, standing with Hank, half a block away. She was standing outside of Starbucks, talking to Hank, and her figure was silhouetted in the setting sun. As Hank fingered her hair and touched her face, Allan stopped walking toward them. Stopped dead in his stride. The light and angle of the sun were perfect to silhouette the side of his wife. He stared transfixed for half a minute. It was obvious. His wife was pregnant. He turned on his heel and left them alone.

Chapter 17

Peter, driving Sue to the Plattsburgh airport at first light on Wednesday, asked, "Ever find out what set Allan off the other night? Barking mad when he called."

"Don't know, he didn't call back, so I just left him alone. But it's sort of my fault. Truth is, I honestly forgot to tell him about Allie going to Atlanta with dad."

"He's still an idiot. I told him to grow up and be an adult."

"He won't like that." Sue turned to face her brother while he drove, and changed their conversation, "Peter, you've been avoiding my questions about memories from childhood." She paused a moment. "Being older than me, you can understand our memories, years back, before my memories were being formed. You know things I was to little to even notice. "

Peter interrupted, "Sue, I don't like remembering my childhood. It's an illusion to think you and I can talk of the past and, magically change it so memories are understood, the confusion goes away, and there's no more pain and regret. It doesn't happen like that."

"It might. Can't you even talk about the little day-to-day things? For me?"

"No. Because you want more. A family's past being like a plate of spaghetti, all mixed together, so when one string of your childhood is touched, then it disturbs part of mine. I don't choose to remember." Peter seemed calm and normal as he continued to drive, but his hands gripping the steering wheel had turned a little whiter. The silence between brother and sister lengthened. Then he said quickly, "If we talk, if I talk, then it will be in confidence and only one time, because you don't realize what you're asking. Do you understand?"

Peter let time and miles clip by in silence, before eventually saying, "Sue, you check in - and then I'll tell you why the past is painful - on one condition, whatever we say stays between us. What I say stays between us." He made eye contact, but said no more.

Sue nodded, almost touched one of his hands on the steering wheel, and remained quiet.

With pre-boarding finished, they found a quiet area in the terminal and Sue opened the conversation, asking Peter, "You were five, the summer mom and dad brought me home from Canada. Can you remember being five?"

"I've done my best to forget it. When mom and dad brought you to Georgia, I was rescued from grandfather. He was a bastard to me. Grandfather was a bully."

"Bully to a five-year-old. Peter, you can't be serious?"

"Shut up, Sue. Don't ever defend him to me. Do you want my story or don't you?"

"He was a sweetie?"

"If you were a girl, he might be soft. With boys, he was a Darth Vader of discipline. It's true. That summer mom left to have you, she left me and Annie with granddad, the sadist. He had a little whip thing, an army baton, and I learned to jump before he even said jump."

Sue realized her brother was talking of abuse. Did granddad hit you, Peter? Did he?"

Peter's hands tightened on coffee, fingers turning white, "Granddad was too smart to hit and leave marks. But abuse is abuse. His favourite trick was to come up behind me, and wack. Wack. Bring the whip down, hard, slap the table right next to my hand. Very effective."

"You never mentioned this."

"I did. Tried to tell dad when he would call on the weekend from California, but a five-year-old can't win against granddad. When dad called and talked to me, granddad would just set the whip by the phone, and I would pee my pants. Granddad flicked the whip, but the abuse was mom's fault. Sue, but I'm serious. Mom knew granddad for what he was. She had yelled at him time and time again - yet she left me alone, knowing he was vicious."

"Took me years to figure it out, that because he hated mom and had to look after her brat of a boy, he hated me. He couldn't whip mom, so he made life miserable for me. And, when granny was ill for a while, he just did his thing with me. I spilled cereal milk once, and he hit the table till I wet my pants and, then made me wear the pants all day. For god's sake, I was five!"

"Dad ever know of this?"

"How could he? Granddad was dad's hero, so perhaps our dad just didn't want to know. There was no escape for me in rural Georgia, where worse stuff still happens. Granddad was a mean disciplinarian, wacking things around me everyday mom was gone. Seemed like years. Forever."

"A funny thing, Sue, those memories weren't painful growing up, almost erased from my mind but, later, when my first wife, Janis, had our son, I was haunted from the day he came home. The fear of 'could I became like granddad' caused me to go inward. That fear, of good and evil fighting within me, caused my little breakdowns for years."

"I didn't know any of this. Peter, just stop. We can do this later?"

"I might cry, but I'll finish. So hear it now for I won't repeat it."

Sue just nodded and Peter continued, "My childhood set me up for divorce. Truth is, Janis has a hyper personality, so we were only compatible dating. But after the birth of my son, Harold, I fell apart."

"Then, why have a child?"

Peter laughed, "Not all babies are planned, Sue. Harold's birth terrified me into asking what kind of dad I would be. A haunting fear - I could be a sadist to my own son. Granddad and his whip were sort of frozen in my head, especially, when I held my son. So, I manipulated my marriage into problems. Until Janis was quite happy to see the back of me. It's true. My fear of raising children destroyed our relationship."

"So that's why you and Maggie aren't having kids. I get it."

"Oh, that's something else you don't know." Peter took a deep breath, "I chose Maggie, deliberately, cause she can't have kids. And everything in our marriage was fine, until you started digging around in old birth questions. Talking of mom got me upset. Talking to dad still does. But you're not to blame Sue, but mom is. Mom, the dithering flake, abandoned me."

"Peter, she didn't make granddad nutty. Mom took care of us."

"Yeah, right? Like driving me to school without shoes. More than once without shoes. Sue, mom wasn't reliable, even with simple things. Remember, when dad couldn't call because our phone was cut off, and mom had a drawer full of unpaid bills. Dad was furious. And the next week she held my birthday party in June, when I was born in the fall. Figure that!"

"Mom never, absolutely never wasted a penny. She knew the value of money."

Peter knew her flight was boarding soon. "Okay, Sue, granted mom improved as she got older, but until I was eight, mom spent money like water. No thought. Just spend. And the Christmas I was eight, mom disappeared for months. That's when I gave up on mom."

"What happened to mom? I don't recall her not being there

for me.”

“Who knows? You were only three. Years later, I figured with dad away there was another guy involved. She was gone. Then, she was back, and the adults talked like it didn't happen.”

“Peter, if you think mom was a spender, just remember she taught me how to save. I can still see the chocolate box she made into a bank, when I was five. Peter, our memories don't match.”

Peter threw up his hands. “Well, we had the same mom. Maybe, she just loved you more than me. But we were kids, Sue, and our memories lacked an adult perspective. Dad should be answering your questions on this, not me.”

“Peter, how can dad remember? He was in California playing soldier.”

“Then give up, Sue. Is the search worth the trouble and pain for you and our family? Leave the past alone.”

“I can't. I feel there are facts to discover. Perhaps, just down the road, when I ask the right question, answers could be found. That's why this California trip needs to be taken. Yet, I'm sorry my search has caused you so much pain. And there is one more confidence to share. Peter, talk to your wife, because she knows you're troubled. I made a deal, Peter, and everything you said will stay with me, but, trust me now, tell everything to Maggie. She already knows most of it, and has guessed the rest. If you don't talk, you risk losing her. Do it. Tonight. Sit her down and talk. As for me, I'll try and keep the past out of your life. Can't promise, but I'll try.”

The terminal intercom announced Sue's flight and as she walked to the gate, she thought, ‘This trip is right. According to Maria, Cecile will have adult memories of my mom, while I view those same years as a child.’ Cecile, you've taken on a large dimension of hope, and I'm counting on you.’

The San Francisco flight went off without a hitch but, the city by the bay, delayed Sue's connector flight to Eureka. A cold front covered the region in dense fog. Sue waited among countless other passengers in a long, crowded, concourse. She waited impatiently - counted the number of stands hawking San Francisco Sour Dough bread, and tried to name the almost familiar opera aria played near an Espresso counter. Her uncle Fred would know the words and music continually drowned out by the noise of steamy milk hitting a metal container. At times, the harsh sound of steam and frothy opera merged into an acceptable beat. Eventually, she knew there was no way to make the flight today, so she called Bonnie Hunter.

"Hello." A now familiar voice answered the call.

"Bonnie, it's Sue. I'm wrapped in your San Francisco fog. It won't lift today."

"New Yorker's always knock our world famous fog."

"I'm from Vermont."

"Close enough. Sue, when will you make Crescent City?"

"Tomorrow. Say your place by mid-morning. And losing a day now means I can only stay with you a few hours to catch my return flight. See you tomorrow."

Next Sue wanted to call her daughter but decided against it. Calling Allie in Atlanta, she will get upset at the end of my call, and dad is left dealing with a sulking granddaughter. But I can see if Hank's home.

"Sue, you picked a good time to call. DNA test results of your mom's brother and his wife are back. No surprises. Fred's mitochondrial DNA, as expected, matches your brother and sister, but not you. While his wife, Maria, as expected, is not related to your family or you. I'll send a copy of these test results to your dad's place in Atlanta just for your records."

"So, I'm still the odd one in the family. Let's hope Cecile

knows something. I need some facts to keep the search going."

Morning dawned California perfect; yesterday's depressive fog replaced with spirit-lifting sunshine. First the connector flight, then an ideal morning to drive along the coast with a calm Pacific Ocean floating to the west. Eventually, US 101 flowed directly to Crescent City, and Bay Street did, indeed, overlook the bay. However, finding number 17 proved difficult. The large, hundred-year-old homes of Bay Street, jumped from number 15 to 19. Only after a careful look was a smaller home revealed. Number 17, partially hidden, set back from the road, and showing years of neglect. No great wealth here. Sue followed a narrow, cracked and grass overgrown cement walk, then up three sagging wooden steps, and moved across a once elegant verandah. She knocked on the front door of the ill-kept home.

A younger woman, with natural looking red hair, greeted Sue warmly, "Come in, right in. You must be Sue, Sue from Vermont."

"Yes, I'm Sue. Nice to meet you, and we haven't met before or I'd remember. Your green eyes are striking. Irish heritage, Bonnie?"

She shook her head, "My dad was English. Come in. Tea's ready in the kitchen, or coffee, if you take instant?"

"Tea sounds nice, Bonnie." Haven't come here to dawdle over tea. "If I can see my aunt, first."

"Would you like that now?" Her host had other plans. "How nice, but best we have tea in the kitchen first. Now, please, tell me why you would come so far to visit an old aunt that has never heard from you until now? Cecile tells me her American relations in the East aren't the least bit social - the kind who never stayed in touch. Last night, Cecile got rather upset that you were coming here at all today. She wants to know why you've come?"

"To chat a little of the past is all. Family-related and complicated Bonnie."

"Almost everything in life is family-related. And complicated. Why are you here?"

"Cecile registered my birth in Canada and may be the only person who can remember the circumstances. Those early days have become important to me and Cecile may have memories of my birth that I need."

As Bonnie remained silent, Sue continued, "Also, I'm hoping my aunt will provide a DNA sample. Just a simple swab or a cut of hair. Now, if it's not too much to ask, can I see my aunt?"

"Cecile is... persnickety today. And she's a clever old bird. Seems she's waited years for contact with your side of the family and, isn't pleased, you came only when you need her help. Can you understand, Sue? Cecile views you as a back-handed visitor."

"Seriously, Bonnie, tell her I only found out about the rift with Cecile a few weeks ago. Surely, she can't blame me for my parents' actions?"

Bonnie nodded, "I agree." Then lowered her voice as if conspiring, "If it were my pick, you'd be seeing the old biddy right now. Except, old or not, she has choices, and we don't want a grumpy Cecile on our hands, do we? I think, if I understand her grumbling, she wants an apology over some old letter, letters sent by John Stevens to American Immigration. Now you're a Charter, but were a Stevens: is John Stevens your dad? She keeps asking me to find out."

Cecile is still thinking of dad's blacklisting her. It's not my fault he wrote the letter. "Yes, John Stevens is my dad, and he's sorry to have caused her any problems."

Bonnie took a deep breath, "Oh god, that won't work. If she asks about him, can you just say no, or pretend you have a different father? Your aunt is obsessed by your dad's meddling, or something to do with revenge. Perhaps you understand it better? Do you know what he did?"

"Oh, can't be much, besides, Bonnie, it's the past now. We're all family. I'd downplay the old thing as no big deal."

Bonnie shrugged again, "True, that's just so true. Unfortunately, Cecile still remembers it as a big deal, so family or not, it bothers her as an insult. Guess when you hurt someone badly, they remember. She says, "How would you like to be labelled anti-American and not be able to work all your life?""

"I've never called Cecile anti-American? Bonnie, it's time to reunite the family, to forget letters written years ago. I'll explain to her."

Bonnie drummed her fingers on the kitchen table and made a decision. " So true. Okay, I'll try... see if she's changed her mind. Help yourself to more tea, while I butter up Cecile."

Sue glanced at her watch, "I don't have unlimited time here... a talk with Cecile, then a fast drive to Eureka and catch the flight home."

Bonnie prepared a drink and a biscuit on a tray, "Your aunt is partial to chocolate." Adding a second biscuit, she winked at Sue, "Let's get her in a good mood." Bonnie disappeared with the tray toward the rear of the house.

Minutes ticked past. Ten. Fifteen. Something heavy banged on the floor. A door slammed and Bonnie returned, "Well, that cuts it; she's never thrown a plate of cookies before. She's ordered you from her home. You'll have to leave, Sue. Not a chance in hell she'll calm down and talk today."

"It's taken two days to get here, Bonnie." Sue pushed her kitchen chair back and stood up. "I can talk sense to her in five minutes."

Bonnie blocked the hallway and directed Sue toward the front door. No force, just her determination to keep Cecile off limits. "Look, your aunt demands you leave. It's not a suggestion. She's adamant and this is her home. So, old or not, she gets her way and you go."

    As the front door was closing to Sue alone on the verandah, she blurted out, "Bonnie, I can resolve this? I still don't understand why I'm leaving?"

    Bonnie held the half-closed door and said, "If it will help you any to understand Cecile, she kept repeating one word, revenge. Perhaps, try again tomorrow, but today, if your aunt wants revenge for hurts in the past, she won't see you. She won't change her mind today. She's lying there calling your dad 'a war mongrel bastard.'"

Chapter 18

Sue was stunned, at how terribly wrong this visit had been. Dad, I could wring your neck to have fuelled Cecile's resentments all these years. When mom said 'war is evil' was she perceptive enough to include the bitterness left when the fighting stops - as in the bitterness of generations after our Civil War. Well, I don't know what to do next, but Peter may have an answer.

When Peter heard her voice, he picked up, "Sis, glad you got my message to call immediately."

"What's urgent? Is Allie all right?"

"She's fine, Sue. The problem is your house in Clearville. Are you selling?"

"Peter, real estate in Vermont is more depressed than I am. Why?"

"It's listed for sale. The bank called me, cause I'm listed on your mortgage as reference, and they say your signature on sell documents looks suspicious. Would Allan pull a fast one and forge your name to sell it?"

"Peter, tell the bank I signed nothing. Then call the real estate and stop the sale.

"Stay on the line, Sue." The phone clicked, she waited five minutes, and he came back, "Done. Any transfer, documents or money will be frozen. However, the bank will likely investigate, and if it's forgery or a sale by fraud, then Allan's in legal problems." He paused a moment, changed gears and continued. "So, if you weren't calling over the mortgage, what's happening in sunny California?"

"Peter. I need some advice." Sue outlined the events on Bay Street, from knocking on her aunt's door to being asked to leave.

"I'm just stunned that aunt Cecile is still so pissed at dad, she ordered me out of her house. If I can't ask questions, then this trip is a loss."

Her brother, always the realist asked, "Does this mean we won't be remembered in her will?"

"Don't make me laugh. It's depressing to leave without seeing her."

"Then be practical. You're there now, on her turf, so try seeing her again. Make a plan. What have you got too lose. Call the airline for a later flight, then go see our dear aunt one more time. Old people do change their mind, Sue. Why give up? Take her flowers and smile a lot."

"Cecile dotes on chocolate cookies."

"Even better. If she kicks you out, then bring them home. I like cookies."

"You're right - may as well try again. Thanks for the talk, bro. And keep the real estate wolves away from my door. Bye for now."

Sue drives back to Bay Street, and parks away from her aunt's home to gain courage before attempting a second visit. It was one thing to make the plan but, quite another, to knock on the door again. While waiting in the rental car, she sees Bonnie leaving Cecile's home, and Sue made a quick decision - I'll talk to Cecile alone. Crossing the sagging verandah, she knocked on the front door, waited, knocked again, and then knocked a third time - no answer at all. She tried the door and it opened at her touch. Well, seems Crescent City folk are more trusting than Vermont country folk.

"Hello?" Sue's voice advanced into the silent home faster than her hesitant steps. "Aunt Cecile? It's Sue, your niece, dropping off cookies before my flight east. Hello. Cecile, shall I bring them to you?" Worst she can do is order me out again.

Walking past the kitchen into a central hall, past a bedroom for Bonnie, a bathroom, to one room with the door closed. Sue tapped lightly, asking, "Are you awake?" Getting no answer, she softly entered a dim bedroom, Cecile's room, by the look of Doulton figurines and lace mats. Doesn't Bonnie ever clean the dust in here?

Sue bumped against a walker before her eyes adjusted to the dimness, "I'll leave the chocolates on your dresser and..." Sue paused in mid-sentence, then continued, "What the hell is going on?" Her eyes could see well enough now to realize she had been speaking to an empty room. No aunt, in the bed or anywhere else. It's an empty room, and the dust shows it's been empty for a long time.

Who was Bonnie talking to earlier, while I waited in the kitchen? And where's Cecile? I spoke to her days ago on the phone. Sue spoke aloud to the empty room, "I'll leave your chocolates in the kitchen auntie, while I go find Bonnie for a little talk."

The mail on the kitchen counter was addressed to Bonnie. The fridge had more wine than food, and nothing indicated Cecile even lived here. Bonnie, I'll make that coffee you offered and wait on the verandah till you return.

An hour later, as Bonnie returned home, she found Sue sitting on the verandah steps. "I've already told you..." she started to say, then stopped talking as Sue raised one of Bonnie's coffee cups in greeting.

Sue attacked, "Welcome back, liar."

And Bonnie responded with venom, "Liar? Some nerve. You accuse me of lying!" She gave a dirty laugh, "Didn't you say the old letter meant nothing? Get the hell off my property."

"Soon as I see my aunt." Sue didn't back down, "Get Cecile, or should I call the cops?"

"Go ahead, call the cops - and then say what? That you

broke into my place. You self-centred bubble head. How will you explain my damn coffee cup you're holding. Stupidity must run rampant in your family."

"Just who the hell are you, Bonnie Hunter? And where's Cecile? I spoke to her on the phone."

"You don't even have a clue." Then, after another dirty laugh, Bonnie put on a show. Speaking in low, frail voice, "Yes, of course, you spoke to Cecile. And don't forget the cookies." Then she reverted to a bitter tone, "You never even cared who I was. Typical of the Stevens' family, a self-centred bunch of jerks. So leave. Just apologize for breaking in, and get the hell off my land."

Sue needed to ratchet down this shouting match. "Can we stop our grade school yelling. Truth is Bonnie, I do apologize for entering your house. Now, can we stop shouting and talk. Perhaps act as adults?"

Bonnie was still willing to fight. "Oh, sure, act like the big people with problems. They settle trouble with guns."

Sue started to chuckle, before saying, "Hey, I used to squabble like this with my sister, and there were no winners then. So I surrender. Now then, who the hell are you and how are you connected to Cecile?"

Bonnie, looking at Sue closely, asked, "Haven't you figured it out?"

"I wouldn't be asking, if I had!"

Then, in a normal tone, Bonnie looked at Sue's tummy, asking, "Hey, are you expecting?"

When Sue nodded, Bonnie continued in a softer voice, "Well, I accept your apology . . . besides, no use me beating up on a pregnant lady. Come on, sit down on the step so we can talk." Plopping herself down next to Sue, Bonnie simply added, "Our moms were sisters, so that makes us cousins. Cecile was my mom."

"Cecile's kid? Maria never mentioned Cecile was married."

"Marriage isn't a prerequisite for having kids in California. My mom had one kid, me. And you're a little late wanting to make friends with Cecile, cause she died four years ago last spring."

"Died? I didn't know." Careful, remember Bonnie lied before. Can I believe her now? "Why did we never know?"

Bitterness edged Bonnie's voice, "Blame your family. Think I'd contact your dad when mom died? Your dad hated Cecile and ignored her in life, so I had no reason to let them know she had died."

Sue, seized another unresolved fact, "Maria, in Oakville, thinks Cecile is still living."

"Ah, right, Christmas cards. That's Cecile's old flair of signing her cards in green ink. As long as I sign cards with a green pen, her old friends remember her as living. Until you blab, of course." Bonnie paused to face Sue directly, "Look, I've got arsenic out back. Would you like another tea?"

A spark of understanding passed between them. "Bonnie, I'd love another cup of tea. From my new cousin."

"We're not friends, Sue Stevens Charter, and, be careful of me, cousin." Bonnie spoke with a gleam in her eyes, "Like the Irish, I still might turn the past bitterness into future revenge. We may have a truce Sue, but it's not a friendship, not yet."

"We can work on it. Get it all out on the table. No more secrets and you can help by telling me why my dad wrote against your mom."

Bonnie shook her head in resignation. "You are something else, lady. Only asking me to set aside thirty years of bitterness just cause you find we are cousins. Something else. I'll get the tea."

When she returned, Bonnie drank half a cup before talking, and then she couldn't stop. "Long before you and I were born, your dad just hated my mom for the way she was close to Joanna. I'm told that mom's sharp tongue easily pulled your dad's chain. But while Cecile lived in Canada, he could only sit and boil at her comments."

Bonnie looked away from Sue, holding painful emotion to herself, as she repeated the past, "Then, after your birth, Cecile's Canadian firm offered her work in the States, so she asked John and Joanna for an immigration reference and went to California before getting a clearance because of her job offer. It was common to do back then. Start the paperwork and finish it down in the States because they made exceptions on working skills."

Bonnie was speaking in a low voice now, holding her emotion in check. "The short version of events is your dad sabotaged Cecile. He wrote a black letter against her and sent it to US immigration. A scathing litany of lies that cost my mom to lose every good job she had while working in the States. Time after time, she would be let go with no reason given. Then, one kind employer told her the truth. The FBI had quietly warned him against her. So despite being a good worker - the smear campaign initiated by your dad - blackballed her. She made a substandard, miserable living, because of your dad. McCarthyism was over, but his ideas stayed on and punished my mom for years."

"I know it happened to many people. It's well documented. And besides, this is exactly what dad admitted, or I'd have a hard time believing you."

"Knowing it took place is one thing, having it happen to us was devastating. Sue, how can you call it patriotism to smear people in secret? I'll stand proudly for our country but not that sad episode in the '50's. Or the next two decades, when our American government bludgeoned our own people over the Vietnam war. The accounts are in our history books. Right wing hawks hated anyone they thought were sitting on the sidelines. So, for your dad, Canada became the goat - cosy with communist, liking Cuba, everything we weren't. And for my mom, she was the target for the lies in his head.

The lies he wrote against his wife's family."

"Bonnie, why would my dad lie and cause the family split?"

Bonnie quietly exploded another bombshell from the past. "You have it backwards, Sue? Your dad denounced my mom for revenge. My mom told me the fight in Canada, when you were born, was just a continuation of bitterness. Your dad wouldn't listen to anyone who told him the truth over your mom's bouts of illness. I'm not kidding. Cecile told me what he was doing."

"My mom's illness? Joanna was ill?"

"Seriously ill. Postpartum depression is deadly serious for many women. Didn't you know your mom struggled with it after each birth?"

"No. Bonnie, this is the first time it has ever been mentioned. I didn't know."

"Well, your dad's folks from Georgia called it the 'woman's blues,' and they insisted she just 'pull up her socks' to be fine." Bonnie, seeing a bewildered look in Sue's eyes hesitated, then asked, "You really never knew this, did you?"

"How could Cecile know this of my mom when I didn't?"

"My mom said it started when your brother Peter was born, and Cecile tried to get medical help for Joanna." Bonnie took a deep breath, "According to my mom, Joanna was ill after her first child, but your dad insisted Joanna was fine and would get better by herself. That's when my mom went to Plattsburgh, dragged Joanna back into a hospital, and tore a strip off your dad and his folks. Apparently, my mom berated your dad, in public, saying postpartum was a treatable medical illness, and Joanna should be careful after every birth. She went so far as tell your dad - 'Tie a knot in it and don't have anymore.' So your dad felt slighted at the interference, incensed that an outsider would try and tell him what to do. That's when he started the family split."

"Years later, when Cecile applied for a visa, your dad penned his infamous letter. Revenge - against my mom for trying to help Joanna."

Sue was thoughtful. Bonnie had lied before. Was she telling the truth now? Her story seemed genuine, and it answered so many questions, but was it true? "Bonnie, I believe you, but I can't just take your word against my dad. If I question my dad, he goes silent. If I take your word, well, it's after you set up the charade of being your mom and lying to me. How can I believe what you say?"

Bonnie stood up, "God, Sue, you're a pain in the ass. When I pretended to my mom, it was just getting a little revenge back for her. You were in Plattsburgh and stringing you along with lies seemed harmless. Okay, childish. How was I to know you would fly here? Look, I lied to give my mom a little revenge against your father, and it felt good."

"Still only your word. Give me a snip of hair to prove you're family."

"My mom fell in love with William Bryan Hunter, a good old English scoundrel, lazy, full of blarney, and a drunk." Bonnie fluffed her hair. "My inheritance is simple - red hair, green eyes and a temper - plus, a very thirst of liking to drink."

The empty wine bottles under the sink. "Is your dad still alive, Bonnie?"

"I don't want to know. Being on my own is infinitely better than having him around. You can never trust a drunk. Never. Even when sober, you can't trust them. They talk a good talk - and nothing else." Bonnie looked directly at Sue. "Harsh, but there it is."

Sue thought of Allan as Bonnie finished talking. "I know just what you mean, cause I married a drunk and spent the last ten years regretting it."

"Well, being a child of a drunk is worse. A wife can always divorce." Bonnie continued. "So my past is better staying closed." She pointed at her watch. "Doesn't your flight leave soon?"

"Yes, soon. Then, if what you say is true, then my dad has lied to me."

"You still question me? Think I'm lying?"

"Bonnie, I've learned to be cautious and check what people tell me. Yes, I still need to check you out."

"You really are a pain, Sue." Bonnie stood up and went into her house, deliberately slamming the door. She returned with small plastic bags and a sewing needle. "Ready to become blood sisters." Bonnie pricked her own finger, squeezed blood onto a tissue, and placed it in a plastic bag. Another tissue, placed in her mouth for saliva, went into a second bag. Last, she wrote her birth date and place of birth and handed the lot to Sue, "This is me in a little package. Now, go, catch your flight in Eureka." Bonnie gave a wry smile, "Who knows cousin, we just might like each other the next time we meet. Have a safe trip back east."

Sue hugged her red-haired cousin, "God, Bonnie, it's been completely different from I figured - but I'm glad we connected. Thanks for talking." Sue was almost to the car, when she remembered another loose end to the story. She walked back to Bonnie. "Want to come with me to the airport? We can talk for another half hour and then I'll pay a cab to get you back home. There's still a question or two you can put to rest for me. Come along to the airport."

"Sue thanks, but just ask the questions bothering you. What do you need to know?"

"How did your mom know it was my dad who blackballed her? It could have been someone else. Why is she certain it was my dad?"

"President Lyndon B. Johnston made the Freedom of Information act back in the '60's. It took mom years to get the papers, but I still have them and will email you a copy. The original three-page letter of complaint against my mom is signed by your dad. John Peter Stevens."

Waving good-byes, Sue drove south to Eureka, made the connector flight to San Francisco, and then faced a long wait before her flight to Atlanta. She made some phone calls.

Sue left a message on Hank's answering machine. "It's me, calling from the FedEx in the San Francisco airport, and sending you blood, saliva, and date of birth from Cecile's daughter, Bonnie Hunter. Can your friend Sam run a quick DNA test? Bonnie Hunter says my aunt Cecile died four years ago. Can that be confirmed? Oh, contact me at my dad's place in Atlanta. Bye." If you're a liar Bonnie, I'll personally break a bottle of red wine over your pretty little head.

There's no point telling dad what Bonnie is claiming. Not yet. "Hi, dad. Yes, yes, doing just fine. How's my daughter? Look, I should arrive at Hartsfield late tonight - and catch a bus home. All right, well if you want to pick me up. Yes, pleased with my birth search, it's starting to make sense. Let me talk to Allie. Yes, mommy missed you pumpkin..."

I believe Bonnie was telling the truth. Mom being postpartum explains the simmering family fights over the years. Explains why Fred and Maria were reluctant to bring it up. The split in the family was a gradual break with my birth the final straw of a major family meltdown. Mom being ill explains Peter staying with granddad, the kids being farmed out at times, and even the tension between dad and mom. And it's the reason my dad reacted so harshly in sending the letter against Cecile. But where does all that leave me. Mom's illness explains those issues, but it doesn't resolve why I'm not part of the family.

Right now, I need to make one more call. Now, where's Maggie's work number?

Chapter 19

Maggie reduced Sue's fear, "Hey kid, you can relax - your house is safe and won't be sold any time soon. You know, in spite of your husband being an idiot, you had no worry of quickly selling a rural property in Vermont. They don't sell fast. Besides, when the real estate firm realized Allan was pulling a fast one, they froze their arrangement, and quietly spread the word to other firms. No one will touch that dead sale. Although Allan's fit to be tied, your equity is safe. Now, when are you flying back east? You need to see what I've found."

"Flying to Atlanta tonight, Maggie, so you can call me at dad's place tomorrow."

"Then, make time for a long conversation with me. I've uncovered a few old medical records in your mom's papers that don't make sense to me. It's a packet of invoices and letters from the American Air Force, asking for confirmation of Canadian medical payments, plus, they want access to Canadian hospital records."

"Maggie, are they the payments covering my birth?"

"Don't think so, Sue. The date is a couple of months before your birth. It's your mom, in a Toronto hospital, a couple of months before you were born. What's it all about?"

"Beats me? Do the papers give medical reasons?"

"It's not a hospital bill and most of the information is in four digit codes. Looks like the Air Force is requesting confirmation on medical procedures already performed. Sent to Joanna Stevens in Oakville, Canada, with reference to your dad's rank, serial number, and location in California."

"Depression. My new California cousin says my mom was

depressed after each child. Do these papers mention postpartum?"

Maggie laughed, "Is that a trick question, Sue? Postpartum comes after birth. Perhaps, your dad will know how this fits with your mom in Canada. Makes no sense on the surface, as the invoices are all dated months before your birth."

"Can you fax a copy to me in Atlanta, Maggie?"

"Sure, but there's more here, stuff I can't explain. For instance, a paper bag with tiny, tiny notes and paper. I have no idea why your mom would keep it. I wish you were here to see this lot and talk it over with me."

"How, Plattsburgh isn't near Atlanta, and Allie needs me in her life. I plan on staying in Atlanta, getting a job, and settling down. Keep looking in those boxes. See if you can find any more on what was happening in Toronto in the months before I was born. Bye Maggie. Love you."

* * * * *

In the months before Susan Stevens birth, Toronto was experiencing a heat wave in the inflamed summer of Nineteen Sixty Eight. The news from Vietnam had been optimistic, the Tet offensive of January was forgotten and the west was winning the war in the cold spring in 1968. After a wet March, the temperature in Toronto climbed to record levels through May, June and July. As the heat wave engulfed the city, swimming pools opened two weeks ahead of schedule, and the kids loved it all.

Women's College Hospital, south-facing windows filled the room with an abundance of sunlight. Brightness everywhere. Starched sheets rustled, stainless steel sparkled, and a nurse spoke softly to a patient. "Good... you're waking up. Take it easy dear, I'll get you some water."

"I was dreaming of water. Everything so white and clean. Dream like."

"I'm Miss Elliot, head nurse for intensive care. You're a very lucky lady... recovering from a tough time in surgery. Just wake up slowly... no need to rush."

"Where am I?"

"Women's College Hospital. We're taking good care of you and all you have to do is try and rest. You're going to be fine."

"But this is wrong. This can't happen to me."

"Try not to get upset, dear. You're in good hands, and it's best to rest. We called the friend you stay with, Mrs. Alhambra, and she will soon be here to see you. Other information can wait for later. But you need rest. Take this medication to help you sleep."

"Wait... wait, so nice. Everything is so clean. The sheets are so white. No blood. And clothes. I'll need new ones. Old ones... burn them... burn it - my old bloody dress"

"That's fine, dear. Sleep now. You can talk later.

* * * * *

While Sue left sunny San Francisco airport, the evening shadows had grown longer over Lake Champlain, and the approaching darkness increased the forlorn appearance of the home squatting at the end of the gravel drive. No light showed, no sign of life, not even Allan's truck was visible. Yet Stu figured Allan was there, so he parked, and loudly knocked. No answer. He knocked again, louder and longer. "Allan, open up. Don't play games - open the door." Moments later, after the sound of a night chain sliding, the door opened a few inches.

From the darkened hall, Allan muttered, "Go away, Stu.

Don't need no help."

Stu forced the door wider, half-pushed, half-stepped inside, "Look, I'm only staying five minutes, so cut the crap and talk in the kitchen" Stu knew the routine. Want the truth on a drunk, then check his kitchen.

He picked up one spaghetti encrusted plate, with a fork embedded in dried sauce, flipped it upside down and watched the fork defy gravity. "You know these things are quite the invention. They're called plates and designed to be recycled. They come with instructions to wash them, once in a while, and then reuse the little suckers."

"Very funny." He grabbed the plate from Stu's hand, "You made the trip for nothing, cause you're not dragging me to a stinking meeting."

"Hell, Allan, you're thinking wrong. I'm here as a friend. Apparently, you got a bank all riled up over placing this house on the market. And now the cops are interested in the mess you started.."

"You stay out of my business. Who told you, anyway?"

"Clearville's a small town, Allan. No secrets."

Allan crossed his arms in thought, then quickly brought his fist smashing onto the table. "Peter told you. Damn Sue's family. And anyone else who crosses me."

"Stu moved a jacket and empty soup cans from a chair, and sat next to the cluttered table. "Great idea, Allan, get even." Stu glanced at the time and continued, "Allan, I'm here for two reasons. First, as a friend. Always ready to have a coffee... any time. That's the main reason I made the trip."

Allan smiled for a moment as he asked, "You buying the coffee, Stu?"

"That's negotiable," Stu replied, and then waited.

Allan let a minute tick by before asking, "All right, what's the second reason?"

Stu yelled, loud enough to take Allan's head off, shouting, "To find out why you went nuts. Two weeks ago, you were laughing and scratching and talking of getting your old life back. Now you sit in the dark, surrounded by dirty dishes and afraid the cops will knock on your door." Stu waved his hands, pointing to the mess, "What are you doing? What the hell happened?"

He waves his hands at the mess in the house, "All this, all of it, because of her. It's my wife's doing. Stu, she played me for a fucking fool, hinting she'd come home, while screwing around with Hank. It's all Sue's doing."

"Allan, I'm getting hard of hearing. Can you tell me again how - you forging real estate papers is your wife's fault? I must have missed the logic."

"I want my money from my house before Hank moves in? Big deal, forging her name, I've done it before. Big deal, big fucking deal." Spite and hate kept spewing out of Allan. "She lied about coming back, lied about me seeing Allie, and the bitch then sent my daughter to Atlanta with her granddad." Allan waved his hands around the kitchen. He could hardly contain his anger, standing and shouting, "She's carrying Hank's baby, and sticking me with payments for the next twenty years. It's my right to get even Stu. I'm entitled to sell this place and damn her brother Peter for stopping the sale. The bank was wrong to call the cops. For god's sake, Sue set me up. If she had made one phone call to let me know Allie was leaving, but nothing. Nada. Zip. Sue pulled my chain just being silent. But Stu, I hold all the aces when I know exactly what she's thinking and doing all the time. Knowing all her plans will make me the winner."

A cunning smile flickered over Allan's face, "Allie tells me everything - going to Canada, meeting Hank in Atlanta, and now she's on a California vacation." Allan smashed his fist against the table, and again and again. "Burns me, Sue's in California on my money, and planning to stick me for supporting her new kid"

Stu was tense, nevertheless, he tried reason once more, "Spending your money? You haven't had enough for a coffee the past few months. What money of yours is she spending?"

Allan sputtered, spewed anger over the kitchen table, excessive black bile, flowing over the edge, dripping on the floor, to infect everyone in the room. "Years of taking cash from my wallet. I'd go drinking, wake up missing big bucks. She'd say I squandered it on drink, but that money she took is paying for her trips."

It was hopeless trying to reason, and he got up to go. "You're paranoid, Allan. Your wife pilfered thousands from you like the moon is made of green cheese." Call me when you think straight, buddy. "You keep in touch, Allan."

Allan's mood darkened, "Might not be around here. Could find work in Atlanta for a while - check on Sue and Allie." Allan glanced at the kitchen knives, "Give Sue one of those. Razor sharp. It's a dangerous city Atlanta - lots of violence, murders, women getting hurt. Sue may not be safe in Atlanta."

"Don't be a fool. Revenge is a stupid idea."

"Hey, there's options, something happens to Sue... no fault of mine. Or take this house... it's got the fire insurance. But again, nothing to do with me."

Stu was getting out. "Allan, guys smarter than you end up being caught."

"There's lots of fools in the world who get caught, cause they don't plan well. But not me Stu... I'm no fool. My plans are thought out very carefully."

* * * * *

Late at night, Sue arrived at the Atlanta airport and hugged Allie as if she had been away a months rather than days. "I'm staying put for a while Allie, so don't worry of me going away again. Main thing is getting work here. Right now, I'm hungry, and tired of travelling. Let's get home, dad."

John drove over to the Camp Creek Parkway and headed north to his condo, while Sue talked of all the small details on the trip, avoiding any mention of her new cousin, Bonnie, or the death of Cecile. And over the next few days, when talking with her dad, Sue remained vague on specific revelations from her California trip. John was aware of Sue and Maggie phoning each other and talking of Joanna. He knew Sue was getting ready to confront him, but John acted first.

When Sue returned from job searching, and the TV was quiet, she asked the obvious, "Where's Allie, dad?"

"Sunny invited her downstairs for baking and staying for supper. And, I figured you might like to go out for dinner and a chat. We need some time alone to talk."

"Good, yes... all for it." She set a few groceries in the kitchen, picked up her daughter's clothes and mess any ten-year-old makes, and collapsed for a moment in the living room's second best chair, "You know, dad, Einstein must have had kids to figure out his theory that older bodies have less energy." Her dad, meanwhile, sat in the best living room chair, sipped a beer, and let his daughter relax a while before casually speaking. "Come on then, first we check on Allie, and then go to dinner."

"Now. This early?"

"The timing is right. Come on."

John drove through downtown Atlanta, picked up the I-75, southbound. By the time he was driving in the dusty hills toward Griffin and Barnesville, his talking had become serious. "I called your brother, today, at work. Had a good talk." By now, Sue was sure where they were headed, as her dad continued, "And I also called your sister, to more or less say the same as I told Peter. So, tonight, it's your turn to hear a story from the past." John had turned off the main road, pulled into a park-like area, found the bench he knew well. Near the grave of Joanna Stevens.

"Figured it best we were near your mom, if we plan on talking of her. I come often, sit on this bench, and run old memories in my mind. "What I told Peter and Annie today is, exactly, what I'll tell you now. I figured we'd be best to clear the family air."

"In that case, dad, you should here of my California trip."

"Be plenty of time later to hear of your California trip. This is important." John looked directly at his daughter, saying quietly but firm, "Everything I've told you is true, everything. I haven't told a single lie. But I withheld talking of mom's illness, because it was so traumatic. Joanna made me promise to keep her problems secret. We agreed I would never mention to our family that she was seriously ill for a long time. But it all needs to come out now. When you were a kid, three or four, your mom went away for a couple of months. Longer than a couple of months. She didn't want the family to know their mom had been hospitalized. Her illness has been kept from all you kids and there was no need to talk of it... until you started to pry apart the past but, now, your unrelenting search has made it necessary to air some family dirty linen."

"Dad, I know of mom being hospitalized in Canada, before my birth."

Chapter 20

"Sue, don't confuse mom's illness in Georgia with trips to Canada or you won't understand anything. The main problems all happened in Georgia. So hush, and let me explain." He moved to be comfortable on the hard bench, "Your mom and I were just a young couple, starting life, and when our first child was coming, the world looked rosy. But then Peter arrived and your mom was seriously ill in Plattsburgh. My folks told me 'baby blues' were common and, wait a week or so, and the mom would be just fine - seemed good advice."

John held up his hand to stop Sue speaking, "Now don't interrupt. You only know part of this story of Joanna being ill from Peter's birth. I took your mom and Peter home at first, then Cecile came down and insisted Joanna goes back in the hospital. What you don't know is the seriousness of her illness. They put her in a locked ward, because the doctors feared she would cause damage to herself or someone else. It was terrible the look in her eyes, seething anger. I still remember those eyes. Then, magically, it passed. One day she was ill. The next she was asking to come home and wondering why they were keeping her locked up."

Annie's birth was a carbon copy of Peter's, only the postpartum, was longer. And that's when I knew the doctors were right. No more children."

"Dad, remember Cecile. She said the same thing, no more kids."

"Don't bring Cecile into this. I'll tell it my way. After Annie's birth, your mom and I decided no more kids because after having Annie, we all feared for your mom's life. Her depression was intense. So our choice was a family of two kids. Unfortunately, when Harry came along, your mom insisted it was a mistake with the birth control pills. It could happen and I believed her, but Harry's birth set off a different postpartum depression. Now, she was in and out of reality for months. So, after Harry, I even considered a vasectomy but being a red-blooded Georgia boy, couldn't bring myself to do it. So we were really careful, although your mom kept insisting she wanted one more child."

John looked directly at Sue. "We love you and have always been proud of you, but now you know why I was furious, when Joanna told me out in California you had been conceived. Sue, we had three kids already. I could go to 'Nam at any time, and she would be alone giving birth to you in Georgia followed inevitably by another depression, while I could be a few thousand miles away. Angry, god, I was angry, for months, so angry, that your mom took off to stay with her folks in Canada for a while."

"Dad, I didn't realize how ill mom was after giving birth, but you told Hank and me a couple of months back. And Maria confirmed mom's postpartum."

John gave a little laugh, "Ah, yes, kids today - they know everything. Sue, you don't know what you think you know. Let me finish. When Joanna had you weeks early in Canada, I told my base commander of her illness and within hours, they flew me into Toronto. Not taking any chances. But this time her illness was insidious, slow starting and delayed for months. It had become invisible. Joanna had you in the Milton Hospital. I brought you back to Georgia and, by god, family life was good. Life seemed fine for months, till we noticed you were not gaining weight and, even then, it took a number of doctors' visits before the obvious was found. You weren't being fed. Your mom's postpartum had distorted her mind - she no longer tried to kill herself - she was trying to get rid of you. You were being starved."

"Dad, you're making me cry. Mom loved me every day of my life." Tears streaked Sue's face as she continued, "Mom loved me."

"Yes, your mom loved you, loved you dearly. But, illness isn't logical. Joanna spent months in and out of the hospital, when you were little. Short stays, long stays, home some weekends, gone for a month - just a mixed-up summer. At one point, Annie went to stay with her grandparents in Oakville, cause mom couldn't handle our three kids."

Sue could only nod, "Annie's drawings were made then. And mom wasn't with her."

"Joanna's parents looked after Annie but were disgusted with me. Blamed me for pushing Joanna into her illness once again. They even laughed when I told them I finally had a vasectomy. Laughing at me having a vasectomy was another bullet between us."

Sue stood up, walked over to her mom's grave stone, composed her upset mind, then returned to her dad, "Why am I the last person to find out mom's illness. Cecile is dead, but her grown kid, Bonnie Hunter, knew this, she told me of my mom being ill. She knew of my mom and I didn't have a clue. Why?"

"Be reasonable. Tell a little girl that her mother tried to kill her? Could you have understood?"

"I'm an adult now, dad. You could have told me while I was searching for answers."

Her dad looked at his wife's gravestone. "There's more to explain and I'm breaking my word to your mom and getting all this in the open. Peter and Annie heard the story this afternoon and now it's your turn. It goes back to when you were three, almost four. Joanna went after my dad with a knife. He was bigger and stronger, but again, she was smart. She had him trapped in the hallway near the stairs in our old home. She was able to trip him, turn the hall table over, and trap him but good. Now I don't like telling the rest

Sue, but it has to come out. Joanna stabbed him once, hard, in his back left shoulder, and told him if he moved, she would cut his throat. No kidding, no exaggeration, this is what happened. And then it got worse."

"My wife, Joanna, stripped my dad's pants down, took his little whip thing he always carried, and rammed it up his backside. She must have hit it hard and rammed the whip handle deep inside him. There was blood all over the hall and..."

"Dad, stop. You don't have to tell me." Sue was sobbing.

"It happened like this, Sue, it has to be known." John continued in a calm, cold voice. "The ambulance came, they took dad to hospital, and, they called the local sheriff. He took your mom to the lock-up, and that's where she spent the night. It was a mess when the hospital contacted me in California, and I arranged things from there. My dad told the cops, it was an accident. That Joanna was trying to help him, not hurt him. Cops knew he was lying but, in our small town, lies are accepted and people look the other way. And the cops knew, Joanna was now kept in a locked ward, and started on her electric shock treatment. Months of it. And it worked. She was calm, stable, dependable, but no longer the vibrant wife of before. She was both cured but changed. And very ashamed. You can't imagine her shame." John, stopped, breathing hard, and continued, "After her treatment, Joanna refused to come home, adamantly refused... until I promised her trying to kill my dad and her shock treatment would forever be secret. You kids would be told nothing."

"So if you lied, then, have you lied about my birth. Any more hidden from me?"

"I never lied about your birth. Never."

"Dad, scientifically, I don't fit into the family and I can't explain it?"

"Neither can I. And it doesn't bother me cause you are my

daughter. Period."

Sue calmed down, moving onto another track, "Look, Hank called yesterday, confirming that Bonnie Hunter is Cecile's kid. And I suspect you knew of her existence all along but you let me travel to California to find out. Why keep them secret?"

John nodded, "We'd heard rumours your mom's sister had a family, but so what? I never knew for certain, and we were estranged by then."

"Bonnie told me you sent the letter that screwed them."

"That's a different chapter of Joanna's illness. Cecile called to ask for immigration sponsorship, but I was ticked off and wrote that letter. I didn't mail it. Sometimes, you write a letter in anger and just leave it sit. That's what I did. And years later, I was surprised to find it had been sent - but I didn't mail it."

Sue replied, "Tell that to Bonnie. She is sending a copy, and it has your signature on it."

John whispered back, "I can't explain every detail of mom's illness. It was a hard, crazy time. We didn't realize how abnormal Joanna was until she set Peter outside the front door once and just left him there. It was winter and hours before we found him. But understand this Sue, what you know of postpartum now, I didn't know anything back then. It took time to see the problem and longer to know what to do."

"Dad, it didn't take Cecile long to know the problem. Bonnie says Cecile knew from the first child, how ill mom was."

John was turning red in the face. "What the hell would Bonnie know. She wasn't even born then. The great Bonnie must paint us as country bumpkins and Georgia rednecks, against Cecile, the hero, who rescues Joanna. That's simplistic thinking, Sue, cause Cecile's legend doesn't match her reality. Truth is, Cecile only made matters worse by charging in and taking Joanna to the hospital. Hell, we were ready to do exactly what she did."

"Is that when you decided against her, to blackball her?"

"No. I didn't like her. Didn't want her interfering in our family. She was a negative influence, but she lived in Oakville. We were in Plattsburgh. I just ignored her."

"You ignored her? What about the letter? You lied to immigration, giving Cecile a blacklisting, so she and Bonnie grew up in hard times. If that's ignoring her, dad, I'd hate to see you doing something against her."

"Sue, you keep picking up the wrong end of the stick - and all we are doing now is arguing. I wanted to clear the air today, tell the truth of your mom's illness. You want to talk of Cecile. These are two very separate issues, very separate times, and can't be linked. Also, you can't judge the past on today's standards. What will you say, in ten years from now, if Allie yells at you for leaving Vermont and her dad?"

"That's different, I'm not lying to Allie. You lied to immigration against mom's sister."

John went silent for a while, before continuing, "After you were three, the only way to treat your mom was with shock treatments. It was a drastic measure - a terrible treatment - but it worked. And if the procedure dramatically changed her personality, at least she lived a normal life from then on. Your mom was never manic again, but she also never wrote poetry. And Joanna was so ashamed of her illness, so ashamed of having the shock treatment, that she begged me to keep it all secret."

"It's medical, not shameful."

"Yes, sure, except tell Tom Eagleton that."

"Eagleton?"

"Goggle Thomas Eagleton ran for vice-president till his previous shock therapy hit the media coverage. Public ignorance of shock therapy made Eagleton resign the vice-presidential spot. Joanna was no fool; she knew people would shun her. Cured, but she, certainly never wrote poetry again." John knew cured was not the right word. But it would do. No use telling Sue that after his dad came home from the hospital, he always slept with his door locked. He would place a chair under the door handle, and it wouldn't be moved till morning. And, occasionally, if his dad was getting arrogant or loud, Joanna would simply hold a wooden spoon, long end facing up, and she would just look at the old man. He never really bothered anyone in the house again. But Sue didn't need to know all this.

"Thanks, dad. It explains a great deal." Sue thoughtfully said, "Peter and I remember mom differently, because she was manic in his childhood but stable for mine." *A flake for Peter yet solid for me.*

Sue could see her dad's shoulders were rounded, and he looked tired. As John relaxed further into shadows creeping over the bench, he seemed to grow even older. Was it only the light playing tricks - or was her dad becoming an old man? *I've been a fool. Thinking only of myself.*

John spoke quietly, yet his voice still had the timber of authority, "Perhaps, after your mom died, I should have told you kids everything. Who knows what's best."

Sue reached over and gave him a long hard hug, "Dad, time to go home. Allie has school tomorrow." And then, as they drove I-75, Sue asked, "After her treatment, why didn't mom reconnect with her Oakville family. Why continue to blame you for planning against them and her sister?"

"That's where you keep getting the wrong end of the stick, Sue. Snubbing her family and friends was your mom's idea. Even sinking her sister was her doing. After treatment, Joanna wanted privacy and secrecy at any cost. Sure I wrote the letter against Cecile, but your mom dictated the words. Joanna was afraid her family would discover her illness. Just, absolutely, wouldn't talk of it. So she cut everyone off. Wouldn't see her brother Fred, or best friend Maria, stopped writing to her folks - and when Cecile asked for a reference to immigrate - she panicked and spoke against her. The reason I knew so much against Cecile is because it was written in your mom's words. One time, Maria wanted to come and see your mom, but just the thought of her coming was enough to start the depression again. So, as the big bad guy, I called Maria and told her the visit was off. We raised the walls again and kept everyone out."

"Why let everyone think you were the bad guy, dad?"

"I loved your mom. Her family wouldn't believe Joanna pushed them away, so I held the blame. It was a small price to pay, if Joanna could lead a normal life. Was I wrong?"

"All along I felt you were covering up secrets of my birth."

"You're the same little bundle I held in Canada many years ago. You are our daughter." John smiled, saying softly, "And I've thought back, from moment one of your birth, through all your childhood, and until today, and there is no point in time, or incident, from birth till now, that you are not my daughter."

"Dad I believe you. Honestly, honestly believe you. But something must have happened." Sue looked toward her mother's grave, knowing there was no help coming. Feeling alone in the universe now, she knew her dad was telling the truth, yet nothing he said had explained her birth. Sue continued, "May as well tell you that Maggie found Air Force letters, questioning some treatment mom had in Toronto, but the dates don't make sense cause they are a few months before my birth. It can't be postpartum, so why would she see a doctor?"

"I don't know." He took ages to continue that it seemed to Sue her dad just might have finished. But eventually he added, "That's a long time ago and I wasn't there, but I seem to recall your mom calling me in California asking for medical clearance or numbers. She was in Canada for a while and pregnant so, perhaps, she needed to see doctors or something?" He shrugged, adding,

"Show me the papers sometime and the dates might jog my memory."

John stood, stretched, saying, "Dreaded this emotional talk with all you kids, but it went better than I figured. Ready for dinner and then head home?"

Sue linked her arm in his as they made their way toward the car. "Thanks dad. Couldn't have been easy for you talking of mom; you're not much of a talker at any time." I'm talked out myself and all I want is getting home and going to sleep.

John continued, "After I told Peter this afternoon, he thanked me also. He figured we should have another family get-together at his place, a celebration, that, no matter what happens in the future we are a family. It makes sense. You should take a day, fly to Peter's place, and you three kids, talk through everything that's just been aired."

"Dad, I'm not going to Peter's again. Emails are fine."

John turned to look at her, "A family conference, just you kids, hashing out all the stuff we've just talked over is what's needed."

"Dad, I'm not spending any more money or time on family searching. Enough gazing at my belly button. It's stopped. That's final." Don't you see. I'm giving up?

"Okay, just think about a family conference." Have a little respect for your old man and stop interrupting. "You head north for the weekend and Sonny and I will take Allie to Panama City Beach and dip her in the Gulf for a while. I figured it all out. And Peter agrees."

"Dad, I'm staying in Atlanta to look for work."

"All right." He hands her an airline ticket. "It's a return ticket to Plattsburgh that you can throw away, when we get home." Her dad kept driving with a straight face and didn't even look over to see Sue roll her eyes and shake her head.

Later, back at her dad's condo, Sue was in bed with her mind racing. All right, so mom's illness can explain why Peter and I see a different mom, but it doesn't even touch the issue of my different genetics. Unless, is it possible that when my mom attacked my grandfather she knew something that still has not come out. When mom was repeatedly hospitalized, would grandfather have orchestrated a baby switch that went unnoticed? He was the one in charge. But all this is mere speculation made up from whole cloth. I can't accuse dad's parents of something unless there's some proof. So, it's time to let go of the past, keep peace between dad and me, get a job, stability, and let Allie and me get on with life. Also, settle arrangements with Allan. I don't want him and he needs to know. So, stop searching, settle down, and forget the DNA mystery. And I can do that.

Eventually, Sue drifted into a restless dream. A magician took her dad onto a stage full of both bright circles of light and dim areas of darkness. Then, the magician slowly rolled a paper hoop across the stage while a beautiful woman, concealed from the audience walked behind it.

With a flourish, John dropped the paper hoop, and Joanna appeared. The audience went wild. Her dad spoke only to Sue, "No trick, Sue, she was there all the time. Don't you understand?" In the dream Sue, with tears in her eyes, could hardly yell, "I don't understand. I don't understand."

Dream, magician, audience, and laughter faded, her mom moved into focus, holding out a hand that never quite reached Sue's face, "Understand the set-up my dear. All in the set-up."

Sue awakened, sitting bolt upright, disconcerted, and drenched in perspiration again. What a hell of a dream. God, I'm tired of this birth search. It's a millstone around my neck.

I'll accept dad's offer, travel to Plattsburgh and return what's left of the money Maggie lent me. I'm finished. Finished with DNA nonsense Harry's death started. My parents are mom and dad who raised me, not some mythical parents that may never be found. It's over. Searching was a damn stupid idea anyway. To hell with it.

Chapter 21

Plattsburgh's airport arrivals concourse had construction in progress. The same expansion project started more than six years ago never seemed to be finished. Maggie met Sue with a friendly hug, glanced at her slightly showing belly, "You look tired. Rough flight, or is the baby affecting your hormones?"

"Both, tired and full of hormones, Maggie. Dad pushed me into this weekend to wrap up my birth search, otherwise, I would be home taking it easy. How's my brother?"

"Still the same Peter, controlling, like your dad." Maggie walked through the concourse while adding, "Frankly, Sue, you surprised me. Giving up your search on the very weekend we meet as a family to brainstorm solutions. Why?"

"Some things can't be solved. If Plattsburgh wants to fix a problem, then find an easier way to fly here. It's ridiculous. Atlanta to Detroit, to Rochester, to Plattsburgh. Waited in Rochester twice as long as the entire flying time."

"Don't complain. You were fortunate today; the bright side is you flew in good weather." Maggie had little sympathy for bitching. "You realize Hank is saying he figures he can solve your damn annoying birth secret."

"There is no solution, Maggie. Hank is kidding himself."

"Whatever, Sue. How is he accepting your baby bump?"

"Wonderful." Sue continued. "He knows I'm carrying Allan's kid and, despite that, he still wants a future with me. He was quiet for a while at first, then said we can work it out. He wants Allan to know, so there's no misunderstanding."

Later, in Peter's living room, Sue was talking to the team:

Annie, Peter, Maggie, and Hank. "Since Harry died, and my family genetics were disputed, I focused on a birth search, but now it's time to focus on us, on our family. The search is over. I've decided to leave it." She looked at everyone in the room. "Good to let it go. And positive. Dad has opened up about mom, and we can better understand both of them. Also, we connected with cousins in Canada, and Bonnie from California is slowly edging closer to me. So I figure this is the final wrap up - then we leave the search alone. Who wants to start?"

Hank started talking like the official he was, "A few months back, we found Sue's DNA didn't match her siblings..." Sue was impatient, "Hank, don't rehash it all. Do you have an answer?"

He refused to be hurried, "Yes. If a child is switched - and it happens occasionally -then, the closer to birth the easier to settle a child in a strange new family. But that isn't the case with you, is it, Sue? No evidence of you being switched after you were settled into the home in Georgia. Now go forward a step. Sue is two, or three, and Joanna is having severe problems with coping. That's a logical point to have the baby switch."

Peter looked at Sue, then answered Hank, "Why around age two. Why then Hank?"

"Because John told me of Sue's mom's sequence of her illness, when they brought baby Sue back to Georgia. Joanna wasn't ill until the second year. Let me go on." He looked at Sue, "Why couldn't your mom have switched you at age two, when a child could be more trusting. Then, after your mom had additional medical sessions, she couldn't remember the baby switch. She did it when she was starting to get ill and when she recovered, her memory of it had gone. By then you're age three, comfortable in the family, and no one knows any different. With your dad in California, your grandparents getting older, your mom being hospitalized during the year, that was the ideal time for a baby switch. When there was turmoil in the home."

Sue was sceptical, "A possible baby switch."

"Sue, when cops want to solve a crime, one thing they look for is opportunity."

Peter spoke, "Hank, we were cared for by my grandparents. Now granddad was a miserable old bastard, but he was also sharp and protective. He wouldn't let my mom walk off with one child in the morning and return with a different one in the afternoon."

Hank raised his hand, "It didn't have to take place at his home. Joanna's illness is the first long-term opportunity since Sue's birth for anything to happen. Didn't happen at the Canadian hospital, or during Sue's first year in Georgia. No opportunity. However, Joanna having treatment for a year is an opportunity for a switch."

Hank, set out supporting material on the coffee table: missing person's sheets, computer printouts, even a time line of events he had produced, as he continued talking, "During your mom's hospitalization, five baby girls went missing in Georgia. Cases never solved. Now, by cross-checking relatives of the missing girls, against your DNA - we might find a positive match."

Peter had looked doubtful, "This is theory, not hard facts."

"With old cases you don't often have hard facts. But everything I've laid out fits." Hank saw doubt on their faces.

Annie spoke, "Hank, without facts to back you up, this idea could expand to every State. Could be hundreds of missing kids?"

Hank was undeterred, "I didn't say this would be simple. But it's an answer."

"Annie's right." Sue said. "What you're saying might be checked, if there were a shred of evidence to back it up, but there isn't."

Hank wasn't quitting, he faced Sue. "You were switched."

Maggie glanced around the small group before quizzing Hank, "Just suppose you're right Hank, then switching means two babies. How could a person get away with switching Sue and someone else? That's two families. And why would Peter's mom do it?"

Hank was prepared for the objections. "We start with missing children of Sue's age who lived near Sue's childhood home. Then check their relative's DNA and, bingo, we solve the mystery." When no one seemed to support his idea, Hank added, "I've already identified possibilities in three families."

"Hank, you're stretching facts to fit the solution?" Sue remained unconvinced. "But if you believe a random someone can be found, then go for it. However, it's time to look at another loose end - Joanna's medical bills. Maggie you take the floor."

Maggie leaned forward, "Medical letters from the American Air Force, sent to Joanna's parents home in Canada, requesting additional information on Canadian medical bills for Joanna. They are all concerned with procedures dated before Sue's birth, so it could be connected..."

Peter finished his wife's sentence, "to mom's pregnancy. But does it make sense that the Air Force would question bills, when they must have known my mom was carrying Sue? She was pregnant, so why question bills? Sue, you need to request more information from the Air Force."

"Peter, I tried. Only dad can access his confidential medical records, and I don't want to involve him in my failed search anymore. Is there another way to get them?"

Hank was logical, "Sue, ask John to make the request."

Maggie understood Sue. "Except, if Sue wants to keep her dad out of it, my vote is leave it alone." Maggie wasn't finished. "Curious, because these old records are all addressed to Joanna's parent's home in Oakville. So, something was happening."

Sue was stretching, tired from the trip. "The medical letters could be simply accounting questions like what is covered when

Joanna has her child. So unless anyone else has a brain wave, it looks like my search is winding down. And that's all right by me. I say we take a break."

"She leaned closer to Hank and whispered in his ear. He smiled and nodded yes. She continued talking, "By the way, this is my treat day. Carvers for lunch and, Maggie, you're getting most of your loan back. Peter promised to drive me over to Vermont, while I get some medical records sent down to Atlanta. I don't expect to return for a while. Hank and I are going out for dinner tonight, and he can get me to the airport later."

Peter tousled Sue's hair as he did when they were kids. She still didn't like it and knocked his hand away. He did it again, "I'm glad your search is ended, sis. I don't intend to lose a sister. So the way I vote is simple - just assume the DNA was one big mistake."

Hank insisted, "But it wasn't Peter, it wasn't a mistake. There was no DNA error. None."

"Okay, intellectually, we're not challenging genetics. But we can set it aside. I say, let science deal with science, and we just get on with life."

"Just ignore the evidence?"

Peter hit back, "What evidence? What the hell do science professors know anyway? They doubted frozen bacteria for years and look at their red faces now over Snow Bacteria."

"Snow Bacteria?"

"Goggle it, Hank. Eskimos always knew spring snow was fragile. Their experience was snow could often just seem to melt away - because of something in the snow. Trappers knew it, anyone in the north knew it - but science dismissed the idea. Now we know, snowflakes trap bacteria on tiny bits of dust, then as temperature rises, single dormant snow bacteria reproduce rapidly, and it's their combined heat that melts the snow. Snow Bacteria. So if science was wrong with that, why couldn't they be wrong about Sue's DNA? I say we just leave her birth search alone."

The great conference petered out. Maggie, Annie, and Sue retreated to the kitchen, while Hank and Peter moved from snow bacteria to spar over Global Warming, oil supply, and why gas prices were out of sight. Sue's brainstorming conference on her identity had whimpered to a close with little accomplished. Somehow, a sour mood descended on the small group.

A while later, as Hank wandered into the kitchen, Maggie asked, "Did you win the argument against my husband?"

"Hell no, Maggie. He's a bulldozer. How do you get him to stop talking?"

"I usually mention sex, Hank. Works all the time."

Annie nervously stubbed out her cigarette and shook her head at Sue. "I'm not intelligent enough to say this logically, yet seems to me there's a possibility you never mentioned, our new cousin Bonnie. She has mom's mitochondrial stuff. Why haven't we considered the obvious? She could have been mom's kid? Did you think of that Sue?"

"Annie, she's six or seven years younger than me. Also, Bonnie has red hair and green eyes, way outside our family criteria. But, anyway, my mind is made up, I'm dropping the search. As I told dad, my searching has reunited us with cousins, especially Bonnie, told us about mom, and given me all the family support anyone could ask for. And a bonus, Allan is history and there's a future for Hank and me. Believe me - it's ending on a high. So stop being glum. Come on inside Annie, everyone is leaving for Carvers Restaurant."

Peter hugged Sue, "Tonight, we're driving to the airport for your Atlanta flight."

"No need, Peter, Hank's driving me."

"Sue," Peter interrupted, "Me, Maggie and Annie will be at the airport just to say good-byes. We want to do it."

Annie lit another smoke, "Sue, Peter's wrong saying to give up. Let Hank search for those missing kids. And have you tried a fortune-teller?"

"Annie, no spiritualist. The issue is dead."

In her quiet way, Annie was insistent. "The fortuneteller might know what mom was thinking." When Annie could see she was not being taken seriously, she added, "All right then, I'll find one myself. You just might be surprised. Something happened all those years ago. I bet a spiritualist would know what happened in Canada the summer you were born. "

* * * * *

Ontario was hot in the summer of 1968. Just baking. The morning dawned warm when Joanna awoke in her parent's home in Oakville. She slipped on a white summer dress that clearly showed her pregnancy, and then skipped downstairs to find her mom in the kitchen.

Her mom smiled, "Have breakfast, Jo. Make sure the baby stays healthy. And it's too hot you going on that darn march in Toronto today."

"Mom, it's an antiwar march. It's important. You know if I were in Georgia now, they would hang me for marching against the US fighting in Vietnam."

"Hanging? That's a bit melodramatic Joanna, even for you. Just leave the fighting to the men, go back to Georgia and raise your beautiful kids. Or bring them here - we have plenty of room. Anyway, it's not right you staying away from them this long. I know your husband doesn't like it. He's always so uptight, when he calls here."

"You think I'm exaggerating, talking of hanging civil rights people down there mom, but you don't know the south. I've heard it's against the law to sell a vibrator to a woman in the state of Alabama." Sue could see the look of displeasure on her mom's face and changed the talk back to family, "Mom, John's happy playing war, the kids are looked after in Georgia, and I'm having my first break in years of married life. So leave me alone. Protesting, marching today, throwing a tomato at the US Embassy, might not be much, but it's all I can do against another damn US-caused war." Joanna waited a moment, then added, "Mom, ever wonder if I made the right choice in going south? What if I stayed here? What if I didn't go back?"

"Now Jo, people can't build life to suit them, it's the other way around. You don't mean to come back with your kids and make a life here? What would you do?"

"University. Write a thesis on American War. Figure out how many people have been killed over all the years by war. Figure out how many lives each star in their flag has cost. Then I could publish the thesis and distribute it to all the Redneck's in Georgia. Millions of copies." Joanna came and gave her mom a big hug, "Just talking mom, just thinking. I'll head back soon, so don't you worry now. John and I will be all right."

"Well, we won't argue, Jo. You just be happy. Canada is great if you live here, and the States are great if you live there. It's not the place, more like it's the people. Just take it easy on anything physical today. Now then, after the march, you'll stay with Maria for a few days?"

"That's the plan, mom. Maria needs me now more than she ever did. So depressed, she can't work. I would be tearing my hair out if my husband was killed in Nicaragua. And the head man down there, Somoza, he and his National Guard, are supported by the States. That alone is enough to throw tomatoes at the US Embassy. My best friend needs me, mom. Maria's always been there for me, and I want to be there for her."

"Watch the heat dear. It's going to be a hot one."

* * * * *

Hank drove Sue to the airport early, paid good money for two cups of bad coffee, then found a quiet place to sit and talk after Peter and the girls left. He listened to Sue rattle on about life for them in Atlanta, and agreed this chance for their happiness might not come around again. Eventually, as it came time for her flight, Hank talked of his concerns over Allan. "You need to be careful, Sue. I know your ex-husband is up to something, because he's been seen with a few shady characters. No idea what he has in mind, 'cept it's not good."

"Is he drinking, Hank? I don't worry if he's sober, but if he's drinking then I'm safer in Atlanta. Least till he gets resentment out of his brain."

Hank shrugged. "Honestly, I don't know. Allan still faces bank fraud issues over forging your signature, so we keep an unofficial eye on him. My buddies in narcotics tell me Allan is moving with a rough crowd. So, if he comes calling, it's best you are careful."

"Problem is, when he calls Allie for regular chats, he's getting nosey about me." They were in a quiet area, and Sue moved closer to him, "I don't want to talk of Allan."

"Hank, you sure of taking me on? Six weeks ago, when you and I drove north, I didn't give myself to you, because you had no idea I was carrying Allan's child." Reaching to touch his hand, she continued talking, "My feelings are more settled now, but you need to decide if we go any further than friendship." Sue smiled, "I won't be going back to Allan, no matter what happens. He and I are finished."

Sue gently brushed Hank's hand, "Now do you understand -

why I didn't sleep with you, hardly kissed you, trying to be emotionally honest?" Sue repeated herself, "You need to be sure of taking me on. If we're going to have a future, it's going to start off right between us."

She stood up, ready to leave, "Time to go. Just be sure of us, Hank. I'm not much of a catch - pregnant with one kid already, no job, not much to offer."

She reached upward to give him a hug, but Hank gently pulled Sue toward him, held her tight in a long slow kiss that had other passengers nearby notice with envy and admiration.

An elderly lady stopped, saying to Hank, "Gallant men still know how to treat a lady. You, sir, must be a true Southerner."

Hank nodded, "Yes ma'am." And gave the elderly lady his best southern Vermont smile and walked away. Sue could have flown to Atlanta without an airplane.

Two weeks after returning to Atlanta, Sue was feeling quite settled in life and pleased with her decision to stop searching. Hank had called every night, since she arrived home. It wouldn't be an easy relationship to nurture, yet they planned on a future together. Each time Sue got off the phone, her dad made the same remark. "Sue, either, move there or get him here. These calls are costing me a fortune."

Sue always gave her standard reply, "Yeah, I know, dad. I know." And smiled.

Working full time in Marietta, just a twenty minute drive north on the I-75, felt exciting. And the firm liked her. With Allie enrolled in school, life was falling into place.

Then the unexpected happened. A City of Atlanta garbage truck misjudged a turn and ripped into the side of her dad's car. In an instant, metal and plastic shredded, from the rear bumper to the front hood, air bags inflated, and Sue's seat belt jammed her tight, locking her into the seat. Cops were shouting, "Get the pregnant lady out now - NOW - could be a gas explosion. Can she move?"

Firemen cut her seat belt, helped her out the passengers' door, and moved her to the side of the fire truck to await an ambulance. In the organized confusion Sue knew she was thinking only of picking up Allie from school, shouting, "Forget the ambulance, I need to get my kid."

"Ma'am, you're not driving anywhere." The burly fireman pointed to an ambulance, "The only ride you're getting is to the nearest hospital. You have to be checked out."

"What did you say?" His words accidentally opened a window on the past. Her surrounding world of noise and traffic faded a few levels lower, as she finally saw a breakthrough in her birth search, because, she now realized, one person had lied. Sue could kiss the fireman, for starting the insight in her mind. But he had moved on, uninterested in the frazzled lady sitting on his fire truck step, crying, and babbling, "They lied." Dad won't like it, but I'm not finished with my search. Not by a long shot." Sue was almost euphoric. Dad's going to have a bird, when he finds out what I know.

Sue called her dad, babbling, almost shouting, "What a fortunate accident. Can you believe it, dad? I'm waiting for the light on 6th Avenue and 'bang,' the city truck wrecks your car, and I make the connection to explain my DNA. It means one more flight. Then, my birth search is over. When I get this last piece of the puzzle, you'll be the first to know what happened."

Later, in his condo, Sue, smiled her little girl smile at her dad, "Can you look after Allie for a few more days, dad? I need to make one more trip next week."

Sue's exuberance caught John off guard. "Sue, you just returned from California and that was to be your last trip."

"Dad, this is critical. God, you won't believe what I've

figured out."

"Then tell me?"

"I need to be sure." Sue shook her head, "Just give me a few more days, dad, to fit the last pieces of the puzzle. Just a few more days."

And on the phone Maggie wanted to know the answer. "You owe me, Sue. Tell me what you've figured out. What's the great insight?"

"One more flight Maggie, before I say anything. But I'll give you a little teaser - this will explain Peter's problems too. It all fits. And this time, it's my game, played my way. I've waited months for this and it's going to be done right."

* * * * *

The summer of '67 in Toronto began and ended with antiwar marches. Peaceful demonstrations didn't take many cops to control the orderly crowd moving past the US Embassy on University Avenue. Tight security would be a thing of the future. For now, these warm days had a festive atmosphere. So a few tomatoes were pitched, no big deal, as no rocks or bottles were tossed and no great damage was done. The march ended a hundred yards north of the Embassy, and the marchers straggled back to the wide grassy median of University Avenue. The diverse group sat on the grass, played in the middle of University Avenue, waved to the passing cars going north and south, and pointed to the marks their tomatoes had left on the Embassy. Joanna proudly pointed to her red-squashed mark against a second floor window.

On this wide expanse of University Avenue as in all of, Toronto the Good, the day was hot. Relaxing marchers took full advantage of the Avenue's fountains, splashed in the water, climbed the monument to Queen Victoria and walked along the wide granite edges of the water ponds, flower banks and tulip beds. Thousands of tulips, a gift from Holland to Canada, cementing a friendship to commemorate the end of the second world war. Joanna walked along the edge of the tulip beds, skipped in the sunshine, stepped on a slippery patch of wet granite, and started her long slow fall toward the sharp stone edge.

Chapter 22

The large jet thundered through the darkness, falling down to the runway, until Airbus tires hit wet pavement, bounced up once, then screeched down again, racing the massive plane toward the end of concrete. Eventually, flaps, brakes, and thrusters combined to shudder the plane load of humanity to a controlled stop. As the plane returned to the concourse, Sue looked west, into a distance, knowing she still had an hour's drive to complete her journey.

Eventually, driving her rental car along residential streets, she parked across from her destination, faced the house briefly, and knew her decision was right - time to confront a liar. The house was, just as she remembered, set back from the street, with a light gleaming in the kitchen. Sue walked down the drive, quietly entered by the back door without knocking, and simply addressed the woman whose back was to her, standing at the sink, washing the dinner dishes.

Sue spoke two simple words, saying, "Hello, mother."

Maria Court almost dropped the dish in her hand, "Oh, Susan, you startled me so. Why didn't you call?" Her voice was questioning, while her smile welcomed Susan. "Always glad to see you, but this is so unexpected. Come in, and sit down." Maria yelled, "Fred, come see who dropped in." Then, in a quieter voice, "Susan, wait till your uncle sees you here. I'll pull him away from his music right now."

"Can Fred wait, until you and I talk? A talk, just between us, mother?"

"Mother? Well, you can call your old aunt, mother, any day you want. Fred and I never had children and since your mom died a few years back, I often thought you and I could be close one day. So, aunt, or mother, or Maria, is all fine with me. You're very dear to me, Susan. Come, sit down."

Sue preferred standing, "Just stop it. Maria, stop the sham, because you either are my real mom or know who is. It's true. I don't know why you did it, or how, but somehow you managed to make a baby switch in the hospital. Did my mom know, or were you the only one involved?"

Maria sat at the kitchen table. "Oh dear child, you're so very mixed up, very mixed up. Sit down with me. What's happening, Susan? Could it be your pregnancy? Sometimes, with hormones, we go a little funny. What's set you off? The birth search, thinking of a baby switch nonsense? Whatever you need - I'll help you in any way I can."

"Just tell the truth. How did you manage the switch?" It all fits. I can't be wrong. I'll not cry till you admit it. "Maria, this search has ripped me apart. I need to know what happened after my birth. Tell me, just between us, so no one else ever needs to know. God, I don't want to cry." The tears flowed. Maria reached over to hold her close, but Sue pushed away, shouting, "How did you do it. Tell me."

"You seriously figured I was your mom." Maria heaved a long sigh, "Oh dear, when you arrived, you truly saw me as your mom." Another sigh, "You need a cup of tea, Susan." Maria was filling the kettle while talking, "Least, I need one." While the water heated, she continued, "Now, sit down and relax, and tell your aunt what confused your mind so."

"Because you lied to me. Maria, when I visited, weeks ago, you said you never drove a car, and lived miles away from the hospital, yet helped my mom every day in the maternity ward. How? How could you travel that distance, from Toronto to Milton without a car? It's too far. But you told a bigger lie. The hospital location.

Milton is an hour away from Oakville. When I had a car accident in Atlanta they said 'take her to the nearest hospital.' The nearest one. Why would my mom have a baby miles away in Milton Hospital, when mom's folks lived blocks from the Oakville Hospital? It doesn't make sense. That was the lie that woke me up. That's how I know you were part of my birth swap. The hospital lie gave you away."

"Susan, honestly, I played no part in any swap."

Sue wiped her tears, "For weeks now, in my dreams, you were always standing in the shadow of my birth. It all makes sense to me."

Maria set the teapot on the table and gave Susan a hug before saying, "Dreams. Why didn't you call and talk to me? You came all this way on a hunch, on a dream?" Maria gave a third long sigh, saying emphatically, "Oh Susan, I can't have children. Tests show I can't have kids. That's why you're so precious. And if you need to call me mom, then I'm your mom - any time you want. I want to help you."

"But it still makes sense to see you as my mom. Don't you see the similarities? You were there at my birth, and you had the opportunity to make a switch. I figured if you lied on travelling to the hospital, well, you could lie about more. If you're not my mom, then, I've gone a little crazy, Maria?"

Maria stayed calm. "Honestly, Susan, cross my heart, there was no baby switch. Honestly. I mean, think of it. Where would I gather another child from to switch with you? Where? They don't just keep them in the pantry. As for travelling, well it was an effort but it just happened. Once, I did bus to see Joanna and you, but, mostly, I hitched a ride each morning from a friend. He lived near me in Toronto and worked in Milton. Often he would drive me home. And twice sleeping at the hospital if I recall rightly. There was no mystery of travelling." Maria took Susan's hand in hers, then brightened in remembering, and said, "I know. Go back home and test my DNA sample I gave you. That will satisfy you."

"Already did. That test shows you're not my parent. But I figured you altered the sample somehow." Sue gave up and felt bone weary tired, "I've had a stupid dream saying 'It's in the set-up,' meaning at the beginning of my life. Explaining the dream now seems silly but, in the dream, I thought you must be my mother." Sue looked closely at Maria, "It still makes sense, doesn't it? We do look similar." Sue placed her arm next to Maria's, "Look, even the hue of our skin matches."

"You can call me mom any time dear but, perhaps, you need a good rest from searching. Now, drink your tea, while I find your uncle. I'll make up the guest room for you."

"Oh Maria, I can't stay, there's a return flight to catch." Sue had no return flight booked, yet her injured pride, at being wrong once again, made her want to leave now.

"Don't go yet, let me call Fred.

"Maria, my crazy thinking - please, let my mistake just stay between us."

"Of course, my dear. Hormones. You tell Fred whatever suits you." Maria went into the den, shouted at her husband, then lifted his headphones. "Come and see our surprise guest."

Thirty minutes later, Sue dredged up her last bit of energy, gave Maria a long, hard hug, and walked dejectedly down the darkened drive toward her parked car. This has been a disaster. Foolish. Nothing to do now but fly home as a failure.

When she started the car, an arm grabbed her neck and a sharp weapon pushed against her throat. The metal point pressed into her skin, while a guttural voice demanded, "Money. Give me your purse! Drive, turn left - do as I say and you won't be hurt."

Sue just wanted this creep out of her car yet, somehow, his

demand for money seemed reassuring. If that's all he wants, then get it over. Five minutes later, she stopped by a river, at a deserted pier, with Oakville's lighthouse in the near distance. Gently bobbing sail boats rocked in the river, their ropes and ties clinking a musical sound in the darkness. It only now became obvious. Her captor had manoeuvred them to an isolated place. She felt afraid and cold. A gut-wrenching terror gripped her body as her abductor yelled through his ski mask, "Get out!"

Holding a sharpened ice pick in one hand, he started to pull her from the car. She struggled away, pressed down on the car horn, and it's blaring sound combined with her scream, as he plunged the ice pick into her arm. The horn and screaming stopped, as he pulled her from the car.

He shouted through his mask, "Stupid bitch! No one can hear you. Now move, move, out on the pier."

Sue couldn't believe the pain in her bleeding arm, as she stumbled backwards on the cement pier. He prodded with the pick, forcing her backwards, closer to the end of the pier and the deep lake. Another jab, and closer still. "Take the money, take it all. Just go away."

His laughed seemed familiar and, when he finally ripped off the mask, she was shocked. Allan was forcing Sue out on the pier, swinging the ice pick, shouting, "You need to die!"

"Oh my god, Allan! Are you nuts? You can't get away with this."

He smirked, "Get away with what, Suzie Q? My wife drowns, cause she can't swim - what's that got to do with me?" He prodded her toward the edge of the pier. "Me, I'm nowhere near your unfortunate death." Her options were terrible - either move backward to the inevitable water or risk running passed his weapon. He read her mind and prodded again, into a narrow space, "Time to get wet, Suzie Q." He prodded her a step closer to the lake.

"Allan, you'll get caught. They'll know you did this."

"Oh, you're wrong. Sure, the cops might discover my little ten-year-old spy told me you were flying to Oakville. And they might think I acted. But what can they prove? A buddy of mine is gambling in New York with my ID, while I entered Canada as him. Allan Charter is spending money in New York City right now. How will I get caught, Suzie?"

"Allan, for god's sake, I'm carrying your child. Allan, this kid is ours."

"Oh, you're good. What a liar!" Allan talked so fast from anger he spewed spit, "You're pregnant, but with Hank's kid." Anger distorted his voice and flowed from a mind full of hatred. He shouted, "You have to die. I won't ever support Hank's bastard." He lunged with the pick and she moved backwards, stopping within feet from the deep, cold lake.

Sue suddenly felt her body change to a cold resolve. All alone. She would need her wits to fight alone. Sue became agitated, then pointed and looked past Allan, as if help were coming, "Grab him, he's nuts." For a moment, a fleeting moment, Allan looked behind, and Sue acted. Lunging forward and swinging her fist, full of car keys, she swung at his face and raked the keys across his left eye. She meant to do serious damage. Now, his scream shattered the night. Dropping the ice pick, he held his hands to a bleeding face. Sue grabbed the ice pick to ward him off, but Allan's anger made him bellow and charge forward pushing her closer to the edge. She took one blind swing with the pick. It hit his neck, on the left side between chin and shoulder. Stuck deep in his neck, blood spraying over his clothes, he fell toward her. Crying, in agony, he pulled the ice pick free, held one hand to stem the bleeding and crawled toward Sue with his eyes glinting hatred. She backed toward the water, her space on the pier becoming dangerously smaller. Then, in pain, his hands coated in blood, Allan slowed and finally stopped crawling.

Now, Sue waited in the dark as he taunted, "Come on Suzie, move past me. Come on, you might make it." His hate-filled eyes glinted with determination to grab her, if she tried to pass him. They waited in the cold as dark hours passed. They waited in stalemate. Only the lake and Sue witnessed Allan's life blood draining away on the cold dark pier. Right to the end, Allan Charter looked at his wife with an evil gleam in his eyes. His glinting eyes were her last memory of the horror.

Near dawn, a police car stopped for a coffee break by the pier, spotted the bodies, and all hell broke loose. Sue was first taken to the Oakville-Trafalgar Hospital, and then back to the police station on Bronte Road. "Ma'am, you being from the States, you need to be held a few hours while this gets sorted out." The few hours turned into a day long session with
Oakville detective, Kimberly Travis, and a representative from the US embassy.

Sue was taken to a comfortable interview room with two women waiting for her. The older one spoke first. "I'm detective, Kim Travis, with the Oakville police," and she pointed to the young, still wet behind the ears, office girl, "and this is Caroline Werger, from the Toronto US consulate. "This interview is being recorded and video taped. I have a few questions. Miss Werger can only listen and, then, you can spend some time alone with Miss Werger. Do you understand what I've just said, Mrs. Charter?"

"Yes, anything to get home. Can I call my girl?"

"That will be arranged. We want to release you to New York law enforcement, but there are a few discrepancies between your statements and the facts that need to be cleared up." Travis handed both Sue and Werger a copy. "Please read what you have told us. Take your time. It's important you be clear on the facts."

In a few minutes, Sue nodded, "Yes, except, for saying I had been to the pier before. That's not true. And I don't know how my husband followed me."

"You were at the pier before as a visitor to Oakville just six weeks ago. We have a photo of you and a little girl being there."

"I had no idea it was the same pier. And how do you know of the photos?"

"We know a great deal, Mrs. Charter. As for being at the pier before... your aunt and uncle have photos from your visit. Now, are you ready to answer a few questions?"

"Look, I'm the victim here, I've told the truth. Allan tried to kill me. All you have to do is look at his identity - he switched it. That will prove he's lying and I'm telling the truth."

Travis stood up, picked up Sue's folder of arraignment and said, "Your story doesn't match the facts. First, your husband had his own identity, Allan Charter, on his person. Second, he travelled on the same flight you did. Separate seats, yes - but the same flight. Three, he rented a car from Budget just as you did. Four, the ice pick has your prints on it, perhaps, it could be from your kitchen." Travis stopped for the facts to sink in. "Now, Canada goes to great lengths to maintain friendly relations with your country - but you will be held in custody while the investigation is ongoing. You're an American, as was your husband so this is not a Canadian concern. Chances are you will be returned to the States for their justice system."

Travis nodded toward the Embassy kid, "Miss Werger, you have half an hour to speak with your client. And remember, your conversation is being recorded."

Sue took a deep breath and almost without thinking said, "You can't send me back to the States for murder, I was born in Canada. I'm claiming landed refugee status."

* * * * *

Now, after a month in custody at Ontario's Maplehurst Correctional Holding Centre for Women, in Milton, Ontario, Sue was told a relative had come to see her. Till now, her only contact had been letters and phone calls from the States. This was her first visitor.

The guard was talkative today, "Says she's your mother. Come along now."

Maria Louisa Alhambra Court sat alone in the waiting room. Her tear-streaked face had aged in the last month, as she said, "I'm so sorry. Susan, devastated and so very sorry."

Sue stood, faced her a long time before stating, "You came today saying you're my mother. Just a month ago, you denied it all and I ended up on a pier fighting for my life. What's the truth?" Sue sat down across from Maria, "Some mother you are! Why should I believe you now?" Sue felt colder than when she had confronted Allan on the pier.

Maria stopped her tears and, in a shaky voice of the elderly, answered, "Don't judge me... not till you know everything." They sat near a window with sunlight streaming across nearby tables and chairs, as Maria spoke, "Joanna raised you, nurtured you, worried if you were sick, and packed school lunches day after day; a million things she did... and in every way, Joanna is your mom. But your birth was unusual months before you were born."

"You see, contrary to what your dad believed, Joanna didn't leave your brothers and sister in Georgia over a family fight. Joanna engineered the fight but came to Canada, because I needed help. I was pregnant, totally alone, and depressed. My husband, Carlo, had been murdered in Nicaragua. He went to see his family, and the National Guard shot him as a Sandinista revolutionary. He was no more political than a potato."

Sue wanted to get this right, asking, "He died before my birth?"

"Yes. Carlo was murdered by an American supported government, months before you were born. He was dirt poor from El Salvador, and we were happy to have married and having a child. He simply went back to tell his parents of our blessings. Then he vanished in El Salvador. Erased. He was taken off a bus at gunpoint, with others, and none of them survived. Innocent victims of American ambition in Central America."

"Leave the States alone, Maria. Finish your story."

"I was, alone in Toronto, pregnant, poor, and deep in grief. So, Joanna left her kids in Georgia, and came north to comfort me. Some days she saw her folks in Oakville, but mainly spent the time watching me cry."

Sue was trying to relate clearly, "All before I was born?"

Maria nodded. "Joanna arrived pregnant, full of life and had named her child Susan, while I was pregnant and depressed over a murdered husband. Such a dreadful, heartbreaking time. But our life was destined to turn worse."

Maria stopped talking. Minutes passed before she could resume, talking in a whisper, so low, Sue had to strain to understand, "Your mom fell. When the hospital called me they said Joanna had an accident on some peace march. She had fallen, hemorrhaged, and her unborn baby didn't survive. In an instant, Joanna's life changed. She had lost the child she hoped would make her marriage stronger." Maria wiped her eyes of tears from long ago.

"So we told no one - just curled up at my place and, for days, we cried. The saddest friends in the world. Joanna's pain was unstoppable. She refused to let anyone know her baby was gone, so, neither family or husband realized. In the hot Toronto summer, in my sticky rented rooms, she had a breakdown. I think we both went nuts. Just cried day after day in misery. Our heartache was ours alone."

"Then, one morning, I awoke to a Joanna as her old bubbly self. The sun had broken through the clouds. She skipped around the room, "Get up Maria, no more depression. There's an answer for us... you're going to be me, and I'm going to be you.""

Sue understood. There had been no baby switch.

"That's how you did it." Sue understood. "There was no baby switch, you damn well switched mothers. No baby switch, no second child to replace, it's just you and my mom switched identities. That's how you did it. My DNA doesn't match my family, because Joanna was not my birth mother. You are."

Maria smiled as Sue understood, "Exactly so, Susan. Exactly so. And your DNA didn't match my hair sample, because it came from the floor of my hair dresser."

"How did you manage my birth?"

"We needed a small town and Milton fit the bill. I registered with a doctor on Main Street, using your mom's ID, and told him I was visiting from Georgia, and only needed a physician here... just in case a medical problem came up. I gave him all Joanna's information including her family doctor in Georgia. He was pleased to take me on as a travelling patient."

Sue needed to ask, "Was it that easy to get around the medical system?"

"Back then, yes. Paying the bills was not an issue as I offered to pay up front or he could wait till the US Air Force sent the payments. So I saw him a few times and then, when my labour started, we sat in the Milton Hospital car park, waited till the last moment and only then rushed to Emergency. It worked. Hospitals don't ask many questions, when a baby's coming."

"And Joanna's sister, Cecile, was in on this deception?"

"Of course not. Cecile knew nothing. Joanna called Cecile after I gave birth as Joanna, and when Cecile came to the hospital, Joanna was in a chair holding you. Cecile filled out the paperwork willingly - thinking it was true."

"And my dad? He's always insisted I was his kid. He never knew any different?"

"You don't quite get it, Sue, only Joanna and I knew of the deception. I had you as Joanna Stevens, and your mom visited every day as Maria. From the start, you were bottle fed, so that never became an issue. Days later, when John arrived at the hospital, I had already checked out of maternity as Joanna, and then Joanna was waiting in the lobby holding you. John drove mother and daughter to Oakville, where Joanna deliberately started a great family fight. It was Joanna who manipulated John into quickly heading for Georgia. She didn't want to stay at her mom's place and risk someone becoming suspicious that she hadn't given birth."

"It worked because only Joanna and I knew the truth." Maria paused, "But then our plan unravelled as Joanna's mind started to become ill and our arrangement got complicated." Maria had her longest silence of all before telling the rest of the story.

"Susan, I had no intention of giving you up. None. Trouble is, I didn't realize that Joanna was very ill. When she conceived the plan to switch mothers it was to be temporary. She wanted a child at any cost and convinced me by saying she could provide a home and loving family, when my prospects were poverty and a dead husband. Joanna also promised me I would be with you. She said, to wait a few months, then come to Georgia and we would raise you as my child. So, letting Joanna pretend to be your mom for a few months seemed part of our grand plan. But she went strange. Seldom wrote me, wouldn't take my phone calls, and never came to visit her parents again. Joanna was ill, and her illness made worse by our secret she was hiding.

Sue was nodding, "Are you saying my birth secret, eventually, drove her into shock treatments?"

Maria shrugged her shoulders and opened her hands, "Who

can say? But, finally, when you were three, and Joanna was finished her shock treatment, I decided to claim you back. I travelled to Georgia and confronted Joanna in her hospital. She threatened me then. If I did demanded you back she, absolutely, would commit suicide. And I didn't know if she would harm you. I didn't know if she would recover her sanity. I didn't know if I had the strength to fight her, and I had no proof. No one knew but us."

"So, god forgive me Susan, but in that Georgia hospital I made a pact with the devil and walked away from your life. I backed off and promised Joanna, your birth was still secret. Joanna knew that if she stayed sane, our secret would never come out. I went home and later married Fred as the only way to be part of your family. If Joanna was your mom, I could be your aunt."

"How could you abandon me? How could you do that?"

Maria was anguished, "Susan, what was I to do. Tell the world you were mine and risk Joanna's sanity. She could take her own life. Perhaps your life? And what if I claimed you, what then? Would you really want to leave your parents and siblings to go live with me, a single mother, in a new country, fighting to claim a child that would have a better life with two parents? And how could I prove I was your mother? Was DNA even common back then? My options were limited at best. So... my choice was silence. Right or wrong, I promised to say nothing."

"But you continued the lie. And then just watched, while my mom cut us kids off from our grandparents." Sue spoke from a racing mind, "No more contact with my relatives. Your silence let my dad ruin family relations. You said nothing while he caused the family rift."

"He didn't cause the rift. Your dad didn't cause any family rift. It was all Joanna's manipulations pushing your dad, her doing, instigating the family rift. It was Joanna's doing. She, methodically, built a wall against her own family. Joanna was the great manipulator. She was the one who told her parents that John hated Canadians and, at the same time, confided in John that her parents despised Americans. She kept needling John, telling him Canadians were smug, they looked down on Americans, and she even told him we were glad to count American dead coming back from Vietnam. None of it true... but she manipulated him into believing it all. To this day, your dad is uncomfortable with Canada because of the lies Joanna planted."

"It can't be that simple." Susan couldn't believe her mom was responsible, "Cecile's kid, Bonnie, insists my dad caused the split. That he wrote the letter against Cecile."

Maria shrugged, "What does Bonnie know. Bonnie, as a child, listened to Cecile, and Cecile was getting her information from Joanna. Joanna pulled the strings. She had all the puppets in the family moving at the same time to her tune. She cut off her family. You kids never visited your grandparents again, and she convinced your dad to write American immigration a nasty letter against Cecile. He didn't mail it, your mom did. She was afraid any contact with her family might expose the secret. To keep you safe, her family had to go."

"Mom was that sick?"

"The mind can do strange things, Susan. Joanna was sick. From the moment she took you from the Milton Hospital, Joanna manipulated events, created facts, and pushed John into doing what she wanted. She created an illusion, because she loved you so much. When she lost her baby, you became the miracle that replaced it. So she ignored her real parents for the rest of her life to protect the family illusion that you were her daughter."

They sat in silence facing each other. Maria reached over to touch Susan's hand... Susan started to return her touch, then slowly withdrew her hand.

Maria continued, "I am your birth mother, and Joanna raised

you. Not an easy truth to face... but it happened exactly so. Now, I can stand by you. I'm here for you, Susan, and I'm not going to abandon you."

"You're too late! Months ago when I came to see you, you said nothing. Even now, telling me Joanna was the manipulator, how do I know that's true?" Susan stood up. "Didn't you keep the lie going, Maria, by switching the hair sample you gave me in Oakville. And that wasn't spur of the moment. You were ready to lie before we came."

"Susan, give me some credit. When John called to say you were coming, and were interested in family, I realized you had become aware of a problem. So I prepared, with a cutting of discarded hair taken from my weekly hair dressers and..."

Susan finished the sentence for her, "...when I turned my back to get the sample bag, you placed the other person's hair in the bag and sent me on my way. Just one more lie."

Maria sat smiling, a little girl smile, perhaps, like the Cheshire cat, "Exactly so Susan, exactly so. They were lies. But now I'm telling the truth."

So I wait. Confined at Maplehurst. The American Government wants my extradition for trial in the US, but I've invoked Canadian citizenship to stay out of their hands for a while. It's not bad here, they treat me well and, being pregnant, gets me special consideration. Dad phones once a week and lets Allie talk. She cries a lot. It's very hard on her. And Hank, well Hank has turned out to be a good man. He's not a letter writer but when he phones, he clearly wants me in his life.

Someday, they will have to let me go, someday. It's not like I'm a criminal, just someone they can't release because I made a mistake with an ice pick. In time, I hope to see my daughter again. So I wait. Only one visitor keeps coming to see me. The guard told me today, "Your mother has come to see you again, Susan."

But I refuse to go see her. "Tell her, she's mistaken. Tell the lady my mother died.... She died many years ago giving birth to me."

How does the old Simon and Garfunkel song start - *Hello darkness my old friend.* Waiting in lonely silence is better than listening to lies.